PRAISE FOR

THE BEREAVED

...Tracey does a masterful job in this novel, developing Martha as a relatable narrator; readers will find that their spirits rise and fall with hers. For the most part, her life in the city is almost too wrenching to witness. The most painful aspect of the story, wonderfully handled by Tracey, is its depiction of the casual cruelty of the righteous folk who think they should be thanked as they break families apart. This novel is based on members of the author's own family; baby Homer became William Lozier Gaston, who's Tracey's great-great grandfather.

An often painful but uplifting novel by a writer at the top of her game.

—Kirkus Reviews (starred review)

• • • •

I worried about, admired, and grieved with the indominable Martha Lozier, the heroine of Julia Park Tracey's exquisite novel. With a sharp eye for just the right details, Tracey brings Martha's harrowing, astonishing, and ultimately heartrending journey to life. This "everyday" mid-19th century American woman is anything but. How right for her story to be told.

—Lynn Cullen, author of *Mrs. Poe* and *The Woman with the Cure*

• • • •

In *The Bereaved*, Julia Park Tracey reopens America's wounds in prose that is propulsive and resonant. Martha's struggles are the stuff of classic literature. Theodore Dreiser comes to mind, but so, too, the fine contemporary novels of Jo Baker and Maggie O'Farrell.

—Christian Kiefer, author of *Phantoms*

• • • •

Julia Park Tracey's *The Bereaved* is a novel that weaves its intimately detailed characters into your soul. At once, heartbreaking, heartwarming, and absolutely beautiful, this is a story that captures the devastation of loss and the power of enduring hope.

—Lauren Hough, author of *Leaving Isn't the Hardest Thing*

What happens when a mother is left with no choices? In *The Bereaved*, Julia Park Tracey casts a stark light on an era in which hard work and devotion simply aren't enough for women trapped in poverty. Vivid, haunting, authentic, and utterly gripping, it's a beautifully written story that will stay with you long after you turn the last page.

—Ellen Meister, author of *Farewell, Dorothy Parker* and *Dorothy Parker Drank Here*

• • • •

This sumptuous, cinematic book is full of heart and concern for women's plights in this era and gets to the bottom of the Orphan Train tragedy in a way that seems just as compelling and heartless as from the children's perspective.

—Erika Mailman, author of *The Witch's Trinity*

• • • •

The Bereaved, a beautifully researched novel by journalist/historian Julia Park Tracey, portrays a courageous woman who suffers similar heartrending losses to the author's own. Based also on the struggles her third great-grandmother faced in the American Northeast during the Civil War era, Tracey's story is gritty, truthful, inspiring, and compassionate. Simply unique.

— Rebecca Lawton, author of *Swimming Grand Canyon and Other Poems* (2021) and *What I Never Told You: Stories* (2022)

• • • •

Impeccable, poetic writing. The care, respect, and fierce love for her ancestors is evident throughout *The Bereaved.*

—Eleanor Parker Sapia, *A Decent Woman,*
2021 International Latino Book Award

• • • •

Julia Park Tracey's work of historical fiction, *The Bereaved,* is based on the life of her third great-grandmother. Tracey's meticulous research reveals Martha's struggles to keep her young family together in such vivid detail that the reader shares her very real fears, her mounting disappointments, and finally, her heartbreaking decisions.

—Nancy Herman, author of *All We Left Behind:*
Virginia Reed and the Donner Party

The BEREAVED

A Novel

JULIA PARK TRACEY

AN IMPRINT OF ALL THINGS BOOK

Sibylline Press

Published in the United States by Sibylline Press,
an imprint of All Things Book LLC, California.
Sibylline Press is dedicated to publishing the brilliant work of
women authors ages 50 and older.
www.sibyllinepress.com

Distributed to the trade by Publishers Group West.
Sibylline Press Paperback

*This is a work of fiction. Names, characters, places,
and incidents either are the product of the author's
imagination or are used fictitiously.*

ISBN: 978-1-7367954- 2-2
eBook ISBN: 978-1-960573-00-1
Library of Congress Control Number: 2023935664

Book and Cover Design: Alicia Feltman

Cover art features "The Watchful Eye"
courtesy of Grove Emporium and available on Etsy

Cover photo of William L. Gaston
courtesy of the Park Family Trust.

Cover photos include:
The Bronx: American Female Guardian Society and Home for
the Friendless Woodycrest Home, undated

An Orphan Train headed to Kansas, undated

The BEREAVED

A Novel

JULIA PARK TRACEY

“Martha, Martha, thou art worried and troubled about many things.”

—Luke 10:41

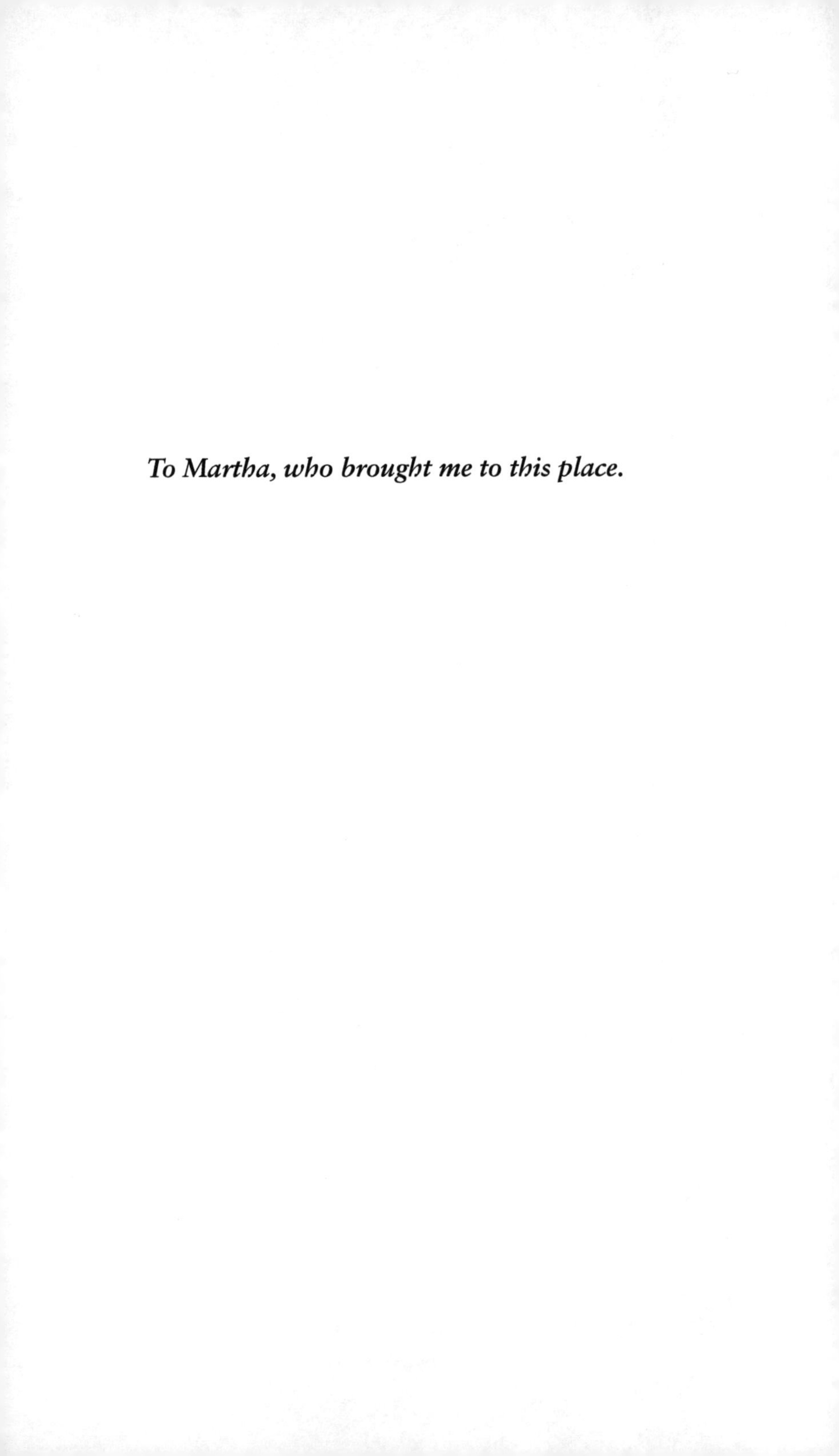

To Martha, who brought me to this place.

Prologue

Newburgh, New York
October 1859

My man Bram died on a Saturday evening, when all the world and its children take their baths. He was just 33. The boys, Ira, twelve, and George, six, were sharing their bathwater at the folks' house, where I'd sent them to stay clear of the sick air, and my big girl, Sarah, thirteen, was up there, too, to keep an eye on them. No misbehaving before the grandfolks, I said. Respect your elders and be silent at table, not like home. Sarah said she'd see to it. Homer stayed with me, as he was still on the teat. I wanted to keep them safe from whatever dread disease crept through Bram's veins and wept through his skin.

Doctor had said he thought it was measles, then camp fever, and it turned out he was right the second time, though Bram hadn't been near any camp. The fieldhands, passing through with help for harvest, mayhap—they were Irish. They might have borne lice, which brought on camp fever—the burly men scratched at themselves when they paused for a drink of water or a pipe, and I suspected nits the time that orange-haired girl came by the little house. I told her to wait outside, fetched the bucket of buttermilk down cellar myself, and sent her, scratching, away. I want to itch my own scalp now, thinking back on it.

Not a week later, Bram came in from the barn, bits of straw fluttering off his sleeves and a sharp pain in his head, squinting at the golden autumn sun. I put him right to bed. Within a few hours, he was fevered and chilled by turns. I sent Ira afoot to the doctor's house, and bid Sarah take George to the big house, to their young aunties. I kept Homer as far away as I could, instead of snug in the big bed with his mama and papa. I laid him on a quilt on the floor with a spool to gnaw while I simmered broth and spooned it into Bram; I sopped my own bread and ate it standing, while dirty sheets boiled white again and Bram moaned and sweated and fluxed. The days ran together while I fought for Bram's life. In those dark hours I prayed and cried, rocked my baby, sponged my husband, begged and muttered to an indifferent God. But before Bram breathed his last, I had known, I heard it coming as clear as the rumble of a train far down the tracks. It didn't matter now where he'd caught this fever, where the rough red rash had come from. The only thing that counted to me and our four children is that Abram Lozier, my husband, their father, was dead.

That Saturday night, I sat with my late husband's body, holding his heavy hand while his dead body cooled at last, my damp cloth no use to him now, my whispered pleas just a hiss of air between my lips, for all the good they'd done. His blue eyes still peeked beneath his dark lashes, and I pressed the lids down again and again, but they would open, his blue gaze upon me as if to say he was sorry. *I'm sorry, too,* I thought, scared and sad so deep I felt faint. *What will we do now, where will we go, where shall we stay?* Must I ask the favor of your folks to keep us? What will become of us in this new cold world? I've been alone before, been Martha to suit my name for all my thirty-one years—but with children now—my heart hammered and then seemed to stop, and I felt my panic rising like foam in a pot.

Homer, heavy as a smoked ham, drowsed in my elbow, a string of white drool at his mouth. I set him on the trundle bed near the wall where he couldn't roll off and tucked the quilt around him. Thank the Lord for this sweet lump, his brown hair mussed, fat fists curled as he snuggled into dreams. Homer kept me anchored. Meanwhile, the bedroom stank like baby flannels and sick, sour as a milk pan left unscrubbed. I had spent ten days attending my husband, barely seeing the children, greeting them through the crack of the door. But work never ends.

When morning came, the women would come; we'd wash and dress Bram in his crisp white shirt, his fine broadcloth suit, and pin his tie in place, every stitch from my own needle. Blue socks I'd knitted and darned, the color of my eyes, he'd called his favorite color; polished boots on his feet, one of my finely hemmed handkerchiefs in his pocket for the hereafter. Charlotte and Malcolm, Bram's folks, would have a coffin made in town, and there'd be a funeral at the Dutch Reform church, and then Bram would be tucked into the family plot, near our two other babies, with a space at his side for me.

Between now and then I'd better sew black bands on the children's clothes, and dye Sarah's plain brown dress black. She was old enough to wear proper mourning at her age, so her dress must grieve with her. And there should be food for callers—we'd offer them doughnuts and pie, cider from the barrel—and me with two floors to scrub before the folks knocked at the door in the morning, and any small thing that Charlotte might fault in the management of my little house, she would notice.

I was tired. Bram was dead. I was still Martha, toiling instead of praying. There was so much for the newly bereaved to do. No time for tears.

Chapter 1

Otisville, New York 1840

I'd been on my own, or alone, in some way or another, a nobody, having to learn what to say and do without much guidance since I was young. I remember a little of my Papa, Ira Seybolt, before he died. I am the eldest of five sisters, with an idle mama. I thought I would be Papa's boy and help him in the fields, but I am not tall, and my figure has always been stick-thin, no matter how much new milk I drank. Papa used to tweak my nose and call me Button and let me drive the horses pulling a big wain of Indian corn from the field. When I was ten, he cut his leg with a dull scythe, and the wound went sour; I can still hear him groaning through locked teeth, his neck cords tight as a braided whip, his harsh cough as he choked on his own juices. After he passed, Mama went home with the three littlest girls to her Greenleaf folks down Hudson's River, and sent sister Amelia, seven, with me to Grandmother Seybolt up in Otisville.

The Seybolts sometimes spoke German to each other if they didn't want us to understand, but I knew they were speaking of my mother, Mary. Amelia was not a strong child, and when we caught the whooping cough, I lived, but she withered and sank too fast. I was left alone in the trundle bed with flickering shadows from the fireplace in Grandmother's house, and Uncle John's loud boots on the floor. The house was warm, but so much quieter than a house full of children. Grandmother, her brown eyes still lively in a lined face, gave me cake with dried cherries in it, hot coffee with thick whipped cream spooned on top, and the juices of her roasted pork with apples and cabbage cooked in a great iron pot. She combed out my mousy hair and braided it up tight in loops to my ears. When I stopped coughing and was well enough to get up, she sat beside me and taught me to sew, starting with a ragdoll, then a doll's quilt of matched squares in blocks of nine, and showed me how the nine-patches could be stacked, with white spaces between, to make a pattern. Mama had not come to see Amelia laid in the ground and wrote to me but infrequently.

I knew how to knit and darn, but I had never sewn a dress by myself, so after the dolls' things, while we were waiting for the fall winds to blow and the windows to frost, we cut through cotton muslin woven in a mill in one of the great cities of the North. I threaded my needle to make the pattern dress before cutting the woolen cloth Uncle John had brought back from New York City. I went to the schoolhouse in the winter and summer terms, helping Grandmother with harvest preserves and hog butchering in the fall, hoeing the kitchen garden in the spring.

Grandmother gave me a silver thimble, and I have used it since that day to sew every stitch of my clothing, and my husband's, and for every one of my six children, including baptism-burial dresses for the babies. Grandmother taught me to stitch a heart inside the neck yoke or placket of every shirt and chemise and gown, to hold my love for the wearer against their necks, their hearts. Sometimes, I stitched in red thread, for my husband and my babies, even though the red might bleed. I still think about those bleeding hearts under the ground sometimes, if my babies are cold, are dank and moldering, or if they are warm and dry and just sleeping in death, as the Reverend Van Horn said.

Grandmother's hands were as gnarled as an old plum tree and though she could sew, kneading dough was too hard on her bones. I learned to bake the light wheat bread and the ryebread loaf the German way, saving the crumbs from each cutting to make the loaf darker the next time. She was a great believer in the Lord and Bible stories, but also remembered many folk tales from her grandmothers—stories of dark woods with hungry witches and greedy dwarves, trolls under bridges and farm animals that played instruments or spoke on Christmas Eve. When I completed a task or threaded her needle, she always acknowledged me, "I thank you, Martha," with a sincerity I learned to trust and revere, knowing she truly loved me.

On an early winter day, before the first real frost, I awoke and found Grandmother was still abed. I thought I would surprise her by making morning coffee the German way, *mit Schlag*, that delicious thick cream, and have it ready when she rose. I cranked the grinder, inhaling the dark savory scent of fresh coffee grounds, while the kettle hissed over the banked fire. Uncle John made the fires so I left it for him to build up, and whipped last night's cream in a yellow bowl with a fork until my arm ached. When the grounds settled in the pot, I poured a jet of fresh *Kaffee* into Grandmother's Dresden cup and spooned a jaunty cap of the whipped cream on top. I could not wait to see her smile when she came to table. She still had not arisen, despite my kitchen noises. Uneasy now, I approached the bedside. Grandmother stared at me from a face frozen and contorted in a grimace.

"Grandmother! Are you ill? Do you hurt?" She could not form words. Her brown eyes blinked and a groan, the kind an idiot makes in the village square, came up from her throat. I ran up the stairs to Uncle John's room, calling him, and he went down faster than I came up.

"Mother! Mother!" I heard him, desperate, saw him rubbing her crooked hand between his. He turned to me, "Fetch my boots and cloak. I'll go for the doctor."

I stayed near and held Grandmother's hands, tried to gently uncurl them from the twist they'd formed overnight. She could only look at me and blink. By the time Doctor arrived with a jangle of cloak and boots and his leather bag, she had fallen asleep. I went back to the kitchen where Grandmother's Dresden cup sat, cold *Kaffee* with a scum of wilted cream. I poured it into my own cup and drank it that way, afraid to waste it, afraid of what was amiss, unable to stop it from happening in our dark shared room.

Doctor called it a stroke of paralysis and said she would get well slowly, or not at all. I baked bread that day because I must keep my hands and mind busy, and served my uncle his meals, tried to get Grandmother to take some broth from a spoon, but it only ran down the sheet. Uncle John paced the floor all the day, and wrote letters, stopping to look at the bedroom door and curse softly into his fist. I barely slept in my trundle next to Grandmother's bed, listening for her breath, her cry for help. There was no sound in the dim room but my own sniffles and muffled sobs. Grandmother Seybolt was dead in the morning, her warmth gone and her dear face frozen in that grimace, unable to say her final prayers, her heart stilled but never forgotten.

Uncle John arranged her burial, quickly before the ground froze, and we stood in the churchyard among all the late Seybolts and departed neighbors and laid her in the grave. Spinster cousins came up from Middletown and Mount Hope to help wait on Uncle John and asked him what he meant to do all alone in the house with a young niece almost 16. The cousins stayed, taking Grandmother's bed, and I knew I was moving on.

• • •

After Grandmother Seybolt passed, I wrote my mother asking if I could come to her at last. She wrote back quickly this time, to say that she had married again, to her cousin Mr. Tooker, and that his house was full of her little daughters, his mother and sisters. He was building a new home in Philadelphia, she wrote, and I might visit them next winter, but in the meantime, I must go to her brother in Newburgh. *Your new father sends his regards.* I had not seen Mama since Papa died, and I wondered if she even remembered me when she wasn't holding my letter in her hand. I didn't know how to feel about my new father; I felt nothing, I suppose. I just wanted a home where I could sit with a needle and thread and with a window on the world.

I showed Mama's letter to my Uncle John and he frowned at her childish scrawl. He didn't curse aloud but he looked thunderous.

"Such a mother," he finally said. "Too busy counting ribbons to keep track of her own children." He chucked me under the chin and promised, "I'll drive you down to Newburgh myself, Martha."

Over the clucking of his miserly cousins, he bought me a new trunk with brass hinges and a lock, to pack my belongings, and gave me Grandmother's silk needlebook to remember her, her yarns and hooks and the two quilts we had made together. The bright nine-patch and the blue and green Ohio Star cushioned the bottom of the trunk; my clothes and sewing filled the rest.

My mother's brother, Uncle Daniel Greenleaf, owned farmland out in the countryside but he worked in the town as an agent for insurance, with chambers on Water Street and a fashionable wife, Aunt Rebecca. They had two young children, Johnny and Helen; I was to help care for the little ones and be at hand for my aunt in any way she asked, for my keep. I was glad to be around babies again; I had missed my little sisters, growing up away from them. Raising babies isn't so hard when you like them to begin with.

A few days latterly, Uncle John drove me and my trunk with a load of hay from Otisville down the chilly country to Newburgh-town, to my Uncle Greenleaf's big house on a cobbled street, pulling up behind the stable on Grand Street to unload. Though Uncle's wagon was a good one, after five hours in the open air on that rattling seat, my hands were stiff and cold and so was my breech. I was relieved to go inside and warm by the keeping room's fireplace.

My Aunt Rebecca, whom I had met long ago but had not seen for years, came into the room gliding toward me like a skater across the ice. She wore a dark green gown with the most elegant point to her Basque waist and a similar vee-shaped opening at her neck. The dress was patterned with black leaves over a forest-colored ground, and the tiny pearly buttons were black as jet. Her sleeves were wrist-length and so fitted, they seemed like long gloves. I could not stop gazing at the magnificence of her gown. My aunt, as short as I am but rounder, with bright eyes and the color of hair they call strawberry, took my cold hands in hers and shook them as if I were a grown-up person. She smiled into my face.

"Are you frozen, my dear? It's positively *arctic* out there!"

"No, not *too* cold," I fibbed. I was so relieved that she was kind and friendly.

"Come in and meet the children and find your bed upstairs. We are pleased to have you, and the children are so looking forward to meeting their cousin." She smiled again, and it seemed that was her favorite thing to do: Be cheerful. I hoped so.

Aunt Rebecca took me by the arm very companionably and brought me through to a downstairs parlor where the children played before a screened fire, Helen on the floor with a cloth book and some rag toys, and Johnny with a Noah's Ark carved of wood. He was setting up his animal kingdom and making the sounds of wild creatures in a low tone. He growled up at his mother and looked at me with mischief in his eyes. "Rawr!"

"Jonathan! Is that any way to greet your cousin Martha?"

"Goodness, are you a bear?" I asked, bending over to see.

"Tiyer!" He held up a carved shape daubed with black and orange stripes.

"Tiger, Johnny," Aunt urged. "Tiger."

"Tijer."

Aunt looked at me and said, "We must improve his speech. You'll help, won't you?"

The tiger began to fight a camel and Johnny's dialogue returned to growls and squeals. Little Helen flapped the cloth pages at her mama and raised her arms to be picked up. Aunt took her baby girl in arms and smoothed the baby's strawberry curls. "This one needs a hair ribbon or a cap; her tresses are most unruly. And look at this face!" The scolding words were spoken in the most loving of tones, as Aunt wiped her child's drooly chin with a handkerchief. I held my hands out to Helen to see if she would come to me, and she looked at me with round eyes, then hid her face in her mother's neck. I knew how she felt, shy of strangers, longing for reassurance.

"Let us go up to your bed chamber, shall we, and bring your coat and cap. Your Uncle Daniel will bring up your trunk before supper and you will make yourself comfortable, the way you like things best. But I am parched for a cup of tea and I believe you must be so? Very well." And as it began, so it continued.

The Greenleafs absorbed me into their household with kindness but I had much to learn. I was a town girl now—no forest walks or farm chores. I could read and write and figure, so there was no more call for school. The household employed Nola, the Scotch girl in the kitchen, to scrub and stew, and I wasn't expected to bake bread or mend fires. I was neither child nor adult; not servant but not quite of the family. I took the children for walks and gave them their baths, and I was permitted to run errands alone for my aunt and uncle, provided I did not actually run. I crocheted lace instead of sewing quilts and gazed out my high window at the wonders of town.

I loved to walk down the streets of Newburgh to take a message to my uncle's chamber of offices, to stop and look in shop windows on Montgomery and Water streets, and to notice every detail on the clothes of women who passed by. Cartridge pleats, white manchette cuffs, *en coeur* necklines, pelerines with a sharp point at the front, silk shawls and the Jenny Lind collar, named for the famous Swedish singer who had been pictured in the pages of *Godey's Lady's Book*. My eyes could not get enough of the rich details that could be sewn into darts, pleats, plackets and piping, much less tassels, fringe and lace. And I didn't even want to *wear* such clothes—I wanted to craft them. Cloth goods were expensive, so I practiced on the rag bag's leftovers, and made wee smocked bonnets and tatted lace collars for Helen and her dolls. I heard Aunt and Uncle speaking of New York City and its stylish salons and playhouses, where well-dressed people filled the halls. Aunt's clothes were made for her by a Newburgh dressmaker, but when she saw what I knew, she allowed me to make more clothes for the children, and then for myself, sparing the expense of a purchased garment or a dressmaker.

Soon it was clear that Aunt Rebecca expected another child and I begged to be permitted to make the christening dress. She bought all the trimmings she desired, and after observing me with the muslin, Aunt Rebecca allowed me to cut into the soft white silk. I spent hours by daylight and by lamplight making the tiny puffed sleeves, the many rows of pin tucks and gathers. Laid out on the big bed, the pearled gown was almost four feet long, enough to drape to the floor in church, from Baby's place in its mother's arms. I could not wait to see it on the new child, boy or girl. The finished gown lay in clean white paper when Aunt Rebecca took to her bed and Doctor came.

But her labor was long, and the infant was not hale, and by the fourth day of his life, I helped clothe the nameless boy in his christening dress just once, for all eternity.

• • •

The Dutch Reformed Church in Newburgh, with its white columns and wide doorways, sat just blocks up from my uncle's home, on the hill where you could see out across Hudson's River to the town of Beacon. I often saw steam ferries chugging upriver and down, floats of cattle or sheep, and the white sails of boats that preferred to try the wind and shifting tide. On occasion I took a message to invite the Reverend Dr. Van Horn to supper, or to deliver loaves of bread and hard cheese for the poor; we went on Sundays to the long service. The Greenleafs had been with the Dutch church since they left Nantucket Island behind.

A well-to-do family from the countryside owned a private pew not far from the Greenleafs' row near the front. I saw their name in the register, heard it spoken in greeting: *Lozier*, a foreign sounding name, with that letter Z scratched downward, curving upward in ink, a pleasant buzz in my mouth when I whispered it to myself. The handsome wife, the jolly-looking husband, and so many young daughters I couldn't keep count, four, five, and another baby on the mother's arm? There was a boy, older than I but not too grown, Abram, they said. Abram Lozier.

He wore a brown hat and even at eighteen bore a shadow on his cheeks, shaven clean for churchgoing, but later, he grew a rich dark beard. Abram was a solid name, a forefather's name reaching back to Bible times, and his family had farmed in Orange County well before General Washington of Virginia quartered in Newburgh. I watched Abram's back, his passing shoulder, but lowered my eyes when he turned. The Sunday glimpse was enough to dream of for six days and nights. First the Z caught my eye, then the dark forelock, deep blue eyes fringed with black lashes looking back in weighted silence, and I wished to be walked home, to be asked to an apple bee, a frolic.

My aunt was not well after the baby died, and she did not see visitors, staying in her own dark parlor with curtains drawn and shutters pulled, rocking in a chair by her fire for hours. She seemed old before her time, no longer the cheerful aunt I had met just a year before; she often gave no answer at all when I spoke. Her illness meant I had more work with the children, and less time sewing or walking in town. One spring afternoon, however, Uncle Daniel told Scotch Nola to watch the children and sent me to his attorney, Mr. Charles Montgomery, with papers inside a leather folder. Relieved to get shut of the dispirited house and my sorrowing aunt, I put on my bonnet and walked briskly in May sunshine to Montgomery Street, where the attorney kept his offices. I had never noticed before that the street and the lawyer bore the same name. He must be influential, or rich, I mused.

At the front steps I passed two pretty ladies wearing new summer dresses; one carried a matching parasol with tiny jingle bells attached to each point. The ladies were so bright and fashionable, and my mind was full of their delightful ensembles when I rapped at the door to see *Chas. E. Montgomery, Esq., Attorney at Law*. A young clerk in a stiff collar opened the heavy oaken door and showed me to a bench by the attorney's private office. I was not important, just a nobody delivering a paper, but soon the inner office door opened and the great man himself appeared. I recognized him from town, from occasions on the square, when I saw him—his silk waistcoat was a glossy green tartan, and his wavy dark hair, parted on the side, drawn across his forehead, gave him a foppish look. His gray eyes seemed very pale in his tanned face.

"Well, well." He looked down at me. "And who are you?"

"Martha Seybolt, sir. My Uncle Greenleaf sent this for you." I stepped forward to hand the folder to him.

He received it and flicked a glance into the folder, set it back on his table. He sat down on the edge of his table in a very casual manner and swung his leg like a country boy.

"Greenleaf's girl, yes. Enchanted to meet you at last." His voice was smooth as a minister's and he looked right into my eyes as if raking my soul. He took my hand as if to shake it, but he was very close and I was not used to shaking hands with gentlemen, or even ladies. He brought up my hand as if to kiss it, as I had heard that foreign gentlemen sometimes do, and instead he nibbled the ends of my fingers.

I pulled away, more than startled. "My—!" His dangling foot lifted, and he was raising my skirt. I stepped back and swished my skirt straight. "Goodness!"

"I beg your pardon, my mistake." His eyes were laughing. "You are older than I imagined."

I didn't know how to respond.

"How old are you, my dear?"

"I'm sixteen, sir." I felt certain that gentlemen shouldn't ask that question of a young lady, but I was just the errand girl, a forgettable niece, and perhaps a gentleman could ask me whatever he would. How was I to know? Who would have told me?

"All of sixteen. Quite the young lady, aren't we?" His way of speaking poked and prodded me for weakness. He twisted words to mean more than one thing.

"Yes, sir." Or was the correct answer no? I didn't like the way he looked at me. It made me feel small—like a rabbit, frozen in fear.

"Fancy that. Miss Martha Seybolt, sixteen years of age. Would you care to stay and have a cup of tea with an old bachelor attorney, just the two of us?" He stretched out his hand as if to take mine again. "I'd like to make your acquaintance, my dear."

"No, thank you, sir. I must be going." I backed away, my hands behind me.

"Another time, my dear. Regards to your aunt and uncle."

I passed through the heavy door and down the steps, confused and abashed. I made my way back to the house without daydreaming of Abram or dresses, only thinking that Mr. Montgomery was a strange man, who could say the wrong word to my uncle or aunt and cause trouble. What was I to make of his behavior—he'd nibbled my fingers, flipped up my skirt, invited me to a private tea? Who would believe that? I must have misunderstood. I rubbed my hand on my skirt as if to clean his nibbling away and walked faster home.

Uncle Daniel was short-tempered, Aunt Rebecca had been weeping, and Nola had supper to cook. She handed Helen back to me, snappish. "Took yer time, girl."

But my fortune was cast. Mr. Montgomery had caught my scent like a bloodhound. The attorney nodded to me in town now and joined us at luncheon or tea after supper at my uncle's house. I served custard and cake, handed around cups of coffee to my uncle's guests, while the man found ways to confound me. He dropped his napkin or his spoon before me, then pretending to pick it up from the floor, ran his hand up under my skirt. I spun away, cups rattling in my hands, and backed off, embarrassed at everyone's attention to my clumsiness. Uncle Daniel gave me a sharp look.

Aunt Rebecca called me in to her parlor soon after. She had the lamp lit despite summer afternoon light, and the curtains just barely opened. "Mr. Greenleaf says I must speak to you about your deportment." I stood on the carpet before her, my hands clasped to stop them shaking. I didn't know if I could tell her how I felt: a mouse between a cat's paws.

"You are a young lady now and you must act like one. No silly games. I don't want to hear of you acting foolishly before my husband's guests. Mr. Montgomery is an important friend, and your uncle says you have been flirting with him, sashaying your skirts when passing, and causing a disturbance when serving. Martha, if you cannot behave yourself, you are no help to us."

"No, ma'am." I could hide my face in my hands if lovely Aunt Rebecca believed this of me. But I did not know how to answer a man's unwanted attention.

"Mr. Montgomery said you visited his office and wanted to take tea with him—alone! He is much too old for you! I think it is best you don't deliver messages anymore. Stay here and help me. You know I need your help, don't you, dear?"

"Yes, ma'am. I beg your pardon." But I felt crushed that Aunt Rebecca thought me capable of such behavior—or that I admired the man. And I had lost my moment to speak up, to say that Montgomery was bothering me. My words would only be defensive now.

She kept me busy at home, and Uncle sent me no more to errand for him. I sang nursery rhymes with Johnny and played with Helen on a quilt under the trees in soft summer warmth. I still saw the Loziers at church, but my daydreams were confused; what if all men acted thusly with women? I kept my gaze on the ground, afraid to encourage anyone without meaning to. Abram at last asked to walk me home from church, and, with a glance at Aunt Rebecca, Uncle said he might.

Our first walk together was all but silent down the hill with Aunt and Uncle chatting behind us, then the turn up Grand Street toward the townhouse. Abram's shirt was well-made, but I would have sewn the buttons closer together down the front and chosen a color for his cravat other than that dull brown. He would look a fashion plate in *Godey's* with a blue ascot. I was too shy to speak now that my girlish daydream was walking alongside me. When we came to cross the street, which was wide with potholes and puddles, he offered his arm and I took it, feeling the knot of his muscle beneath the cloth of his coat. I knew I wouldn't fall if I held onto that arm. At the dooryard he held open the gate for me and waited until my uncle and aunt had also passed through. I watched this gesture of civility with an almost bodiless feeling of watching from above.

Abram touched his brown hat. He nodded towards my guardians, and then looked into my face with such eyes, such a direct gaze, that I couldn't keep it. I felt a shiver, recalling the same kind of keen glance from Mr. Montgomery.

"Good day, Miss Seybolt." He turned and walked out the gate.

"Goodbye," I said to his retreating back. He wouldn't ask me, a silent, shivering ninny, again.

• • •

Montgomery, however, did not walk away. He shadowed me in plain sight, acting the benevolent friend of the family; Uncle Daniel and Aunt Rebecca thought him charming and so attentive, and did not see his effect. It would be awkward and embarrassing to react to him with anything other than a polite answer or smile. But he haunted me. Anticipating his appearance at our house or in town made me so anxious that my hands trembled. A rash bloomed on my inner elbows and behind my knees when he was due to arrive. My hands shook as I poured the tea or coffee, and I became paralyzed under his eye, that roaming gaze that feasted on my body. When he could, he'd nudge or bump by accident, and when he couldn't, I felt the pinpoint of his attention. I longed for him to go away, but eminent citizens cannot be ignored, and I was forced to be polite and shake his hand many times, my innards quaking, my skin bright with rash.

After one Sunday supper I went outside in the bright starlit night, pegging damp dishcloths to the line, glad to be out of the room where he laughed and chatted with Uncle. The dooryard was dim, and suddenly Mr. Montgomery was behind me, his arm around my chest, his hand cupping my bosom, his bare member in his hand, pressing it into my hand, pushing it into my hip. It was a hard thing, not the soft curl of flesh like a child's; I smelt his tobacco breath whispering, "Not a word, my dear. Just hold that, there, and I won't tell your uncle about you." He ground into my hand, crushing my chest with his other arm, pinching my teat. I tried to cry out but he jerked me tighter toward him; I could do nothing but sob as he did this thing in my hand, pulling away with a gasp and shudder, and then he released me, blotting his brow and his hands with a handkerchief. I staggered away, choking through tears, and ran toward the kitchen door. He caught my arm in a painful vise.

"Not a word, or I'll tell him you aroused me." I jerked away, and stumbled indoors, holding myself in the dim, cool passageway between the woodshed and the kitchen.

Who would believe me? How would I even explain what happened—a young girl loitering behind the house in the dark, where the men went to the privy? If Mr. Montgomery told his version—I was sick to think what could happen. I had no other home. Nola found me in the back stoop, sobbing into a rough towel. She saw my stained dress and got a wet cloth to clean the spot. She didn't even ask, just made me a cup of very sugary hot tea and sent me up the back stairs. "Go on, girl, I'll tell 'em ye had headache. Try to forget it."

I lay in the dark weeping quietly into my pillow, his tobacco breath and his shuddering member haunting my sleep.

Why did I not speak to my uncle? Because Uncle Daniel didn't see me as a person; he saw only his foolish sister Mary's offspring, a household helper, not a girl needing protection. He thought his attorney friend a fine fellow; they enjoyed their brandy and cigars and talking of business and politics late into the night. If I said anything against Mr. Montgomery, Esquire, I would be opening a creel of hooks. Aunt Rebecca was weak and needed help, and so did the children, but if I were tainted by scandal, they'd have me out of the house quicker than a trap snares a rabbit. And my aunt was so melancholy that I dare not bother her with my troubles.

Nola saw me, though. "Will ye help in the kitchen," she'd say as if asking, when in fact she was offering escape from those pale eyes, his unwanted attention. Instead of taking the dishcloths out at night and risking a meeting by the woodshed, we did them in the morning. She accompanied me to the privy if he were visiting. She stood with me when she could, to bring out the cakes or carry cups into a dining room of men, standing between us when he ventured near.

One crisp autumn evening, Uncle Daniel brought his gentlemen acquaintances home for conversation after hearing a political speech about the upcoming presidential election. The men were full of opinions and objections to both Mr. James Polk and Mr. Henry Clay. Nola and I served cakes while

Uncle brought out his decanters. Aunt Rebecca stayed in her upstairs parlor. Mr. Lozier and Abram had come this time, but so had Mr. Montgomery. We set the platters of cakes on the sideboard, then Nola and I retreated to the kitchen. She stirred her soup and prepared the children's supper of bread and warm milk in Aunt's pretty dishes. I set a tray with the bowls, silver spoons and extra cloths, and took it upstairs to her parlor, where she was sitting with the children.

"I'm ready to feed them, Aunt."

"No, my dear. I'm feeling better just now. I'll feed them supper and put them to bed tonight, and you may go. I hear that young Mr. Lozier has come. Perhaps you'd like to stay down and visit with him." She gave me a wan smile, one that almost rose to her eyes. "Go be a good hostess."

"Thank you, Aunt Rebecca." I could not enjoy myself with my tormenter in the front parlor, but she didn't know that. I slipped down the back stairs toward the kitchen, and almost bumped into someone in the unlit passage.

"Where are you going, my little ghost?" Mr. Montgomery quickly snared my hands together in one of his, tight as a manacle. "Are you sneaking out to see your lover? He's still in the parlor, so perhaps you have another young man waiting by the woodshed?"

"I'm going to the kitchen."

He leaned in against me and whispered into my hair. "Why the hurry? No need to run away." He sniffed at my hair like a hound.

"Please let me go." His grip tightened. "You're hurting me," I said through burning tears. "Please."

"Yes, please. Let her go." Abram Lozier stood right behind Mr. Montgomery, his voice low and hot as a red-tipped poker.

Mr. Montgomery released my hands. "Eh. This little cat was asking for cream," he said. "She's a spitfire, boy. Don't know if you could handle her."

I ducked under his grasp.

"Don't you ever speak of Daniel Greenleaf's niece that way, or I'll see you're sorry." Abram, eyes blazing, jerked his head toward the front parlor. "Get back to that meeting now. And I ain't your boy."

The attorney started to reply, but instead smoothed his hair. "Enjoy this little piece. She's plenty of good time."

Abram lunged at Montgomery as if to punch with a fist hardened by work, and Montgomery startled back into the wall with a thump, alarm showing on his sharp face. Abram pulled his blow at the last second, leaving the attorney to straighten his cravat and back away, scuttling toward the parlor door.

"Miss Seybolt, are you hurt? Did he injure you?"

I still stood, quivering, teary, and astounded that someone had stood up for me. Not just someone—Abram. "I'm—fine." I reached for my handkerchief, but Abram had his out first. I tried to think of a plausible reason that Montgomery would talk so cheaply of me in the hall, or anywhere, without me saying what else had happened.

"You're *not* fine. You're frightened as a hare. What did he do to you?"

I couldn't forestall him; in one mad moment, I broke down. "He's been—bothering me," I said in a low voice. "He's an important man. My uncle's friend." I swallowed. "I don't like him. But he won't leave me be."

His dark blue eyes grew steely, his jaw set. "He will from now on. Leave it to me." He smiled down at me gently. "Trust me, Martha. Don't you worry."

I felt, for the first time in ages, that someone would take care and I *could* stop worrying. That I could, perhaps, sleep without fear, and that my tormentor—that monster—would go away. "I thank you, Mr. Lozier." I had never meant it so deeply in my life.

"My friends call me Bram."

"Bram."

He nodded. "Martha."

We were wed some three months later, on a cold, bright January forenoon in the year 1845. And I saw Montgomery but rarely in the years thereafter.

Chapter 2

Newburgh, New York
October 1859

Work was a poultice to my wounds. Now, without Bram to oversee it, the hog-butchering took place at the big house, and all the flurry was over there instead of in my kitchen. I did my part, and at night, folded letters to Mama, my grown sisters, my uncles and the Seybolt cousins over to Otisville. If I kept busy enough, I could keep my grief tucked up a sleeve, in my pocket, balled up like a child's wilted handkerchief. Worry, instead, pushed grief to the side of the fire, and came to a boil.

Bram, as the eldest son, had expected to inherit and manage the farmlands and the family as Malcolm slowed into age. With two sisters already married, unless the last two married, we'd care for them and my mother-in-law just the same; no one was a burden. But now, brother Jesse at seventeen was still too young to take over our little house without a wife of his own. Jesse and my Ira—if he left school now—would henceforth butcher the hogs, thresh the wheat, run the sheep. Ira chopped wood and could plow a straight furrow by his ninth birthday. George and Homer would grow into strong men, Lord willing. But now instead of inheriting, my three boys would be no more than helpers on the land, would have to find their own places in the world.

And what of me? What could a widow offer her husband's family, already full of womenfolk? And Sarah's place in the family? Instead of landed family, my children were half-orphaned, and we were all dependent on Malcolm for whatever came next. That made me and my brood the burdens.

I worried on, knitting new socks for George, with red yarn so we could find them when cast off around the house. Without a grown man to farm Bram's portion and his own, Malcolm must hire new hands, and probably house them in our little home. Which meant we'd perhaps move to the big house, live under Charlotte's reign. I don't complain of her treatment: Charlotte was always correct with me, but never warm; she thought me a nobody, not a true Lozier. She spoiled her girls, preferring a servant or two, keeping her daughters' hands white and soft. Perhaps my Sarah would be absorbed into that sphere, and I won't say I liked it, but having her treated like a servant would be worse. Once again, I felt stuck between two worlds, neither fish nor fowl. I couldn't be certain which way the clock's pendulum would swing. I would help in the big house, as I always did, but I feared to become their maid of all work, a Cinderella—what a shame to have become this hanger-on again. No one would put us out, but keep us in our familiar little house? Unlikely.

I must speak to Malcolm alone and see what was to become of us. I left the stew hanging on the crane over the fire.

"Sarah, I'm walking to the big house to speak with Grandpapa. Stir the stew, and mind the baby and the boys, please." I ran my hand down her fine gold hair, tight in its mid-back braids. Her hair looked even brighter against the black of her newly dyed dress.

"Yes, Mama. Homie, come to Sarah." She tried to get Homer to stand but he wasn't ready to walk just yet. She sat on the quilt with him and chanted, "Ring around a rosie…"

George was settled his corner where he liked to sit on an old bit of cowhide and play with his stick people, although I say *play* as a catch-all for George's pastime. Bram had whittled a brown man from walnut wood and a red one from a stick of maple; George clacked these together for noise as he played in the corner. He brought in plain sticks from the kindling pile to round out his armies, laying them in rows, picking them up, laying and arranging them with the tiniest touches to be perfectly aligned. George hadn't talked at the age when my other babies babbled. He could still scream the house down, though he was six already, and we had yet to hear conversation from him. He had not gone to school, unwilling to leave his corner without a tantrum. The boy lived in his own little world, one that relied on most things coursing the same, every day. Jenny, the kitchen maid at the big house, called him a fae boy.

I talked to him anyway, knowing he wouldn't respond in words. "Georgie, Mama's taking a walk to Grandpapa's. Listen to Ira, now." Ira was most able to wheedle his brother into doing what we wanted. George rocked a little on his round breech and aligned his sticks.

I wrapped myself in my coat and black woolen shawl and went out from the warm kitchen into the autumn wind. Ira was at the woodpile, chopping enough kindling for morning. The axe was still large in his boyish hands. He shook his hair out of his eyes and paused. "Where you going, Mama?"

"The big house. To speak with Grandpapa."

"About the house." His face, pink from exertion, looked both babyish and ancient at once, caught in mute grief. "We have to move out, don't we?"

My heart hurt, knowing how much he saw what went on, and how he wanted to step into his father's place. He was still just twelve.

"I don't know, son. It's up to Grandpapa. He's your guardian now, so we'll do what he says." I tucked the ends of my shawl a little deeper under my coat, blocking the icy knife of air that had slipped in. "I may be a while. Go in and help George eat supper if I'm late?"

He would. Ira swung the axe again and the *thunk thunk* of his effort followed me through the barnyard and across the first field toward the woods. The big house was a ten-minute walk from the little house. Rain hadn't fallen for some days. In late October, the leaves of the woods had browned or gone, their glorious golds and russets fallen to earth in a rustling carpet for my feet. I recognized the crunch beneath my laced boots, a childish pleasure remembered for an instant, then tucked away again like a strand of windblown hair. Wood smoke hung in the air, and I heard the *chip chip chip* of the cardinal before I caught his red flash in the canopy.

Malcolm and Charlotte Lozier lived in the big house with its Dutch barn, standing strong at the top of a rise since before the War for Independence. Their house was older than the barn, built from the bluestone of the Hudson River Valley by Malcolm's Huguenot forebear Le Sueur and his Dutch wife. At some prosperous point the Loziers had added another story to the house, and then more rooms, and the different shades of bluestone, outlined by the additions, stood out clearly from both east and west ends, as if the larger house had swallowed the smaller one. The grand front door, freshly painted blue, held its place in the center of the south side, its black hinges and handle shining like polished boot leather.

I went to the kitchen door and let myself in. Charlotte, wearing black like me, stood speaking to the kitchen girl about supper and saw me enter.

"Goodness, Martha. You should have used the front door. We're not country bumpkins here." She dusted her hands off as if they were floury, but of course her hands were clean and smooth. "Supper at half past six o'clock, Jenny. No later." She glanced at me. "Come along. No need to stay in here."

I saw Jenny take a deep breath as Charlotte turned away and I met the girl's eye. She raised her eyebrows at me. Charlotte went through the door ahead of me. I closed it behind and followed her to the hallway. A large brass cage stood on a stand in the corner of the room holding an aged green parrot with a yellow head named Sandy that Malcolm had brought to his wife when Bram was a child. The bird watched with a gimlet eye as we came through.

"Take off your coat, for mercy's sake." Charlotte's commands, though they were not quite rude, always felt like a reprimand. I dutifully hung my coat and shawl on the ornate hat stand in the hall. "Did you come with a purpose, or were you out strolling the woods by yourself of an evening?" Before I could answer, she walked into the parlor where her two daughters sat with sketchbook and tambour frame, approved before-supper activities. "Girls, your sister Martha is here."

Emily, fourteen, dropped her sketchbook and rushed to hug me, tears spilling down her cheeks. "Oh, sister Martha, what are we going to do without Abram? I miss my brother!"

Mariah, seventeen, tucked her needle into the frame and pulled a handkerchief from her sleeve. "Emily, for pity's sake, don't be so theatrical. Martha has lost a husband and that's worse than losing a brother, however hard it is for us."

"But not as hard as for Mama." Emily turned back, hands on her hips. "Mama misses him more than anyone!"

Charlotte pressed her hand to her bosom and cried out. "Girls! Please!" she sank into her cushioned chair and covered her face with her hands. Emily hovered over her mother and stroked her back.

"Don't cry, Mama."

"Don't cry, Mama," the parrot called from its perch.

I wanted to run back out to the cold, dark woods where I could feel my heart beating, feel Bram within me, instead of watching this mincing scene. Everyone had sorrow, but whose was the deepest? What did it matter? These women still had a home, a future. I fisted my hands in desperation, but forced myself to remain calm.

"I must speak with my father-in-law—is he in his study?"

Charlotte didn't answer, although she wasn't crying. She just sat with her face in her hands, with Emily, tears running freely, seated on the arm of the chair.

"He was there a while ago." Mariah answered me. "Writing letters."

"Please excuse me, Mother Lozier." I walked up the hall to the passageway where Malcolm kept his study, away from the chirpings of his wife and daughters and sometimes the bird. My low boots sounded loud on the shining floorboards as I passed years of crewel- and silk-floss samplers made by the many Lozier daughters, framed and hanging on the papered walls.

Malcolm's door stood open, the man himself seated at the walnut-wood desk, its pigeonholes stuffed with letters and bills. The study held his books, his farm records, newspapers from New York and London. Malcolm, telltale ink-stains on his right fingers, looked up as I stopped in the door frame. A Delft pen-and-inkstand, inherited down the years, took pride of place before him; little blue figures on its side went mutely to their work, dancing with palm fronds or poling a barge.

"My dear." He set down his pen and stood to greet me. "I've been writing to my cousins up Saratoga way—about Abram."

"Good evening, Father-in-Law."

On the creamy plastered wall hung an oil painting of the farmstead Malcolm had commissioned from an itinerant artist some years before. The landscape showed a cluster of sheep with a small shepherd, who we agreed was Jesse, apple trees in fruit, and a man seated on a wagon, wearing a brown hat. That was Bram, but the face was a mere pink smudge, the hands a smaller pair of dots, nothing more than a hat on a scarecrow instead of the man I loved. At least it was a likeness. I wished I had a miniature of him, never thinking to want one before.

"Everything in good form at the little house? Children managing all right without—" He didn't finish the sentence. How could any of us be all right without Bram? He cleared his throat, an embarrassed cough. "Do sit, please."

I closed his door and took the straight chair near him. "Father-in-law, may I speak plainly?"

"Please do, child. You know I like things straight and true." He smiled without light in his eyes, revealing his own unspent sorrow.

"What shall we do, the children and I? How shall we—" My voice thinned and caught in my throat. I swallowed. Balled the knot a little tighter. "Forgive me—I can cook and sew for the field hands—make myself useful. But the children." I left it unasked.

"My dear." Malcolm reached over and laid his hand upon mine, his brown eyes sad. "Please do not exercise yourself about the welfare of the children. Abram ever had but one request of me, that I care for his family. I will pay for their education and clothing, until Sarah is married and the boys are of age. And you will always have a place with us, never fear."

But I did fear.

"Shall we stay on the farm, or move into town, give up the little house?" Malcolm owned a small townhouse he sometimes rented out, down near Water Street. Perhaps we could avoid sharing the big house with Charlotte that way. It was a straw to grasp at.

"Oh, no, too damp, near the river." He coughed again. He patted his chest as if to say, *this is why*. "Much too damp."

"Of course."

"I think it might be best if you moved up here. You can have the little boys with you, upstairs in Nella's room. Ira can go in with Jesse, and Sarah can share Emily's room. Perhaps next year we shall send Sarah with Emily to the Albany Female Academy—wouldn't you like that for her? Ira must go back to town school to master his figures."

"He needs that," I agreed, but silently bemoaned the change in household. "Sarah longs for her education." At least she would have it, whatever the cost to me personally.

"The land, of course, all of the farm, should be Abram's, but now Jesse will have it." Malcolm sighed, rueful. "I'll put something aside for Ira—some land if I can get it at good value. I'd like to do better by my grandies. I'm better able to afford such now than I was for Abram when he was young. I must sit with Montgomery and remake my will."

I stiffened when Montgomery's name passed his lips.

Malcolm *tsked* at me. "Why do you harbor such dislike of him? He has never spoken ill of you. Charles Montgomery is a generous donor to the almshouse and to the churches, even to those he doesn't attend. His grandsire was a Patriot!" He huffed. "Such a man is an ally. You don't know him as a gentleman, as I do, that is your trouble."

I could not agree, nor could I argue. My family's fate was in Malcolm's hands. "Pardon me, Father-in-Law. I shall try to like him better." I should not try, but if it pleased Malcolm to hear it, I would keep peace.

"That is all I ask. Now, toward the other boys."

"George and Homer."

"My dear." Malcolm rubbed his inky fingertips together, but the stains remained. "I think we all know that George has no such future. He has his brother's face but not his brain. We'll keep young George on the farm and he'll turn out well enough, I'm sure. A strong worker, that's what we'll make him. The babe is too young for me to see his future. You keep him at your bosom until he's in knee breeches, and we'll make a Lozier out of him."

Malcolm got up to mend the fire. "Are you satisfied, my dear? No need to fret. Your husband and his old father have taken care of you." He coughed again. "Blast this catarrh!"

"Let me stir a hot brandy for you." I went to the sideboard for the glass decanter. "It won't take a moment."

"That is just what I need." He smiled and sat back into his chair to pick up the pen again. "You're a good girl, Martha."

"I thank you, sir. For everything."

• • •

Too soon I was writing to my mother again.

October 28, 1859

My dear Mama,

I am writing with the sad news of the passing of my dear Father-in-Law, Mr. Malcolm Lozier. We had but returned to our home grieving the loss of my beloved husband when my Father-in-Law became ill with a sick fever and Doctor said it was turned to pneumonia. Being that the illness took him too soon from our lives I am at present at a loss; my Father-in-Law was intended to be the children's Guardian had he lived. Now I know from my young Brother-in-Law Mr. Jesse Lozier that the children are to be placed under Guardianship of Mr. Chas. Montgomery, Esquire, Attorney at Law in Newburgh town, N. Y.

I ask leave to come to you for a visit of some weeks or longer if we may; for my widowed Mother-in-Law Mrs. Malcolm Lozier is prostrate with sorrow and unable to assist us. My Brother-in-Law Jesse being too young to support us as well as his sisters and Mother, and having no direction on how we are to live, I ask that we may visit and I speak with my Step-Father your good Husband for his counsel.

Your loving daughter,
Martha Seybolt Lozier

I felt as if lost in one of our Northern blizzards. I could barely stand the death of my husband and the attendant difficulties that presented, but without Malcolm, there was no safe haven at all. The Rev. Dr. Van Horn came to the big house daily to condole with Charlotte and the girls, who truly were lost souls, and poor Jesse, a lad who had only just begun to shave his chin, was to be their support. I knew Malcolm had written a new will, and I knew there was something in it for the children, but I had not expected that Mr. Montgomery, a jack-in-a-box springing out with a fearful grin, would pop back into my life again so plainly.

The married Lozier girls and their husbands arrived and filled beds; we took the bachelor cousins from upstate into our little house. Malcolm was an important man in Newburgh, and his funeral was well attended by the gentlemen of the town. It was written up in the *Newburgh Gazette* and the *Telegraph*, even published as far away as the *Albany Evening Journal*. I kept to the big house kitchen, rolling out doughnuts and kneading bread alongside Jenny, who kept kettles of water on the boil for more coffee, more tea. The first snow had fallen and travelers were cold and hungry. We had a turkey in the bake-oven and a pork roast on the spit for the evening meal. The grave had been dug despite cold weather; the morrow would bring the burial, for menfolk only. Charlotte had decreed that the women would stay away, it so upset her to face Malcolm's death. Back at the big house, a formal reading of the will would follow, by Mr. Montgomery himself, and I was not ready to see his smirking face.

"We must get a good night's sleep before tomorrow," I made excuse, and instead of the long table and all the family feasting mournfully, I dusted and dried my hands, wrapped myself warmly, and took out through the woods with the whale oil lamp and Ira. The bachelor cousins could follow when they wished. Tomorrow, Jenny's sister Orla would come to stay with the little boys while Ira, Sarah and I went to hear the will, and our futures, read. Tonight, while we still could, I wanted to savor the safe little house I'd shared with Bram, the home we had made together.

I did a baking of gingernuts to take along in the morning, filling the house with the comforting smells of nutmeg and ginger. George loved to eat gingernuts, nibbling like a chipmunk on as many as I would give him, and I couldn't help but indulge him. I didn't have the strength to deny them just now, as we mourned. Discipline would come, and order, when we learned our new path on the morrow.

Ira and George slept together in their straw-tick up in the loft as usual, and so had Sarah before now, with a slatted partition between them. But Sarah was in my bed with me and Homer, while the cousins had the trundle by the fire, and Sarah's tick upstairs.

"Mama." She spoke softly over Homer's sleeping head. "Why is Mr. Montgomery our new guardian? What does that mean?"

"It means he makes decisions about your money, if you had any, where you might go to school, and if you could marry if you weren't eighteen. Lawyers often take on this role for half-orphans." I kept my tone very practical. "He's your Uncle Jesse's guardian for another year, and also your aunts Emily and Mariah. That's what Grandpapa wanted in his will, and we have to do what the will says."

"It seems peculiar that a—well, a dead person can tell people what to do, and then a stranger would have power over our choices." Her voice, near to my ear in the dark of the bedroom, voiced my private opinion particularly well.

"It does seem peculiar, but that is the law. I think Grandpapa had hoped to live a long time, and he made these plans just in case. He never thought he would leave so many young folks behind." That much I knew was true. My voice quavered, however. I felt desolate in the bedroom darkness.

"Mama."

"Yes, daughter?"

"Are you afraid? Of what the will might say, about where we shall live?"

Oh, this perceptive girl. I pulled myself together. "Afraid? I try not to be. But concerned, yes. I love our little house and have loved it for fifteen years. I don't want to move any more than you do. Let's see what happens tomorrow and try to face it with courage and a cheerful heart." Courageous words, anyway. I was quite afraid.

Sarah reached out and stroked my arm. "You're so brave, Mama. I hope I will be as brave as you."

"Pishhh, daughter. We'll all be brave together."

"Mama?"

"We must go to sleep, love. Goodnight."

"One more thing, please? May I wear my braids pinned up tomorrow? I want to look grown-up when we go to the meeting. My life is about to change."

"Yes, daughter. I will be glad to pin your hair before we go—if you haven't changed your mind by then. Now, please, to sleep."

• • •

In the morning jolly Irish Orla arrived at sunup, to take over breakfast for the little boys. I had already cooked for the bachelor cousins and they were gone ahead to care for their horses. Sarah, Ira and I drank our tea and ate our fried ham and potatoes while Orla stirred up a pot of oat porridge for the little boys. I had nursed Homer early but left him still sleeping to her care. I pinned Sarah's two braids across her head, leaving the nape of her slender neck white and exposed. We bundled into coats and scarves and caps and walked through the woods toward our destiny.

Ira put his thumbs together and tried to whistle on a dry grass blade, and shied tiny hemlock cones at Sarah until I made him stop.

"I'm an excellent shot," he boasted. "Uncle Jesse is going to give me his squirrel rifle when he gets a new one, and I'm going to shoot game for our supper pot." Once he got going on rifles, he turned the topic to soldiers and cavalry, and that could go on for an hour. "I'll sling it over my shoulder like a real soldier."

"I'll crochet a nice sling for you," Sarah promised.

Ira laughed and laughed. "I don't want no crochet holster. It has to be rawhide, or leathern, something rough. Can you see me heading off to war with my rifle in a crocheted bag? They'll shoot me at sunrise!" He slapped his knee. "Wait 'til I tell Jesse."

"*Uncle* Jesse, and there's not going to be another war." Sarah corrected her brother before I could get the words out. "The soldiers licked all the Indians, and the British are afraid of us now. And so are the French-Canadians," she added, showing off her schooling.

"Let's mind ourselves, both of you. This is a serious day, Grandpapa's burial. And the will. Squirrel guns and war can keep for another time."

I rapped at the kitchen door and handed my basket of gingernuts in to the hired daygirl, nodding a greeting to Jenny. The children and I walked around to the front of the house. I reminded them, taking them in hand, before we went into the big house. "No fiddling and laughing today. Pay attention and have your best manner, or I'll send you home with the babies." I dropped their hands and we entered the wide front doorway as a family.

The menfolk, including young Jesse, returned to the big house by wagon after the burial in the churchyard. The house, already busy, was soon full of tall hats, pipe and cigar smoke, the scent of boiled coffee and the rosemary-and-creosote scent of macassar pomade. Charlotte, in a high-necked gown of black moiré silk, sat in her chair in the parlor with a bevy of cousins and in-laws fanned around. The Lozier daughters held each other's hands and whispered, their eyes roving the room as if seeking out their next subject for gossip. Jenny wove her way into the room with a tray of little cakes and shortbreads, cheese fans and jam tarts, and left with several empty teacups and saucers.

Cousins from across Orange County and as far as Albany and New York City, Long Island and Scranton, had come to comfort their relatives, and perhaps see what crumbs might fall to them from Malcolm's last testament, which was rumored to be lengthy. Ira slipped away to stand with his Uncle Jesse, down the hallway where they could take shortbreads off the passing tray and show that they were ready to take on adult responsibility. Sarah was absorbed by her aunts and cousins, her golden head visible among the many brunettes in the room.

A bustle at the door announced the arrival of Mr. Montgomery, Esq., and his newest clerk, in dark clothing as befitted the occasion. No garish waistcoat this day, I noticed. Perhaps he had stopped being a skirt-chaser and a fop after all these years. I stayed as far away as I could, wary that he might approach from behind in his old way. I could not shake my fear of the man, even fifteen years later. Leopards don't change their spots, so they say. The room thickened with heat and voices, and I saw him down the hall speaking with Jesse and Ira. Ira stood straight and held out his hand to his new guardian for a proper handshake. I hated that my son must speak to him; that Ira was too young to have learned from his father what a man like Montgomery was, that my sons were the lawyer's wards now. Malcolm's will decreed it so.

Another fist rapped the door, and I opened it to allow the minister to enter after his cold ride from the churchyard.

"Such a brisk day. A blessing we had no snowfall upon us." The Rev. Van Horn shuddered out of his cloak. "How do you do, Widow Lozier?"

I took his coat, greeting him somberly, and remembered that I had unwillingly competed with Charlotte for the title of Mrs. Lozier, and now we were both Widows Lozier. How we were to share a single house, I did not know, and the very idea made me queer with dread just then. I ushered the minister into Charlotte's court and slipped back to the kitchen for a sip of cider, water, coffee, anything to quell my nerves and avoid Montgomery.

"How goes it, miss?" Jenny had her hands full preparing food for after the meeting, while her daygirl Elsie washed and dried dishes. "Yer wanting tea?"

"Perhaps some cider? I'm nervy as a cat today."

"Ye look it, green as a ghost," she said, pouring a tot of sack wine from a jug near her baking table into a tin measuring cup. "Sip this and it'll soothe yer tripes." She handed me the cup. "Just this once. Ye've had it rough, miss."

I am not a drinker of strong spirits, and ordinarily I would balk at the very idea. But I was not myself that day. I swallowed the two gulps of sack quickly. The liquid burned down my throat into my breadbasket. I wiped tears from my eyes, with a little gasp. I sat a moment and then shook myself. I felt a little surge of bravery course through me. "Gracious. I suppose I had better go back out."

"Good luck to ye, miss!" She was already stirring up her next receipt.

I squeezed through the hallway past Ira and Jesse and the bachelor cousins, past the cage where Sandy bobbed and preened, past the passageway toward Malcolm's study and into the second parlor, what Charlotte called the morning room. The room was bustling with relatives, but quieter than the front parlor. I didn't see Sarah in the front parlor, either, so I went down the other way and climbed the front stairs to the bedchambers. Sometimes Sarah went off with her young aunts, who were close in age; they had grown up together, as close as cousins, if not quite equal as sisters. Nella's door was open, as was Jesse's and Charlotte's, and Mariah's as well. The last door on the second floor was closed. I expected to find Sarah and Emily telling secrets and wanted to scold them that the day was not yet over. The reading of the will might start at any time.

I opened the spare chamber door to see Sarah perched on the canopied bed, her frightened face, her legs spread on either side of a man's body, whose face I could not see. Her high shoes and black stockings stuck out from under her black dress, all akimbo, but her white split pantaloons were clear to view, her sex shockingly revealed. I ran forward and jerked my Sarah's arm, pulling her sideways off the bed. She landed on the floor in a heap, sobbing into her hand.

Charles Montgomery turned, smoothing his hair across his forehead. "Well, here comes the cat. I was looking for you."

"What did you do to her? What did you do?" I sank with my arms around Sarah.

"I was merely telling her about the guardianship. You have a lovely daughter, Mrs.—ah, *Widow* Lozier."

"How dare you?" I spat in my anger, rising to face him. "You would never—if Malcolm were here! If Bram—he would kill you!"

"But that's just it. They aren't here. The children are under my protection, to do with what I wish." Montgomery flicked a glance at Sarah. "Poor little orphans."

"I'll call the sheriff, I'll—"

"There's nothing you can do." He all but licked his fingers. "The will is explicit. Your husband left you nothing, and Papa Lozier left me guardian of everything. You have nothing—except me, between you and the street."

I sank on weak knees to Sarah, but he grabbed my arm, pulling me near until I was right in his face. He sniffed deeply, as he used to do, a wolf at the door. "Why, Widow Lozier. Have you taken to drink?" He clicked his tongue. "As the guardian of your children, I have to see that they are safe from—." He sniffed me again. "—the bad influence." I jerked my arm away.

He pulled out his pocket watch. "Alas, it is time for the reading of the will. I shall see you when you have finished primping. And we shall talk again later. I've missed you, Martha. Cheerio!" He pulled the door closed behind him.

"Sarah—Sarah." I sank to the floor next to her again, my knees unable to hold me up.

"Mama!" She dove into my arms, sobbing. "Mama, is it true? Must I go live with him? Is it true?"

"Listen to me, Sarah. Did he get inside—your clothes? Let me look." She sobbed. I gently pulled up her skirt and looked beneath, expecting to see torn fabric or a bloody spot, but I saw nothing like that. So it would be only my word against Montgomery's if I called on the sheriff, and the Montgomery name was golden in

Newburgh town. I cursed myself for taking that sip of sack wine. He was slick as a serpent, and I was a quivering fool.

"Child, wait here a moment. I need to get Ira."

"Don't leave me alone!" She clawed at me.

"I'll just go down the back stairs. If anyone else tries to open this door, you scream as loud as you can, you hear?"

She nodded, all but hysterical already. I got to my feet and checked the mirror. Despite my inner havoc, I looked unchanged from when I arrived that morning. I passed through the door, pulling it closed quietly. There was no one in the hall but I could hear Montgomery's voice, charming them, talking over the buzz, calling the heirs to gather in the morning room, and the rest could wait in the parlor. Ira still stood in the back hall, looking for me.

"Ira. Go get our cloaks. Mine and Sarah's. Where's your coat? Get it."

"What's wrong?" He brought his voice low like mine.

"Sarah's ill. We have to take her home." He looked as if he might argue to stay, but I added, "I'll meet you at the kitchen door. Now!" He nodded one sharp nod and went for our coats. I sped back up the stairs and called her softly from outside the door, "Sarah, it's Mama." I opened the door and she had stopped crying and had wiped her eyes. Her hair was unpinned now, her two braids hanging like lank straw on her shoulders.

"Ira's getting our cloaks. I think it best we went home now."

We went quietly down the back stairs again, as the front of the house continued the scraping of chairs and men's and women's voices. Ira met us by the kitchen door and we put on our wraps. I opened the kitchen door to tell Jenny, "Sarah has taken ill. We're going home. I'll send Ira back with a message soon. Tell them," I nodded at the front of the house.

Jenny gave a sympathetic look but had no time to pause just then. "Yes, miss."

Ira and I took Sarah's arms and walked her, as if she couldn't walk herself, through the woods and back toward our little house. I shushed Ira's questions and told him we would speak later. When we got to the house, I sent Orla on her way with a five-cent piece and a loaf of new bread. George was in his corner playing and Homer, who was teething, gnawing on a knotted rag. I let Sarah lie in the bedroom and told her to howl as much as she wanted.

"Better to cry it out. I'm sorry. But please tell me—did he hurt you?"

She took a deep sobbing breath and let it out. "He forced me to open my legs and he pushed up against me. Am I going to have a baby now?"

Oh, my child. "No, you're not. You're a good girl. He's an evil man." My gut was roiling. "Sarah, when I was a girl, a little older than you, he did such things to me as well. I didn't do anything to encourage him."

"He said he wanted to talk to me privately about the guardianship and took me upstairs. He said I was his ward now. And before I knew it, he was over me—trying to—mate me." She started to sob again. She rubbed her arms and said, "He grabbed me, held so tight." Later, I saw the fingerprints, the purple thumbmarks he had left on her arms.

"He's a man who—he preys on helpless girls, with no protection. That's what he did to me—and he thinks he can do it to you, now that Grandpapa—he's a bad man." I wished I didn't have to explain it all to her. I wished she could have lived without ever knowing. "Women have to watch out for such men, Sarah, when we go into the world. You're a good girl," I said. "Rest now, while I think on what to do."

I stepped outside in the icy wind with Ira and explained to him what happened. "It's not safe for us here now. We can't put Sarah under his power. Even though it's the law." Another thought had occurred to me. What would Montgomery do about George? Would he leave him be or send him away? It would not stand.

Ira's jaw was tight, his teeth shut tight on a quiet anger, his eyes a dark fire, his father in miniature. "I'm going back there and tell him what I think of him." He looked around and saw the ax head half-buried in a chunk of oak. "I'll keep him off Sarah. I'll take care of Georgie. And you and Homer."

"No, son—we can't go near him. We have to plan—."

"We have to get away. We have to run away!" His eyes were fiercely blue, like his father's. "Where can we go?"

"I've been thinking, son. I'll need your help. I'll need you and Sarah to help me. It's the only way."

Late afternoon, the bachelor cousins returned to the house. They said we were missed at the reading of the will, that Montgomery was indeed the children's guardian. They betook themselves back to Saratoga; nothing in the will for them, so no reason to stay behind, it seemed. I waited all the day for Montgomery to knock at the door, while the old familiar rash prickled out of my skin behind my knees and inside my sleeves. Finally I sent Ira to the big house kitchen, to tell Jenny that Sarah had the grippe, avoiding the family entirely, and to play the innocent if he saw the family.

When he returned the daylight was gone and I had lit the lamp. "Jenny said Mr. Montgomery said that we're moving to Grandpapa's townhouse to be nearer to him. Grandmama thought that was a good idea. She said we should commence packing," Ira said, peeling off his icy muffler.

Of course she did.

"Where he can 'watch over us,' is what she said," Ira reported. "I told Jenny to tell them you would call on him at his chambers, when Sarah is feeling better."

"Well done, son." But we had no time to lose. In the privacy of our little house, I told Sarah what was to come. And while George played and hummed tunelessly to himself, and Homer banged wooden clothes pegs together, we made a plan that would, if all went well, save my children from Charles Montgomery's clutches, and keep us safe, and together, forever.

Chapter 3

New York City October 1859

How we managed to get ourselves down to the ferry in the dark for its first daily run to New York City that early morning, me carrying Homer and my carpetbag, I can't bear to recall. Ira held George's hand and in his other arm, a blanket roll, another bundle on his back; Sarah carried a tied-up bundle of clothes in a muslin sheet in both arms. We looked for all the world like a passel of bog Irish off a coffin ship. I would have said at least our faces were clean, but by the time we landed at the Albany & Troy Steam Line's wharf at almost the toe of New York City, we were as filthy as any other newly arrived family. Ahead of us rolled the mighty Atlantic Ocean, and all of Europe beyond, but I scarce had time to notice, as the sun was already low in the west and we scrambled to find a boarding house. I had but forty dollars and a handful of coins in my reticule; the journey had cost a whole dollar for the day's travel.

Hostels cost too much but we had to find a place to stay, to think what's next, somewhere I could get some sewing work and put the children back in school. A young Negro man drew with his finger in his hand the way to a rooming house and told me to ask for Mrs. Lander. It was the first time I had spoken with a Freeman. I gave him a penny for his help, and we dragged ourselves the few City blocks to said house. Mrs. Lander gave us a narrow room off a crowded hallway, with two stacked bunks we could share for ten cents a night. Meals for the family were another ten cents a day, and she served just morning and night.

George, who had stared like a ragdoll into space most of the day, eating mechanically and wetting himself, flew into a screaming fit when we finally got to our bunks. My fae boy liked his routine, and it had been nothing but strange disruptions all day. Neighboring boarders pounded the walls. It was all we could do to shush him, and out of desperation I gave him a piece of sugar I had tucked away from my kitchen. He sucked on it and fell asleep on the top bunk. I fed Homer until he, too, slept, then we put him in the corner of the bottom bed. Sarah and I sat on the edge and sighed. Ira leaned against the wall.

"Well, Mama," he said. "We made it."

I started to laugh, but also cried a little, so exhausted was I by then. "I don't know how."

"You changed our name." He and Sarah exchanged glances. "Are we still Loziers or are we all 'Seabolts' now?" I had changed Seybolt, my maiden name, to Seabolt, and it seemed to suit us. We had, indeed, bolted toward the sea.

"Seabolts, just for now, just to keep ourselves lost for a while," I said.

Sarah leaned against me and said, "May I wash my face? I can't bear being dirty as a schoolboy." A pitcher of water in its small basin stood on a little table with a lit candle; a chamber pot lurked under the lower bed.

"Use your handkerchief and do your best. Ira, you, too. I'm going down to ask for some bread and butter for the three of us tonight." I washed my hands and face and smoothed my hair, wishing for a glass or even my comb, I felt so frightful. My dress, being black, hid most of the grime. "I'll come back soon."

I passed other boarders behind doors, heard the front door closing, and somewhere in the house, the noise of a spoon scraping a pot and dishes clinking. I followed the sound through the entry hallway, where walnut cubbyholes for mail hung above a wide desk with a brass bell on its countertop. Through the dining room, empty of whomever had eaten supper, to the swing door to the kitchen, I rapped and pushed the door to. Inside, a Mulatto woman washed while Mrs. Lander wiped dry the plain white dishes.

"I beg your pardon, ma'am. Might I buy some bread and butter for our supper?"

Mrs. Lander wore a pink and cream cameo pinned to a froth of cheap lace at her breast and a long chain of keys that fastened to her waist. Her dress was stylish but severe, maroon and brown stripes but no adornment save the lace and the keys. Her still-dark hair was pulled back in a tight knot. She could have been forty or seventy; her unlined forehead told no tales, but the set of her mouth, prim and a little sour, did. "That's ten cents. Just this once. I don't like food in the rooms; it brings the rats. No crumbs, now." She said to the dishwasher, "Nancy, will you?"

Nancy dried her hands on her apron and cut several slices of bread, then scooped a knob of butter from the ball on a dish. She buttered the bread herself and piled the slices on a white plate for me. She pushed the plate toward me, flicking her eyes at me, then away.

"Much obliged, Nancy," I said.

Mrs. Lander held out her hand. "Keep that child quiet up there."

I dropped the two five-cent pieces into her cupped hand and retreated without argument. "Good night, Mrs. Lander."

Upstairs, we three shared the bread, every last crumb, and didn't spill. Ira climbed up the foot of the bunk to sleep with his brother, while Sarah and I tried to share at opposite ends. With a knot of worry under my ribs, unfamiliar City noises, the movement of unknown neighbors, and my hunger not really sated, I lay exhausted for a while before sleep. We were in the pickle, but at least we were safe. *We are safe,* the last thought in my head that night, and every night, if I could help it.

In the morning Sarah looked out at the City between calico curtains and called her brothers to see the many rooftops and black coal smoke hanging in the air. George awoke full of energy, bouncing; we left his shoes off, so at least he wouldn't thump. I sent Ira and Sarah first for their breakfast at the communal table and nursed Homer; they brought back bread and jam for George. I then hurriedly downed my black coffee and hashed potatoes as the long table was being cleared. The day looked gray and cold, but that kind of cloud wouldn't snow.

I wrapped Homer in a shawl and his red and white cap and mitts and took Ira with me that first day. Sarah stayed in the little room to play with George, although they had my permission to play in the hallway if George got too restless. He had his two wooden men, and she had her workbag, and George seemed content. We would be back before supper.

Ira took a turn holding his baby brother, resting my arms as we waited for the horse-drawn streetcar. It cost five cents to ride, but the conductor didn't charge for Ira. We headed uptown toward Harlem village, to find one of the new tenement buildings that would house us for less than we paid at Mrs. Lander's. Each City block showed me a different wonder—a bank building with white Grecian columns like those on the Dutch Reform Church in Newburgh; a bronze statue of President Washington with his wig and grim expression; a pushcart with fragrant meat and apple hand-pies, a Negro man selling oysters, a portly scissor-grinder. An old man in a brown apron pushed a broom on the sidewalk, while a spotted dog sniffed something foul in the gutter. Horses trotted past, as men in dark suits that had never seen country muck spoke in twos and threes on the sidewalks.

Ira had never seen a newsboy, but such a one held a *New York Advertiser* and called out, "Newspaper here! Get your weekly!" The boy's youthful voice was breaking into manhood's deeper tones, and he couldn't help how comical it sounded. His tweed cap was pulled down over his brows and his jacket and breeches were black with grime. His fingers were black, too, from the ink on his papers. His shoes were coming apart at the seams. I wanted to put him in a bath and scrub him, wash and sew up his torn clothes, and wondered where was his mama.

"Broome Street," the conductor sang out. "Bowery Street next." We alit and stepped over puddles to the cobbled sidewalk. The horsecar went on up the wide avenue. We looked both ways at street corners and, as other did, held an arm straight up when crossing so wagons and horses would see us, like City folk. Brick and marble buildings several stories tall blocked the wind, but when we came to a corner, that fierce east wind returned, slicing through as if we were unclothed.

Homer had fallen asleep on my shoulder and we had an hour or so before he wanted feeding, so we walked as briskly as we could. It helped keep us warm, too. "We're riding shanks' pony," Ira noted, "so Papa said."

"It will do us good to see the town and learn our way."

"I hope I see a soldier. A whole mess of soldiers!"

"A whole brigade of soldiers," I offered, to which my boy laughed.

"No, ma'am. That would be thousands. I'll be glad to see just two. They almost always travel by two, Grandpapa said."

"He would know. He fought back in the War of '12."

Ira took off chattering about wars and soldiers and particular skirmishes and what he would have done in Malcolm's place, which carried us to the first iron railings and festooned clotheslines on Mott Avenue. We looked for the telltale sign of "Rooms to Let" or "Tenancy," and tried our luck knocking at doors. One no, three noes, then another, and Homer awoke. My feet ached in my City shoes; I should have worn my lace-up boots instead of these pointed toes and heels. Homer bellowed.

"Let's sit here on the steps while I feed him." I tucked into the stoop of a house with my back to the wind, my shawl over Homer's head while the neighborhood rolled by. Another meat-pie handcart with a jangling bell rolled past and I dug pennies out of my reticule. "See what you can get for that, son. Something warm, perhaps?"

Ira palmed the coins and trotted down the sidewalk, while I crooned to Homer under my breath and he held my thumb in his dimpled hand. "You're a good boy, my dumpling." He struggled to sit up and burped. I rubbed his back and waited for Ira's return.

Soon enough my eldest trotted back with a hot mince pie cut in two pieces, all wrapped in newspaper. We ate that dry meat pie, feeding bits of potato and soft carrot to Homer, thinking of the pepper, gravy and a glass of milk that it needed. As we finished our picnic, we heard a drummer beating a cadence, and soon a platoon of some thirty-six United States soldiers in rows of four marched past. The drummer boy at the back could have been just Ira's age. We watched as they reached the next corner, precisely turning in a swift movement so that they rippled along like a caterpillar.

"My wish came true." Ira flashed a wide grin. "Did you see them?"

"Let's wish for a new home and see what comes?"

"We've had luck so far. Let's go. Back on the pony." He slapped his thigh.

"Shall we?" I held out my hand and Ira pulled me to my feet. Homer pointed at Ira, who clapped his brother's little hand.

"Let me take him a while, Mother."

I gave the bundle that was Homer to Ira, hiding a smile at the big boy's switch from *Mama* to *Mother* in a single hour. That which makes boys turn into men never ceased to amaze.

• • •

We got home hours later, exhausted, no luck with housing. We washed up and joined the household supper, folding extra bread and jam into a handkerchief for George's breakfast. Sarah had asked for bread and butter at noon, and Nancy had given it; the cost was added to our bill in the end.

We looked for rooms for three more days, farther and farther up toward Harlem, and closer to the East River. At last we found a small set of two furnished rooms for twelve dollars a month—an astronomical sum, it sounded—on the Friday that week. We all rode the horse-car uptown with our bundles on Saturday to Twenty Sixth Street, then walked to Third Avenue, where our new home staked the corner. Our place was on the third floor, so up we went. Ira led the way carrying two bundles. George climbed the steps like a dog on four limbs, sometimes barking; Sarah toted the satchel, and I carried my sturdy, heavy boy Homer. The hallway walls were papered but very dingy; soot from the gas lamps and coal heaters had dimmed their cream and brown striped beauty.

"Keep going, my lamb." I nudged George before me with my knee.

"To the end of the hall," I told the children as strangers poked out of their doors to see who we were. I smiled tersely, unsure how to act yet in our new digs. The door to our new home was locked; I gave Ira the key from my reticule.

With a little wriggling, he got the door open and there before us was our new world.

Our kitchen contained a coal stove for cooking and heat, a table built into the wall, and two wooden crates to sit on. The kitchen boasted a window on the backside of the building, and another window was set between the rooms, so light would reach the bed chamber. Our new bed was built into the corner of two walls, leaving a narrow space along one side to get in and out, and space for storage underneath. A very thin canvas palliasse, much stained, served as a mattress atop the wooden base. For laundry, a clothesline on a pulley was attached to the wall out the window, three stories up from the privies and water pipe in the yard below. The table flipped up on a hinge and there was the wash tub for clothes or small children. The floor was painted brown, and a board over the stove could hold dishes or bread. We might add a crate for storage. No chamber pot revealed itself for relief, only the privies down three sets of stairs plus another down to the yard. I must buy a chamber pot or poor George would be wet from dawn to dusk, and Homer might never learn.

I set Homer down on the palliasse and sat next to him myself. The bed was as hard as no mattress at all, but it was wide enough for four of us. "Ira, I thought you could make a bedroll like a soldier and sleep near the stove?" It wasn't really a suggestion. He understood that and took it like a man.

Next thing was coal. We had newspaper from our meat pies, and matches to start a fire, but no other fuel. The rooms were chilly, as cold as outside. While Sarah and I undid the bundles, I sent Ira out in the street to buy coal for the stove; a boy outside had said where to go. I was used to a wide-hearth fireplace and wall oven. An iron stove for heat and cooking was new. Sarah took the bucket downstairs for water, with George to visit the privies out back. There were three privies for a dozen or more families to share, next to a standing pipe for fresh water and a communal mangle. When Ira brought back the coal, we learned how to get it lit, with much failing and just the one success that we needed. Coal smoke was not a wholesome smell like woodsmoke. We'd get used to it.

It was too late in the day to get milk. I used leftover bread to make a little supper for us all: toasted with farm cheese atop, warmed on a tin in the small oven, with a little left for morning. We took turns sipping water from Ira's tin cup. The children trooped down to the privy, Ira managing George, and Sarah standing by. I made a bedroll for Ira with my Ohio Star quilt and a sheet, and told him, "This is yours. You take care of it and roll it up in the morning."

Muslin sheets and my nine-patch quilt dressed the bed, with our coats for pillows. George lay across the bottom by our feet. It was hard as the floor, but better than the boarding house. We'd already improved our lot in New York City. We all fit into the little apartment. Rain began to fall that night and we felt the chill, but we weren't freezing. My children were little coal ovens themselves, and Ira was before the heater, so I didn't fret too much. I began a tally in my head of all the things to do next day but fell asleep counting them.

New home, new list.

Chapter 4

New York City
November 1859

It took some getting used to, this City life, for the children as much as for me. I had lived in Newburgh town but it was nothing like New York City. I paid the first whole month's rent, then paid it weekly, never knowing if I would have enough to make the next week. We started an account at the corner grocer and the butcher, paid in half-dimes and pennies to street vendors. George liked to climb up the stairs like a dog, then slide back down on his front. I couldn't understand the appeal, but I am not a boy living in my own dreamworld, so let him be. Ira quickly made friends among the boys in the building and found that he must learn to play marbles; it seemed one was a dolt and a blockhead if one didn't carry his shooter in his pocket, ready for a challenge. Alas that Ira did not own even one marble, but he was on the lookout for a good street pebble the right size and shape to challenge his cohorts.

We often left the two boys in the hallway. Sarah came with me to shop, either carrying the market basket or lugging Homer. We traded off on the way home. The first few days we supplied ourselves with the tin chamber pot called a johnny, two tin plates and bowls, an iron kettle and fry pan, and two tin mugs. Tea was cheaper than coffee, beans were less than meat, but I tried to buy a stew piece for soup when I could. Turnips and potatoes rounded out our diet. The coal stove was so small that I made biscuits instead of bread, with a pinch of *sal aeratus* instead of yeast, mixed up right in the flour sack so as not to waste it. Water was free from the standpipe, and I reused those tea leaves until there wasn't a trace of color left.

At the very bottom of the stairwell a door opened down to the small yard behind. A gate led to a small alleyway beyond, called Broad Way Alley like some kind of joke; it was narrow and smelled of animals and damp. The privies stood there, shoulder to shoulder. Grayish sheets, much mended, hung to dry, flapping in the chilly breeze, and when I tilted my head back and looked up the canyon between buildings, the view was festooned with wet clothing hung like garlands of bunting at Independence Day. Stockings and baby flannels, shirts, skirts, and unmentionables: men's crotch-stained drawers and even a lady's discolored monthly cloths, hung out where anyone could see. The yard was splashy with puddles rimed with mud; the small space would become a midden to walk through in the wet. The crowded privies were misery enough in cold weather, but I imagined the flies and stench to come in summer. There was no laundry green to help dry sheets and underthings and bleach them white.

"When can we go back to school, Mama? I miss my lessons." Sarah handed Homer back to me and took her turn in the privy.

"Y're new folk, airn't ye?" A woman about my age or older, as sturdy as a newly cooped barrel, her dark hair graying but her face unlined, spoke from the first-floor landing looking down at us. She held a wicker basket on her hip and stared with frank curiosity. She pulled at a sheet on the line and the sheets came toward her, the line on a pulley.

"Yes, we are. I'm Mrs. Seabolt and this is my daughter, Sarah." I managed to say our new-old name without a hiccup.

"Ye've got boys, too. A big boy, the bairn, and the foolish ane."

"I beg your pardon? Mrs.—?"

"Tavish. Me husband's publican at the corner. I've a wean, too, Jamie. He's seven. Like to play with yer foolish ane—is he troubled, or jest soft?"

She meant George. I stiffened. "My boy's not soft."

"Do he speak?"

"Not much. He likes to play on the stairs. He's no trouble. His name's George."

"I seen yon boys on the stair. Send them down to play; Jamie'll show them the games, the street. All the weans run the streets. All the world is their play-yard. Let them run!"

I still didn't know what to say to strangers about George. He wasn't an idiot. He just didn't speak. He could if he wanted, I'm sure. It had been easier in the country, when he could run in the yard with the dogs, with Ira, and speak his own language, not displayed to all who might come up the stairs. Mrs. Tavish pulled the last sheet from the line.

I asked before she went in, "Is there a schoolhouse nearby?"

"Oh, aye, few blocks away. Don't know how ye'd manage without the weans to help ye. School," she scoffed. "That's fer toffs."

"Toffs?"

"Rich folk, leddy. Not for our like." She sang out her opinion over her shoulder: "The new leddy's a toff. Good day, *madame*!" She went in the door laughing at me.

Sarah rejoined me. "That was unkind."

"Never mind. We'll see about the school." We hoisted our skirts and climbed the stairs.

The door was open to the front apartment downstairs and I could see pieces of fabric and a pile of sleeves on a table, the back of a woman's braided head, bent over a length. I recognized the sweep of her arm, minute stitches made quickly, tightened, the same sweep over again. I knew that motion in my own arm, in my mind's eye, and hesitated a step by the open door. Then I heard German spoken, words I didn't understand, but recognized from Grandmother Seybolt's house long ago, where German still lingered in the scratchy print of the Bible and the sturdy ryebread, in pork and cabbage and pickled beets, in certain songs at Christmastide, even after five generations in America. It warmed my heart.

Up the narrow hallways, gaslight was turned off during the day, despite the clouds and gloom outside. A red-haired man, clean-shaven, his tie knotted, flat cap under his arm, rounded the top of the flight and clattered toward us instead of politely waiting for us to mount the stairs. I pressed my back against the wall for him to pass. He squeezed by, indecently close, and met my eye, making a click in his cheek at me and at Sarah, winking. "Morning, ladies," he chirruped, then caught the newel post and fairly skimmed around and down the next flight. He looked Irish but didn't sound like one.

At the landing of the next floor, two identical small boys, no older than George, played at marbles, their haunches in the air and elbows on the scuffed floor. An older boy about Ira's size leaned against the wall, his stockings slumped over the tops of his unpolished boots. His dark hair stood up like newly shocked oats. A galaxy of freckles covered his round face.

"Good morning," I said in passing. "Are these your brothers?"

"Yes, ma'am. I'm keeping my eyes on them. Mam's busy." He rolled his eyes upward at a higher floor in the building. "We play out until dinner."

Sarah opened our own door and Ira and George popped

out. "Mother," Ira said. "We need more coal. I can go buy some! And then—?" He looked at the boys in the hall.

"I'll get my coin-purse." I looked back at the hall. "Where do you live, boys?"

"Next one up," said the elder. The younger two played their game. "Tommy," he thumbed his chest. "Willie and Freddie. They're twins, they are." He jerked his thumb at his brothers.

"Ira and George will be out presently." We went in and pulled the door just ajar. With a half-dime from my coin-purse, Ira promised he would be careful and scooted out the door to the coal-yard on the next street. I heard him gallop downstairs, still talking to the other boys. Tommy leaned over the railing and shouted downward, "Pull foot, Ira!"

Ira returned with a hessian sack a quarter full of coal, enough for a day or two, and ran off with his friends, a raw turnip in his pocket to eat. I made George sit on the pot, changed Homer's flannel, then put navy beans to soak, and split some biscuits in half to toast for our noon meal. Sarah dusted the rooms and straightened the bedcovers before Homer's nap. George went back on the landing to play, gradually sitting nearer the marbles game but still playing his own game. It almost looked as if he were making friends.

After Homer went down to rest, I brushed my hair and twisted it tight in its knot, then put on my City shoes. "Sarah, mind the boys. I'll be right back." I bit my lips and slapped my cheeks for some color, checking my reflection best I could in the window glass. I took my sewing shears, point down, slipped the silver thimble on my middle finger and descended to the first floor. Residents habitually left open their doors for light and air, and to see the comings and goings of the neighbors. I felt folks' glances as I passed. The door to the German family's room was still open. I tapped at the door, trying not to stare into the room where partially sewn dresses lay in piles.

Three women and two girls about fifteen years old, all with some variation of braids or twists across their heads, sat upon a low sofa and a hassock, bent over their work. Their blonde heads popped up when I knocked.

"Good afternoon." I couldn't remember the German words for a greeting. "I am looking for sewing, a job of work. May I speak with—" Was it *Mutter* or *Vater* or the tailor? I hesitated, but one of the women came forward, speaking brusquely in German.

"Was möchten Sie, gnädige Frau? Wir sind sehr beschäftigt. Der Auftrag muss bald fertig sein!"

I held out my shears and thimble, then patted my chest. "I sew. Dressmaker." I aped sewing with an imaginary needle. "*Ich—*" But my memory failed, and I could say little more than that. *"Bitte?"*

"Nein, nein, wir haben keine Arbeit für Sie." The woman wagged her head emphatically, swishing her hand to erase the pantomime. *"Nein!"* That much was clear. The woman, barking in her foreign way, gave me to feel like a scolded schoolgirl. My cheeks burned.

"I beg your pardon. *Danke schön.*" I stepped backward into the hallway. How many of my neighbors had seen or heard, I did not know. But I must have work. I started up the stairs, then turned about and went down and out into the street.

I had no coat on, and though there was yet no snow, the wind whistled across Twenty-Sixth Street with a bitterness that would freeze my very marrow if I stayed out long. I looked around, and, seeing a tailor shop across the way, and what looked like another beyond that, I took myself back inside for a coat, to look proper if I was to venture to those establishments, as well as the haberdashery nearby. Surely there was some tailor somewhere in this district who spoke English, who needed an able seamstress.

On the stairs above the first floor, a woman younger than I, with a baby on her hip and frizzy carroty hair bound in a loose knot stood blocking my way.

"Looking for work, are ye?" Her accent revealed her Irish birth. She looked down with frank curiosity. "Ye'll never have no luck with them folk." She gestured with her chin. "They only take their own. Whyn't ye try the factor, at Clewett's near Madison Square? He's all the time lookin' fer workers. Ye sew, don't ye?"

"I was hoping for dressmaker work with a tailor." I took a step forward, hoping the woman would move. I hadn't considered alternatives, but before I could amend my statement, I had offended again.

"Weh-hell, too fine for piecework, are ye? Yer royal highness, I beg yer pardon!" The woman stepped aside and let me pass. I continued up the stairs, smarting over slights I received, and those I hadn't meant to bestow. I did not want to make enemies but I was not making friends so well.

I could not go running back out to look for work anyway. In the kitchen, George had spilled the soaking navy beans on himself and the floor. Sarah was picking through the spilled beans and George sat wet and blubbering in the corner where Sarah had put him to think about his crime. Homer, wakened from the noise, had found a rubbery bean on the floor and put it in his mouth, and Ira was nowhere to be seen. I swiped a finger through Homer's mouth and felt his sharp little teeth scrape my knuckle. By the time both boys were cleaned, the floor scrubbed and drying, and the beans rinsed and soaking again, it was time to prepare our supper—not beans, since they were still hard. I wanted a cup of hot tea and a cool cloth for my aching head, but I couldn't imagine when or how. I fried an onion and boiled potatoes, then mashed them together with a sprinkle of salt, and made Homer's a bit moister with the potato water. He gnawed on my finger and the spoon and drooled endlessly, poor lamb. Ira came in with day-old newspapers he'd picked up and I asked Sarah to find something worth reading therein after supper.

Every day felt like we were a hundred years away from Newburgh and the farm, though it was less than a month. And each day we became a little closer to penury. When the little boys were gone to bed, I went through the depth of my carpetbag, while Sarah read more items from the news near the candle. Ira, on the floor near the stove, practiced shooting with his thumb and fondled his round pebble shooter, probably thinking of proper glass marbles.

I pulled out treasures from our Newburgh house, items that had belonged to Bram and me, and his family before him, that I had grabbed on our headlong dash away. I drew out a very small clock, with a japanned casing and small brass gears, brought from England. It was a lady's clock, and it was my own, a gift from my in-laws when I married in. The Lozier silver spoons, six of them, stayed wrapped in a square of velvet. I suppose these items should have stayed with the family, but we had needs, and Bram would have sold them to feed his children any day of the week. I brought out a Belgian lace tablecloth still in its white paper and a two-handled silver flagon with Bram's name engraved in it. The cup had been a gift for his coming of age, his most prized possession until his first child was born. After that, he said, I could put flowers in it, or rocks. His treasure was in my arms, little Sarah Delaphina, or Ira Seabolt, or George Frederick. I owned a pair of earbobs that were made from a seal's teeth, dangling on gold hoops, and a bar pin with a seal's tooth, etched with a scrimshaw castle. I had no use to wear such gewgaws now, so I laid these aside. A leather-bound two-volume set of Waverly novels, *Ivanhoe* and *The Monastery*, lay at the bottom of the carpetbag. My earrings and pin and the spoons, I would take to a jeweler or a pawnbroker, someone who would weigh the metal and assess their value. I could sell these things on the street, to be sure, but I was neither bold enough nor so desperate to sell my wares that way. Not yet, anyway.

In the morning I took George and Sarah, along with Homer on my hip, to find a pawnbroker. George needed fresh air instead of crouching all the day in the dim corner of the landing. I put his mittens on a string through his coat sleeves so he wouldn't lose them, golden-yellow so he could find them in case he dropped them. I had spun the wool myself, dyed it with onion skins two summers ago. I had knitted this very pair of mittens at the end of January, just before Homer was born, in long sleepless stretches when false labor pains had wakened me. The little creature inside had kicked my ribs and stepped on my bladder while Bram snored, and the year then had not yet made itself into a trial and a tempest.

We asked a costermonger wheeling his applecart for a pawnbroker and he directed us up several blocks. It was a clear sunny day, but bitterly cold when the wind knifed across. Sarah held George's hand and counted horses with him.

"There's one white horsie, and one black one. Two horsies. Georgie." He looked but didn't respond. "That one's a bay and there's another bay. That's like red. Two red horsies, Georgie. Look at their pretty black socks!"

"There's a piebald," I suggested, looking at a black horse spotted with white. "It looks like a cow!" I showed Homer, chuckling. "See the cow?"

"The cow says moo. Can you say moo, Georgie?"

He barked.

"That's right, moo! Did you hear him talk, Mama? Moo!"

"Moo," I said in Homer's shell-pink ear. "The cow says moo."

The building, listed as *Rosenblum's Pawn* with three gold

balls painted on the window, smelled like a saddlery, with the leathery scent of books and harnesses. The proprietor stood behind a nicked and polished wooden counter leafing through a book. "Good morning." He didn't ask why I was come.

"Good day. I have brought some items to sell." I handed Homer to his sister and opened my reticule. "Silver spoons, and this jewelry."

He knocked on the partition behind him and said something in a thick tongue, not German. "My nephew," he gave explanation. "From Holstein, just came on the boat last month." A youth about Jesse's age came through the door in rough work clothes of a foreign cut—a baggy shirt, an oversized black vest, leather suspenders on his breeches, wooden clogs—he looked like a peasant from my Grandmother Seybolt's *scherenschnitte* cuttings on her wall, lacking only an Alpen pipe. He brought a folding chair to me and I gave it to Sarah. "Stay with Sarah, George."

Rosenblum fitted a monocle in one eye and opened the small velvet box. He looked at the gold clasp on the seal's teeth jewelry, examined the silver spoons for a hallmark. With each item, I felt a twinge of reproach from—whom? My children? My in-laws? The choirs in heaven? How was a widow to feed her children without money? But the goods were mine no more. I took his paper bills and silver coins with relief. Rent was paid and we'd eat this week.

Our tenement was on the corner of Third Avenue and Twenty-Sixth, so instead of going right in, though it was cold, we walked along Third past Keeler's Haberdashery, with men's hats and cards of buttons, a pair of gloves, in the window; then a shop with lettering in German and a festooning of sausage ropes and a pig's head in the window declaiming its purpose, past the chandlery, to the grocery store on the next corner. The street was thronged with children, as many on this block as I'd seen fill a schoolroom in Newburgh, some at play, some clearly at work, either minding their siblings or sweeping, carrying, or selling small items for a penny apiece.

"Needles and pins, pins and needles."

Two white boys with a bucket in each hand shouted, "Fresh fish, fresh today. Hard clams, oyster clams, striped bass, fresh today!" The clams were tightly shut, still fresh, but the small bass in one bucket were slimy and the eyes sunken.

"Not fresh," I told Sarah.

A Negro man with a cart sold ears of corn, freshly boiled, with salt, and red-hot pepper sauce in a shaker if you wanted, while his child collected the eaten cobs and papery husks from the street into a basket. A sturdy red-faced woman, her thick dark braid down her back, carried a shallow basket of browned bread twists covered in crystals of salt. "*Brezeln, Brezeln! Frische Brezeln!*"

A young white mother, shivering in a ragged shawl, with two thin daughters in patched gingham dresses, sat by a handwagon, calling, "Apples, penny apiece!" Another cart was piled with books tied with twine, with newspapers and magazines tucked alongside, pushed by an old white man with shuffling feet and shoes with worn soles.

Sarah kept up a steady monologue with George, listing each new sight, hoping to catch his attention. He always loved animals. A white dog with spots trotted along under the red fire wagon. "Doggie, George. See the spotted doggie?"

George, perversely, would not bark.

A strange, gurgling music around the corner past the grocer reached our ears. George cocked his head and before I could stop him, he had slipped Sarah's grip and run. We ran after him over damp cobblestone, around the corner. The noise turned out to be a bulky box-organ, an olive-skinned man cranking a melody I had never heard, a warbling country-dance tune from another land. The man held a small black monkey on a leash. George skidded to his knees on the muddy cobbles before the man with the monkey, no doubt scraping holes in his newly patched breeches.

The little creature chittered at us and opened its red mouth full of sharp yellow teeth in a yawn or a laugh, perhaps. Its hat was made of red felt and its wee waistcoat was trimmed in black satin cord. Its short trousers had a little hole for its curled tail. It looked like a miniature soldier, only missing its saber.

"Goota morning," said its owner, a gentleman in a black striped coat, his words thick as if speaking through a mouthful of honey. The gentleman smiled with very white teeth and a very black mustache, and put out his hand to the monkey, extending a finger. "How dooya do?"

The monkey grabbed his finger with a tiny pink hand, with such wee fingers, and they shook hands like stockmen at the agricultural fair. George gazed, entranced as if seeing an angel, or a slab of his favorite candy before him. He put out his own small hand and the monkey took George's finger and shook it.

I tensed, expecting a shriek or tears, but George was silent. Suddenly, he said, "How do you do?" his voice like an old man's croak.

"Mama!" Sarah squealed. "Georgie talked!"

I was swept with chills and sudden tears to my eyes. I fumbled in my reticule for a coin. "Give him the penny, George," I managed to say, hiding the quiver in my voice. I nuzzled in Homer's baby head, holding back tears.

Sarah took the penny and placed it in George's hand. "Give it to the monkey, Georgie!" The boy pinched the penny between his fingers and, like a kernel of corn popping, that fast, the monkey had the penny in its hand and had raced up to the man's shoulder, *chit-chit-chittering*. Sarah squealed and so did Homer, with his baby laugh. George stood still as a scarecrow and watched.

The man pocketed the penny in his striped coat and gave the monkey a roasted peanut in a practiced movement. "T'ank you veddy much, leetle boy!" He bowed to George, who stared with eyes like full moons, fingers in his mouth; the man tipped his hat to me and bid us good day. The monkey cracked and ate the peanut up on the shoulder, bits of shell falling away. The box-organ wheezed into action again.

"Georgie, you can talk," Sarah gushed, hugging him, but he pushed her off. He watched the monkey man stroll away. Sarah petted his hair. "Wasn't that marvelous? Oh, wasn't it just?"

I tried to collect myself. "That'll do, now. Good boy, George." I went into the grocery store through its corner door, a little bell ringing as it shut behind. I looked over the groceries arrayed before us, gulping down the lump in my throat, my hands shaking. If George could speak, then bringing them here was no mistake, it was *better* than remaining back on the farm. George might be more than just a worker now after all. He could talk. I could hardly believe it. He wasn't dumb, he could speak!

I bought a cut of bacon, a dozen eggs, apples and a piece of cheese to celebrate. And because I was a foolish woman with a bit of ready money, I went on to buy a dozen glass marbles for Ira, a piece of candy and two tin soldiers for George, a skein of white crochet thread and a very small mirror for Sarah.

It was a happy supper.

Chapter 5

New York City
December 1859

I took some time in the morning to find a scrap of muslin and sewed it into a small bag using blue darning thread. I asked Sarah to crochet up a string as long as her arm out of the same heavy thread, and I pulled it through to make a drawstring. Ira's marbles would be safer than a pocket, and he was glad of it. He ate his cold dinner, then put on his coat and went out to the front stoop with his friends, marble bag in pocket. Sarah took her new thread and a small hook, and tucked onto the bed next to Homer, to keep warm; George played with his new soldiers in the chilly hallway by himself. I put on my coat, took my thimble and small stork scissors in my reticule, and left the long shears at home this time.

I waved and put my finger to my lips at Sarah, pulling the door partially closed to damp the hallway noise, then stopped to tell my son, "Stay here, George. Mama will be back soon." He grunted a little, so I knew he heard me. It was more of a conversation we had ever had, and I tried to stroke his hair, but he bobbed away. He didn't like his head touched. I was pleased with him, though, and felt proud of our progress.

A little bell jangled at the door of the haberdashery next

door when I entered. A middle-aged gentleman, his pot belly straining at the center buttons of a well-cut woolen waistcoat, came from the back room forward to greet me, in an accent definitively American. "Good afternoon, Madam. How may I assist you?" This must be Mr. Keeler, the owner.

"Good afternoon." I was so eager to present myself, without pause, the door still closing behind me, I blurted, "I seek employment in any kind of dressmaking, the sewing of men's shirts, and the like. Do you have need of a seamstress?"

His eyes drifted down my form. "Perhaps."

Oh, one of them. I immediately recognized his ilk. My heart went out of the venture, wanting only retreat, but I'd come this far. I needed work. "I sew quickly. I can do fancywork, cut patterns and the like."

"And where is your husband, Mrs.—?"

"Mrs. Seabolt. My husband has passed." I still wore black, I always wore black, head to toe. How could he not know? He was making time.

"What a pity. My condolences." He stepped around the cutting table. "I might need assistance with shirts. Where is your home?"

"In the neighborhood." I hesitated to tell him any more, this insinuating scalawag, which building, which floor. Better not to say.

"Do you live alone?"

"I live with my family." I didn't want to say more.

He made a snorting sound. He turned and rifled through some white shirting in a mound on the cutting table. "I was going to send these shirts down to Cohen on the corner to make up, but he's too slow. And too expensive. And you speak English." He scoffed again. "If you can piece them, I'll pay a dollar and twenty cents for the dozen. A dime each. Provided they pass muster."

Of course I could sew them. But he hadn't seen my handiwork yet. The rate was enough for our food for a week.

"I will piece them." Just do the shirts, quick and right. He'd see, and he'd give me more shirts to do, and the dollars would come in. That was being a businesswoman. And I needn't take sauce from a harpy on the stairs.

"Come look at these pieces."

I stepped reluctantly closer to the table. He leaned near, nearer than he ought. He showed me sleeves with the cuffs that would pinch together and take a double buttonhole.

"These are gentlemen's shirts. Ever seen that cuff before? I doubt so. It's called a kissing cuff." He said the word as if it were an intimacy between us. "You press them together with a link to fasten them." He turned and breathed in my ear.

I leaned away. "I see." It was Charles Montgomery all over again, a thicker feeling each moment. The sample had a band collar and several rows of accordion pleats down the front. That would take time. I'd have to work very fast. The shirt also had buttons down the front.

"But don't sew this top button. All but this last one." He snapped the fabric sharply and folded it, then counted out buttons for a dozen shirts and folded them into a square of paper like a doctor packing a medicinal powder. He pressed the packet into my hand, his eyelids lowered in the look I recognized as hunger. I'd have to play cat and mouse with him if I wanted work.

Mr. Keeler wrapped the shirt pieces in clean brown paper and tied the bundle with a muslin selvage strip. "Remember, now—I need these Tuesday, at nine sharp. I have customers waiting. Don't disappoint me."

I thought of the first dollar and twenty cents, and more dollars ahead. Perhaps working for him would not be so bad. He would have more respect once he saw my work.

• • •

That week was a brutal blur of nonstop running stitch through underarm seams, hemstitching the bloused bottoms of these shirts; setting the collar band just so, both pinching and stretching the bias at the same time to fit the curved neckband; buttonholes each whipped with tiny stitches, identical one to the next, spaced evenly between hem and collar, eight buttons per front, two buttonholes per cuff but no buttons there. If it were Bram's shirt or Ira's, I would have sewn a heart or a star into the neck or placket, but shirts for a stranger merited no such attention. Impersonal perfection was demanded. I did my best, counting on the clink of coins in my hand at the end of a week's work, putting it toward rent, buying potatoes or tea.

The kitchen with the window offered the brightest light by day, but on the days when rain came, even the window light was too dim, and I had to use up penny candles to see the white on white. Coal kept us warm but it was dear in price, and it put soot on every ledge and sifted through the room. I foolishly left shirts on the table the first night and soot speckled over them like black snow overnight. I tried to blow it away, shake it out, but coal dust only smeared, and I must needs wash, dry and press the garments on a sheet on the table. The finished shirts I returned to the brown paper to keep them clean; but still soot smudged everything. I sacrificed one of our bedsheets to cover my work, protecting it from sooty fallout and the predations of small hands, as Homer was now pulling himself up where he could, and George couldn't touch a thing without breaking or soiling it.

Sarah did yeoman's duty keeping the room tidy and the children busy. She made the bed and watched Homer, took his hands and bounced him on her knee, picked him up and sang to him when he fell. George played in the hallway with his own muslin bag of soldiers and wooden toys until the day, chilly but dry outside, when Ira took him along to play marbles. Then nothing would please George but to follow his brother and mimic Ira's thumb-shot, his one-eyed squint when he aimed, and muttered to himself, all harmless enough. He had spoken aloud, and he was growing into an ordinary boy, I hoped.

I took to preparing the midday meal early, to simmer bean broth at the back of the stove til the noon hour, and supper stewed as long or longer, to free my days of so much cooking. I must finish the shirts, all twelve, to earn the fee, the sooner the better. So much work for so little coin would not sustain us, but what could I do? On the farm, in maple sugar season or hog-slaughter, I'd felt the hot breath of time at our necks. When a baby was imminent and there were still flannels to cut and milk-tea to brew, I had perspired in the face of the looming deadline. Now my lower back ached, I had a sharp pain behind my right shoulder blade, and my neck was stiff from looking down. I could pause long enough to roll my neck and shake out my wrist, then stabbed the needle back through the cloth.

I worked across the Sabbathday while church bells tolled across the City and the good and pious flowed out the front door to church and home again after. Sarah took care of the baby, and with the boys busy enough in play that a biscuit and apple butter would satisfy them, I finished the shirts in six days. I cleaned and pressed the shirts, and rewrapped them in the paper so that Monday, as the new week began, I could meet Mr. Keeler at his door at 9 o'clock.

I am not wont to smile unwarranted, but I couldn't help feeling accomplished. I carried the wrapped shirts in the basket, planning to carry groceries home. I was thirty-one and had never worked for my own money until this very week. Is this how Bram had felt when he sold cattle or a load of hay? No wonder he had been so quietly pleased. It was a good feeling.

The front door was already unlocked and Keeler behind his table. He watched I came through the door and into the sanctum. I set the brown paper package before him on his table. "That took the week," he said. "You'll need to work faster."

"Six days, if you please, Mr. Keeler. You said Tuesday week. It is just Monday."

"Don't be impertinent, Mrs. Seabolt. I can count as well as you can." He reached into a pocket for a pince nez, settled it on his nose, and untied the muslin strip. He lifted each shirt and examined the seams. He tugged a little on each sleeve, on the collar band, flipped the cuffs out and back again. His eyebrows told the story: My buttonholes were faultless. So were my bias strips. He snapped the last shirt and refolded it along its pressed lines. "A pity you didn't sew all the buttons. I cannot sell these."

I gaped at him. "You told me to sew eight buttons on the front. You gave me only enough buttons—"

"I cannot sell a shirt that is incomplete. I'll have to attach the top buttons myself."

"I would have if—"

"But you didn't. You didn't complete the work. Substandard. Who would wear a half-finished shirt?" He snapped the fabric at me. "This is what I get for hiring someone off the street, without a reference. Huh."

"You said you'd pay—"

"For satisfactory work. Which you did not return. Good day."

"That's not fair—"

"Who are you to question me?" He was enjoying his power game. "You haven't earned the dollar, much less further work. Now go on."

I still stood there, my mind incapable of gathering all the threads. He came around the table toward me, so I turned around and went toward the door, my mind reeling for a rejoinder. He reached around, I thought perhaps to open it for me, though my thoughts were muddled. I was confused and so tired. His hand on the door pressed it firmly shut, and there I was, between him and escape, trapped in the space between.

Panic rose in me, and I froze in place.

"I like you, Mrs. Seabolt." Mr. Keeler pursed his lips, like a man about to taste a fresh plum. "You're a pretty woman. And your stitches are very neat. I should like to use your services." I could see the little places where his razor had missed a few hairs, smell breakfast coffee on his breath. His pot belly was touching mine.

"I could use a quick little woman to finish some shirts I have here, a sloppy job that someone failed to complete. If you'd sit here with me and sew buttons on a dozen shirts, I would pay you a penny apiece for those buttons. Will you be my quick little woman?"

The rage rose inside me, steam blowing the ferry's shrill whistle—of all the outrages I'd endured thus far, this one was the vilest. He had planned all along to trick me, to use me, then cheat me of my wages. Twelve cents for a week's work. Or nothing at all, and groceries needed, and the bill to pay them overdue by two days. More coal needed, and soon the rent came due. No to Montgomery, no to Keeler, no to every cockalorum that strutted the earth. I had four hungry children to feed, and no time for this fimble-famble.

"No!" I stamped hard on his instep with my sharp City shoe, and when he cried out and winced downward I twisted and yanked open the door, knocking him away. No dollar was worth that, and no pennies, either. Quivering in anger, I stormed to the corner, through the black door and up the stairs at our tenement, daring anyone to block my way, and only before reaching our own open door did I pause and breathe once, twice, shake out the rage, step inside and smile to the children. They mustn't know.

"I forgot my coin-purse! Who wants to come with me to the grocer? George, want to come look for the monkey?"

I still had some paper money, and a few more valuables to sell. I would find work. We would be fine.

Chapter 6

JANUARY 1860

~~Seamstress~~
~~Dressmaker~~

Patterns copied. Alterations. Mourning.
Inquire Mrs. Seabolt, 358 Third Avenue.

In the New Year, I wrote out a card and posted it at the grocery on the corner. I visited two tailor shops nearby and both times was told no sewing, once in German and once in English. A dry goods store where I bought white thread to replace all I'd used on the dozen lawn shirts also offered no leads, but the merchant took my written card and placed it in the window. His canny wife caught my arm and whispered, so I left with one crucial fact. A dressmaker worked for herself. A seamstress worked for anyone; in fact, it sometimes happened that an out-of-work seamstress might lie back on the cutting table and let a tailor have his way. I had all but invited Mr. Keeler to take his pleasure, according to my informer. A narrow escape there for a country mouse, and a mistake I'd not make again.

Mulling what else to do, when I saw Mr. Schmidt, the old man with the used book cart, I asked him to look for a back number of *Godey's Lady's Book.*

I took out my ragbag again and pieced out a dozen little muslin sacks, like the ones I'd made for the boys. While Homer napped, I sewed the bags and cut yarn in lengths to tie them closed. I sent Sarah to the grocery for two eggs, a finger of gingerroot, and a scant handful of cloves. I had Sarah peel and mince fine the ginger, and when Homer awoke, George helped me by pounding the cloves to bits in a muslin bag with the sadiron. With butter, flour, sugar, and *sal aeratus*, and Sarah and George's contributions, I stirred up a bowlful of gingernut dough, the recipe Bram had enjoyed so much, rolled them into logs, cut them into knobs, baked them well in the oven. The gingery scent filled our rooms and made the day special, somehow, festive.

Ira took a handful outdoors to eat while he went for coal. George put them inside his mitten and ate them one at a time, nibbling like a squirrel with a nut. I made a teething biscuit out of the remaining dough and baked it extra hard for Homer, who enjoyed his treat as any teether would: by gnawing it and rubbing crumbs over his face and into his hair. Sarah and I ate our share with cups of tea, while we tied yarn bows on the little muslin bags, now filled with freshly baked gingernuts.

But how to proceed? I had planned to go out to sell these in front of the building, then wondered if I could sell them door to door in the building itself, to some of my neighbors. But that only advertised our desperation. And perhaps not all the neighbors had a dime to spare. Better not. Better walk a bit and sell them away from the house. As I was considering what next, Sarah interjected. "Mama, may I try to sell them? I think a young face would make a difference."

"Sarah. I could not send you out there—." A young face. That stung.

"I want to. Please let me? I can take Georgie, too."

Little waifs selling sweets in the street. It was a trial to my spirit, it was a test of my faith, to accept the humility, or was it humiliation, of asking folks to buy my wares. To admit my face wasn't young any longer, and my daughter was the comely one, with a face to draw buyers. It was almost like that crueler vice, selling ourselves in the street.

"No, love, I won't have you playing sutler for us. I'll go."

"I'll mix up the biscuit for supper while you're out. But I must go outside sometime! Please."

"I know. We'll go walking tomorrow, get some sunshine and fresh air, if the weather holds."

I had a coat pocket to hold the money but left my reticule safely in my carpetbag. I fastened my hood around my hair and neck and pulled on my gloves. Taking the basket filled with bags of gingernuts, I descended to the street, passing the open doors with my head erect, eyes averted, asking them for nothing—and then, on the street, beginning a quiet refrain.

"Ginger cookies, fresh gingernuts, ten cents a bag!" I had to be bolder. No one even turned a head. I called more loudly. "Just one dime, spiced gingernuts!"

In the street, the crosstown wind whipped my front hair loose from its tight knot and nipped at my nose. In January, night came early, and though it was just four o'clock, I saw gas lamps in the street being lit, and lights coming on in upper windows. Before long, Irish girls from their servant work, Scotch and Irish lads returning home from the cabinet workshops, Germans leaving the piano factory, soldiers marching along a side street toward their garrison on Fourth Avenue passed me by, with nary a taker for my sweets at ten cents.

"Too dear," an older man with a walking stick said in an accent from the Southern states.

"Five cents, one half-dime," I returned, and he paused.

"I set store by my mammaw's gingernuts, ma'am," he said. "Did you bake these?"

"Just made, fresh this afternoon. One half-dime." Oh, how the mighty have fallen.

He fingered out a coin from his breast pocket and handed it to me. "Thankee, ma'am. Beminds me of home."

One sale begat another, and at a half-dime, the bags of sweets sold out in the next hour. By then, my feet and my back hurt, my cheeks were raw from wind and cold, and I had to use the privy. But the basket was empty, the gingernuts were sold, and we were fifty cents richer, if you didn't count the fifteen cents I'd spent on the eggs and rare spices. And the muslin and other ingredients I already had. I'd left my children to fend for themselves for almost two hours. Sakes alive, if I were going to bake and sell items on the street, I'd have to choose between leaving the children home alone, or sending them out, or all of us going together. With George and Homer on my arms, how would I carry the basket, and if Sarah and Ira were to sell, why would they even need me, except to parade our penury for all to see? There was no dignity in selling on the street. I walked home, limping, meeting Ira on the stairs.

"Mr. Schmidt says he has the *Lady's Book* and it's five cents. He says to bring the money if you want it." Ira, his blouse untucked beneath his coat, his stockings falling down, had a dirty face but I kissed him anyway. "Mother." He blushed.

"I sold the gingernuts and they're all gone." I pulled one of my hard-won half-dimes from my coat pocket. "Give him my thanks, son. You're a good boy."

Ira gave me his dirty paw. "We'll make some money and be rich soon," he predicted.

"Go, now, quick as a deer, and watch for wild horses in the street!"

"Yes'm."

The gas lamps were on in the hallway. I went through and down to the privies and pulled the door shut by the fingerhole. There was barely enough room to lift all my skirts and hover over the wooden seat, which was filthy. I knew the hem of my gown was damp and I didn't want to think what slop might be soaking in. I heard others in the yard, someone hauling a squeaky pulley of laundry in, a child squealing, a dog barking, a hacking cough. A scrape and slam when someone went indoors. I straightened my drawers, shook out my skirts, and pushed open the door. It was dark out. A red glow signaled the presence of someone smoking a pipe. I could smell the sweet tarry scent of Virginia leaf and found it familiar and comforting, a reminder of my father's pipe, long ago.

"Did ye sell y'r wares, missy?" The man's voice had a Scotch burr and the gravel of one who had smoked for many years.

I didn't want to converse by the privies, nor be rude to first-floor tenants. I guessed it was Mr. Tavish. We had never been introduced, but I must answer.

"I did."

"Next time come by the pub. We all like a bit of something sweet."

This chilled me, the words behind his words. Perhaps it was only man-talk, jesting, but I disliked it. I had to pass his shadow, the glowing pipe, to reach the stairs.

"Good night." I swept up my skirts to mount the stairs. I felt his grasp, a man's broad hand squeeze my haunch as I passed. "Sir!" I turned, swatting at his hand. I clattered up the stairs, leaving him chuckling in his dark corner.

I hurried upstairs and into our rooms, closing the door behind me. It was too much, a body wanted only to use the privy and to work by the sweat of her brow—it was too much, it was, to endure the humiliation of manhandling as if I were a common guttersnipe. And the thought of Sarah caught unawares—my golden girl. It scared me. My hands were shaking, but I blew on them as if I were cold. I would talk to Sarah later about such dangers.

"Supper is ready, Mama, and the biscuits are hot." She covered the pot on the stove and mashed some potatoes with a fork and pot liquor on a plate for Homer. She had lit the candle and tied a napkin around Homer's neck. He chewed his wooden spoon and said, "Mama mama mama" when I picked him up.

Ira came in with the back number of *Godey's Lady's Book* and after he cleaned up, after we ate, after wiping down the boys again and washing the dishes, at last I sat on the edge of the bed and soaked my feet in hot water and salt. I flipped through the pages, waiting 'til morning to read the words in brighter light, seeking some sort of inspiration or hope. With men in dark corners, with hunger and filth, with exhaustion and debt awaiting at the end of each week, I must try something else.

There must be someone who needed new clothes who could pay for them.

• • •

I sold my City shoes. My feet could not bear walking cobblestone streets in heels, and my back ached, so I sold them for two dollars at the second-hand shop down Twenty-Sixth toward the East River, near Bellevue and the charity House of Refuge. My country boots would suffice. Rent was due weekly, and we were buying coal at an alarming clip since it had snowed.

The boys were so hungry. Sarah and I managed with a biscuit and tea in the mornings, or a scoop of porridge, but Ira and George wanted eggs, milk, meat, an extra serving of beans. They were growing. Ira would be as tall as his father, and sturdy George was as heavy, though not as tall, as his elder sister. Homer ate a little, and nursed; as long as I could make milk, he'd grow up fat and happy. But, oh, how the money drained away.

Ira played outdoors with George and the band of boys from the stairs: Jamie Tavish, Tommy, Willie and Freddie, Nat when he could wangle out of his father's carpenter shop, and others: German boys, Russian Jews, Irish and Scotch. All the redheads from the top floor came down in a clatter in the mornings at five to go to their servant work. The cheeky young man with the flat cap was a waiter somewhere; I'd seen his white aprons on the line, then rolled up under his arm as he jigged down the stairs. The frizzy-haired mother and her carrot-top baby looked after their rooms and chivvied me when we crossed paths.

"Too good to speak to the likes of me, are ye? I suppose yer johnny's filled with gold nuggets, is it?"

I had made an enemy somehow and didn't know how to fix it. I just didn't know how to make a friend, so I stayed in with my children, fighting with my worries and fears, missing my Bram. I kept waiting for a reply to my card in the grocery window.

"A little bird might snip off yer nose, Mrs. High and Mighty," I heard on the hallway. "I hope it don't shit in yer gob, too." I longed to ask about the factor giving out piece-work, but now I was afraid to ask her.

The back number of *Godey's Lady's Book* provided the family with many hours of entertainment. Sarah learnt several of the poems, and Ira liked the woodcut illustration of three American boys launching a little boat into the river for high jinks.

I scored the page and carefully tore it out, and Ira hung it on a protruding nail in the kitchen.

"That reminds me," Sarah said. "Listen, George:

Rub a dub dub, three men in a tub,
and who do you think they be?
The butcher, the baker, the candlestick maker.
Turn them out, knaves, all three!"

"Rub a dub. Rub a dub." George loved nonsense words and would sometimes repeat them.

"Bub!" Homer copied.

"Good boy, Homey! Rub a dub dub."

"Bub!"

"Rub a dub, rub a dub." George repeated.

"What's a knave, Mother?" Ira wanted to know. "Is it like a knight?"

"A knave is a naughty fellow. Not a gentleman. A knave would pick your pocket or cut your purse. Don't be a knave."

"I won't. I'll be a general and lead the troops to victory! I wish I had a horse. Remember Brown Bess and Old May? I miss—the farm." He missed his father but he bravely wouldn't say so. His eyes told me.

Another page declared the beloved truth that, "The fate of a child is always the work of his mother." A sonnet on blessed motherhood followed. I preferred not to read that guilt-full sop.

Page after page showed the newest fashions in color plates, as of the month and year of the publication (it was printed the previous year), which we could still see on any street, near or far. But the rest of the book was timeless. Patterns for crocheted edging, for hair safes and fancy alphabets for a sampler, gifts to be made of pasteboard, then covered in silk or velvet, and schematics for a pair of carpet slippers gave me a pleasant diversion while I waited for water to boil or the sadiron to heat. A pattern for paper roses caught my eye. It said one could purchase silk leaves and ready-made stamens, glue, and papers of pretty colors.

If I could afford those, I wouldn't need to make paper flowers myself. Exasperated, I wondered how to make something else to sell, lacking anyone who wanted a dress made, or even mending or darning done. What if I could make up my own piecework for sale? I could do it, with the children's help.

"Ira, will you go up to the stables, you know the place, the streetcar depot up Fourth Avenue? Ask the hostler for some horse hooves. I mean the trimmings from the farrier. Not many, just a few pieces? A handful."

Ira made a face.

"I know it's queer, son, but I want to make some glue. Will you help me?"

"I can shin my way up there and be back in no time!"

"Ira, don't use slang! It's low and common!" Sarah chided him, but he was out the door and shinning down the stairs even as I scolded. "Isn't it just, Mother?"

"He learns it from the street boys." I read the instructions over again.

"At least George doesn't talk that way."

"Indeed, that is a silver lining." George played silently with his soldiers on the floor, ignoring our palaver.

Sometime later, Ira brought back a pocketful of hoof trimmings and I set them in a little water to a low boil on the stove. The stench was revolting—cooking rotten meat would have smelt as bad. I closed the hallway door off the kitchen, hoping the neighbors wouldn't complain, and opened the front window, fanning the air with a shawl, then shutting out the cold again.

"Mama, I'm taking Homer for a stroll." Sarah spoke in her most diplomatic tone. "Just up and down the halls."

"Go on, stay out til the boy wants to sleep, if you've mind to." I didn't blame her. "I am sorry, it won't take much longer." The resulting gunk ruined my cooking pan—a dollar to replace it for all my effort—but left me with about a pint of glue. I cooked beetroots in the new pot for supper, boiling roots and greens together and then frying them with bacon fat. I stopped Sarah from washing the pot until I found some way to store the red juices.

"I saw some tin cans down by the privies." Ira went down and fumbled in the dark mews, returning with three empty cans that had held herring or oysters, something fishy. I washed those clean and hammered the jagged edges flat with my sadiron and was able to pour the red-staining juices into two of the cans, and the glue into the third. I could sell the glue pot for scrap.

I wiped sticky fingers, faces and dirty bottoms and put the little ones to bed. Ira and Sarah washed themselves. As Ira unrolled his bed and shook out his blanket, I laid my hand on his shoulder. "I am grateful for your help, son. I have in mind to make some flowers."

"How can you make flowers?"

"Paper roses, for decoration. For hats, perhaps. I need some paper. I'll have to save some from the butcher, I think."

"I can get newspaper. I know where there's a big stack."

"Ira, can you? That might just work. Do, if you can." I hesitated. "What would it cost?"

"Nothing—there's a dump on Fourth Avenue to'rd the river. Nat and Tom showed me. I can pick up coal and wood chips from the road, too, down to'rd the docks."

"*Toward,* son. To-ward." His friends' diction was contagious.

"To-ward."

"Let us have some newspaper, then." I didn't want to scavenge, didn't like the path we were taking, but it would be a savings not to spend five cents every other day for coal. "And if you see anything we can use for fuel, bring it home. Anything helps."

"I will, Mother."

"That's my boy."

On the morrow, when he returned from play for his dinner, Ira dragged in the damp and dirty hessian bag with smaller bits of coal, sawn ends from the lumber yard and many chips and curls of wood from the cabinet factory. As well, he brought a stack of newspapers three inches thick—many days' worth, for my flower-making or for the fire, whatever we needed. George immediately picked out several sticks and cut blocks from the pile, and we let him have them. George sat and built towers with his new wooden toys.

"All of this cost nothing?" I praised Ira. Nothing but the work of fetching and carrying it home, it seemed. He brought so many newspapers that we added some to the hard bed, increasing its cushion by a fraction.

"I'll fetch even more tomorrow," he vowed.

Using the stiff back cover of my *Lady's Book*, I cut a pattern of rose petals in different shapes and sizes as the pattern inside directed. The stiff magazine cover made sturdy patterns and I could trace around them many times before they folded or wore down. I cut newspaper into petal shapes and followed the directions to glue petals together in a rose form, shaping some into buds and others into full-blown blossoms. With more newspaper spread across the table, I dunked a paper flower into the beet juice to tint it, but the newsprint clumped and matted almost instantly. Experimenting with ways to color with the beet juice, I found that a bit of wool roving from the ragbag, held in a bunch, worked as well as a paintbrush, although it dyed my fingers deep crimson. I practiced wiping, dabbing, and pouncing the wool for effect, and finally settled on a brushed-on method to color the petals dark to light. The newsprint underneath almost disappeared under the dark red and showed a pleasing effect where the beet juice was thinner. The petals dried with a crisp, realistic effect. By the end of the afternoon hours, before suppertime, I had produced a creditable paper rose deeply colored by beet juice.

Who would buy such a novelty, for home or fashion? I didn't know, but now that the technique was settled, I need only buy beets once a week to make color for my roses; newspaper and glue were free for the intrepid.

I looked at my purpled hands with some rue, smelled them and didn't mind the earthy scent of beets in my stained nails. I enjoyed beets as a supper dish, especially with bacon or ham, and—something in the newspaper beneath my ministrations caught my eye. I read,

STATE OF NEW YORK,
CITY AND COUNTY OF ALBANY:

The people of the STATE of NEW YORK on behalf of Malcolm Lozier, who resided in the town of NEWBURGH in the County of ORANGE in the State of NEW YORK, and Charles W. Montgomery, Esq., attorney at law, who resides in Newburgh, aforesaid, the special guardian of Emily Lozier, Mariah Lozier, and Jesse Lozier, of Newburgh; Sarah Delaphina Lozier, Ira Seabolt Lozier, George Frederick Lozier, William Homer Lozier, lately of Newburgh; Malcolm Evans and Martha Ann Evans of Kingston, minors; the heirs at law and next of kin of Malcolm Lozier, late of the Town of Newburgh, in the County of Orange, deceased, greetings:

You are hereby cited to be and appear before the surrogate of the County of Orange, in his office in Newburgh, in said county, on the 30th day of December next at ten o'clock in the forenoon of that day, to attend the probate of a certain instru-

ment in writing, purporting to be the last Will and Testament of said deceased, bearing the date of October 22, in the year of our Lord one thousand eight hundred and fifty nine, on the application of Jesse Wood Lozier, claiming to be one of the executors thereof which said Will relates to and is offered for probate as a Will of real and personal estate.

I scrambled at the papers to find the date. This notice ran on November 12. What was this thing? What did it mean? I read it again. Had Jesse, or Montgomery, sent this to the newspaper, in search of the children but not of myself? Which newspaper? *The Albany Argus.* They perhaps thought I had gone south to Nyack to be with my mother; except by now they surely knew I had not gone there. My mother would have written back to say I had never been. Now they were seeking me north in Albany. Was this announcement in every newspaper? Must I go? Or they—the children—alone, without me?

We already knew what was in the will. Malcolm, from beyond the grave, or Montgomery on this side of it, were reaching for me. The legal guardian of Jesse and my young sisters-in-law and my children stretched out his slimy hand to grasp at us. Must I go? Dare I defy such a summons?

I dared.

I bathed Homer and George on Saturday night in the tin tub in the kitchen. I rubbed the cloth on the bar of soap and cleaned each ear, rubbed the ticklish bottoms of their feet, the backs of their necks, made certain each nail was cleaned and pared with my tiny stork scissors if need be. I knew the whorls of hair on their heads, the freckle on George's right shoulder and the same on Homer's left foot. Sarah's freckle was under her right eye, a tiny beauty spot. Ira had one on his jawline. Someday it would be covered by a beard, by the tanning of his skin when he worked in the sun.

By rights, he should have been a farmer, tilling the fields of rye and oats, cutting the hay, milking his herd of cows, and sending butter to market. He should have a good wife to help him, and he would have run the Lozier lands as the eldest son of the eldest son. But the Lord had mysterious plans, and Heaven only knew why Abram and Malcolm were called at the same time. I thought of my three sons and wondered if Homer would succeed where Ira would fail, or if George would surprise us all and reveal himself to be some sort of captain of industry. He could speak, he could repeat, he could be taught.

I know my children as I knew myself, as extensions of my own limbs, my inmost heart. I read and reread the newspaper notice and wished I had someone I could ask, someone who knew about legal papers and laws, like Malcolm, like my uncles Seybolt or Greenleaf; I felt myself very much alone in the world. The way I read it, the notice was an invitation, not a command—*Greetings,* it said, in a friendly way. But then it took a grave turn, citing and ordering to appear the minor children. There might be some inheritance money from Malcolm for the children—it couldn't be much, because the land was the wealth, those 400 acres. If I took the children back, Montgomery would surely whisk them away as punishment because we'd run. His legal guardianship eclipsed my role as mother; they were, after all, half-orphans. I had no rights to manage their money, if any.

But no mother would send her children away without her, into the jaws of the lion. It was imbecilic to think I would fall for that. I spent a restless night, turning my dilemma like sticky dough, kneading and tossing it over and over. By morning, I had resolved that while the boys might not suffer under Montgomery, Sarah must go nowhere near the man. We would stay together. No one was going anywhere without the others. I could only pray that they wouldn't send the law after me, find me somehow in the hurly-burly of the City.

Early Sunday morning, with drying paper roses on every level surface of two rooms, I decided. When I stirred up last night's coals, stepping carefully to avoid the sleeping Ira, I twisted the newspaper announcement and used it to fuel the fire. While my children still slept like cherubs in bed-clouds, I hummed a psalm for the Sabbath day, nodding on my kitchen crate, waiting for hot water to boil. With every iota of strength and resolve I had, to my dying day, I would fight and forestall and resist and obfuscate, whatsoever it took to keep my children safe.

Chapter 7

January 1860

I couldn't sell my paper flowers for love nor money, and eventually we used them to start the fire. We tried to keep the drafty rooms warm, but the new year brought blizzards and sickness.

Homer and George coughed wet and coughed dry until nearly February. Ira was as healthy as a Berkshire hog, and he ate like one, too. He was not afflicted with the croup and fever, perhaps because he slept in his bedroll on the floor and not in the miasma of illness in our bed; he ran countless errands to the grocery or the butcher for a soup bone, for expensive dried cherries, honey, and a yellow onion for Grandmother's old German remedy for coughs. Sarah went down with a fever for two days, and then returned to health, albeit with pinker cheeks. Soon thereafter she had her first monthly visitor and I wondered if the fever was her womb's way of announcing itself.

From the bed we shared, fever-soaked sheets made extra washing. Our woolen clothing dripped in the kitchen behind the stove, steaming the kitchen into a summer-like fug. Our sheets hung out on the line in the freezing air, and I didn't bother ironing them anymore. George coughed in my face, as did Homer, and although mothers are not supposed to catch their infants' colds, after the first week, I awoke to a pain in my throat that grew by the hour until it felt like I had a dry bean stuck in my gullet. I dosed myself with a cup of hot tea with honey and wished for a slug of medicinal brandy, but I could feel illness coming—like too much snow gathered in the high branches of a pine tree, bound to slip. I started another pot of beans, baked biscuits to get ahead of the next day's cooking, and by end of day slipped into bed with George and Homer, while Sarah slept across the foot. I could scarcely open my eyes in the morning, my head was so thick; I was too ill to get up and fell back into a fog of exhaustion. I couldn't breathe. I couldn't stop sneezing and coughing, explosions that hurt inside my ears, my head. I rocked myself like a new mother rocks an infant, while Homer and George lay listlessly next to me. Sarah and Ira did their best to bring tea, to feed soup to George and put Homer at my breast, to keep our supply of handkerchiefs washed and dripping dry, and to keep the fire burning.

I was freezing, shivering so that the bed shook. Homer whimpered and fretted at my exposed teat. George kept his tin soldiers in hand and sucked quietly at what was left of the lead paint. I couldn't rouse myself to tell him to stop, that he was too big to suck on things like a baby, but it kept him quiet. I fell into unreal dreams about fire in the chimney and crops that wouldn't grow, mice in all the grain sacks and then under my very hand in the floursack, under my knife at the chopping block. I awoke drenched in perspiration and my nightdress clinging to me as if I were drowning in the river, the weight of the cotton, the dampness of it, the sour scent of my own body, the sudden chill. Sarah was out of sight, and I couldn't hear Ira; the rooms were cool. Was there a fire? Where had they gone?

The two little ones curled together, asleep, their noses caked with green crust, their eye-corners grainy with dried tears. I rolled from the bed, put my feet onto cold wooden boards, found my threadbare carpet slippers, shuffled to the corner where the johnny should have been. It was missing, as was Sarah. The stove was warmish, but I peeked inside and saw the coals cooling gray, and nothing in the woodbox, no coal sack in sight. Outside it was snowing lightly, night falling, the fallen snow purple in the shadows and black in the lee of the buildings. Ira must have gone for fuel. I poked at the coals and doubted there was enough heat to boil water. The kettle was warm but not hot enough for tea. I found my cup of cold medicinal tea, swished it in my mouth, swallowed with difficulty. I must get well, I must stir up some biscuit, make some mush for supper, but I couldn't move from the crate, just sat there staring at the cooling stove.

The door clattered open and Sarah came in with the clean johnny and a full bucket of water. "Mama—why are you up?" She set down the bucket and the pot, shut the door, and came to feel my forehead. Her hand was cold and felt so good on my face. I held my daughter's hand for a moment, savoring the cold against my skin.

"Back to bed, Mama!"

"I will, after I use it." I nodded at the johnny. "Where is Ira?"

"Out for coal. He took the last dime." She lowered her voice. "The rest of the money is paper."

"I know." Ten greenback dollars, in fact. I had counted and recounted them in my mind so many times, I had made myself dizzy. My head felt soft yet full, like a sandbag, and when I turned my head, the sand shifted heavily and I needed to lie down. I took the johnny into the corner and used it, then limped back to bed. The sheets were damp still from sweat. "Will you fetch my shawl, Sarah?"

Sarah wrapped me gently and then pulled up the sheet, the blanket, the nine-patch quilt made long ago with Grandmother. "Are you still cold? I can put my coat over you."

I shivered again, quaking like a tin lid on a boiling pot.

"Yes, just for a moment. Until I warm up, thank you." I was freezing, I was on fire, I was wet with rain and river water and birth fluid and blood. Voices came into my head, and a banging like doors, thunder, drums. A wailing cry, the smell of piss-damp flannel, a croupy baby. Someone helped me to sit and take a little broth from a cup, wiping my chin where I spilled. Sarah helped me to the chamber pot again, then back to suddenly fresh sheets, a clean nightgown. However could I have managed that? Hot tea with whisky in it, some of my own cherry and honey syrup, the scent of cloves from my gingernuts strong in the middle of the night, or was it morning? The room was dim but I heard voices, and the babies were gone, but the bed was warm, and I slept, dreamlessly at last, deeply, and when I roused to life again it was morning and there was hot tea and crisp white bread toasted over the coals, and more broth to follow.

Sarah sat on the bedside with her own mug of tea. "Good morning, Mama. Are you feeling better?"

"I'm sorry I've been ill."

"We were worried."

"You and Ira had to do the work. I'm sorry," I said again, but Sarah said, "No, we didn't, really. It was Mrs. Hearne, from upstairs. She took the boys upstairs so you could rest, and she washed and cooked."

"Mrs. Hearne." I did not recall meeting any such neighbor. "Mrs. Tavish?"

"No, Mother. Mrs. Hearne. From the top floor. She has a baby like Homey. She's ever so kind. She talks funny but I understand her."

A bump against the door, then it popped open, Ira hoisting the dirty hessian bag, followed by a red-haired boy the same size, carrying a stack of newspapers and a candle. "Cut the noise, Jimmy—me ma's asleep!"

"Sure, she's asleep, an' she's sleepwalkin'," the boy sauced him, casting an eye at me in my nightclothes. I pulled the sheet up to my neck.

"Gracious!" I began, but a cough took my breath away, and I hacked for a minute before trying to smooth my bed-braid.

"That's Jimmy, Mrs. Hearne's big boy," Sarah explained. "Jimmy, say how do you do?" She seemed to relish having another youngster to instruct and order about.

"How d'ye do?" The boy gave a charming little bow to me. Ira looked on with a grin on his face.

I wanted to laugh but burst into another long cough instead. I lay back, rolling to my side, when I realized the boy's mother must be the shrew I had met on the stairs, the one who had scolded me endlessly. I nearly choked again. "Where are the little ones, did you say?"

"They're with me mam, up the staircase, there. Mam's feeding them just now." Jimmy was not in the slightest bit embarrassed at my ill health or state of undress. He must be used to a large family and close quarters. *Irish*, I thought. But then—*those Irish just took care of me and my children while I was ill. Who am I to criticize?* The thought of that fierce woman scolding me on the stairs, and then seeing me with my hair down, in my nightgown soaked with sweat, or undressed even further—it was mortifying. I wanted to rebrush my braid and sit up or get up before she arrived again. I felt weak as calves' foot jelly and hadn't even put my foot back out of bed.

"Don't worry, Mama, we're here." Sarah took my hand. "We're all helping, and you'll feel better soon." She soon mended the fire and poured me a cup of tea, laced with brandy from who knows where.

Oh, the shame of being seen like this! I burned with alternating embarrassment and wonder—at myself. What kind of Christian spurns the helping hand of the Samaritan?

I thought, round and round. The warm drink was working in my chest, making me sleepy again. I slept another day and night, finally awakening with Sarah and the little boys in the bed next to me, Ira on the floor, and a knock at the door.

I raked my hair with my fingers and wrapped my shawl around the nightgown, one I'd never seen before and yet I had slept in it. I opened the door a crack. Outside, in the dim hallway, my antagonist-turned-nurse, Mrs. Hearne, stood with a cloth-covered plate.

"Oh, ye'r up already, are ye? Time to eat some't, face the world again, missy!" She came forward through the door. I stepped back without argument. "Water on for tea?"

I coughed hoarsely into my hand and croaked, "Not yet, I—"

"Na matter, na matter, I'll get it. Ye were sick, there, wi' th' grippe. Thought ye'd die. The little 'uns worried." Mrs. Hearne, her orange hair twisted and pinned, frizzing out like sheep's wool, had a brusqueness to the way she moved, talked, looked, and it brooked no argument. But somehow, I could see now that she wasn't angry. She was abrupt, all sharp corners, no nonsense. She was one of those furies I had heard about in fairy tales long ago. An Irish hurricane.

"Sit ye there, I've brung the bread." She indicated the napkin on the plate. "Take a nibble, it won't bite ye." I lifted the napkin to see a large plate-sized biscuit, rough edges, dotted with currants or raisins.

"Han't ye ne'er seen soda bread before? Nuh? We eat it morning and night, easy as nothing to make. Ye make biscuit? It's the same. A child could do it." She gave me my own knife from the shelf over the stove and ordered, "Cut a slab, go on."

She rattled at the stove, pushing in coal and rolled newspaper, clattering with a spoon in a pot, sifting oats into water. "Ye'll need t' pay grocer when ye can. I put't on yer tab there, and at t'butcher. Shouldn't be too much; I pick cheap cuts but I know how to cook 'em. Ham and beans, mutton broth, good for ye when yer ailing. Ye came out of this one just fine, ye did. Back on yer feet no time. Here's yer tea, drink while it's hot, will ye?"

I took the steaming cup but before I bit into the still-warm bread, cleared my throat. I was filled with shame and weakness. "Mrs. Hearne. I thank you for helping me. I am in your debt."

"Eh, fiddle. Don't think of it." She was flustered by my thanks, waving them away. "Women. It's what we do. Don't suppose a darlin' man would ha' lifted finger, nuh?" She broke into a laugh that showed her white teeth. "Anyway. Help me sew a bit when yer feeling strong like. I have six men to darn and sew and wash fer, me man and his brothers, me own brother, plus me Jimmy, me girl Mary, and the baby—me hands'r full! And me name's Lizzie."

"I shall."

I bit into the warm bread then, sweet with plump raisins and light with *sal aeratus*. It beat my light biscuits any day. These Irish. What strange, wonderful folk. She had saved me and my children when she could have let us freeze, let us starve. She didn't owe us a thing, and yet—how many days had I been ill? A week? I didn't even know. I might have died. But the rooms clean, the children fed, a nightgown not my own? Someone had dressed, changed, fed me and the children—this woman. Lizzie Hearne was a true Samaritan. Who was the better Christian, incense and idols, or none? The debt was real.

• • •

I was slow to gain back my strength. Whatever malaise and fever it was had knocked the wind from me, and it took weeks of stopping to rest, of asking the children to help, of being unable to climb the stairs without shaking limbs and a sudden headache, before I felt anything like the vigor of my old self. I helped Lizzie Hearne with her sewing and mending for her family, and though their loud voices and backchat took some getting used to, I found them cheerful and humorous despite dark days, and grubbing as hard as I was. Alas, I was in the same place, or worse, as before: No paying work, and my reserves running low.

By the end of January, we could no longer afford the luxury of two rooms, though I hated to say so. I asked Ira to look out for the landlord, and soon enough, the man passed through the building to collect his rents of a Saturday.

"Mr. Scott, may I have a word?" I invited him in. Known for bright brocade waistcoats and Cuban cigars, a gold watch fob and keys that jangled wherever he went, Mr. Scott was a man of property and of influence in the 21st Ward. He was not unkind but had grown accustomed to poor families leaving him flat. He met this with charm and a way of making the pieces fit so he came out smelling like a rose in the end. I meant to coast on his good graces to my advantage if I could.

"Would you care for some tea?" I handed him a small dish for his cigar ash.

"No thankee, ma'am." He sat on the crate and sucked at his cigar. Blowing from the side of his mouth away from me, he asked, "Have you got the rent?"

"I have it in my purse, but I want to offer you a better bargain."

"Eh? What's that?"

I set my own tin mug on the table and perched on the edge of the other crate. "I heard some unfortunate news. The Quinns have vanished, we heard this morning."

"Absquatulated? If that don't beat all. They're the third ones this week." He jingled his keys in his hand. "I'm down a double sawbuck, and that's the bottom fact!"

"Perhaps I can help. This place is so large for us. Too spacious. We were thinking to move upstairs, if only there were a smaller place." I sipped my tea, the question hanging between us.

"There is now, lady! But my problem's the same. Who takes this'n?" He squinted one eye, assessing the problem. "I'll bet you have an idea, don't you? You womenfolk always get the best of me. Haw haw!" He brayed like a billy goat.

"The Beckers were saying they have family coming from Germany. I cannot speak for them, of course, but perhaps?"

"P'raps they might." He stubbed his cigar into the dish. Ash floated gently onto the tabletop. "Hmm, indeed. Well. You want the upstairs? You may have it. I'll take the new rate starting today, and we'll call it even, you doing me a good turn like this. Now, if you'll just fetch the rent now? Two bucks on the barrelhead, haw haw!"

The new apartment was a single bedsitter, the bed built into the wall like before. It also had a sawhorse table and a couple of wooden crates for seats, as before. Sarah and I began packing immediately. The Seabolts now lived on the top floor in Quinn's old lodging. The Hearns were across the hall. An extra flight of stairs was hard on the arms with full johnny cans and wash water, and the light was dimmer in the halls. I had to watch my step under my skirts when taking the stairs to avoid a nasty fall.

Somehow, word filtered out, probably through Lizzie Hearne, that I would sew mourning clothes. Mr. Scott asked me to sew some mourning for his wife, who had suffered the loss of a nephew from the recent wave of grippe. His wife, the bereaved aunt who had boarded the young man in the past year, came with her dry goods in a basket up to our door and, after measuring her, I bid farewell and started the dress. But I found myself tiring, fatigued still, and wondered if I would ever feel hale again.

In Newburgh, midwinter, after New Year's, the children had played outdoors with much-polished sleds from Bram's childhood, and came inside with red cheeks and bright eyes. Though here in the City the boys went out in dirty gray snow, Sarah hadn't been outdoors to play, and thought herself too old for snow forts and snowball fights. She had no experience of social life in town, but I knew we were missing sleighrides, snow candy, crisp apples, plaiting straw into dolls, quilting bees. Days were still short for us, whose winter days had been bountiful from my root cellar, my smokehouse, my corncrib, my dairy. Every creek froze in Newburgh, and sometimes even Hudson's River itself froze over. When the temperature dropped and the wind was too chill to venture out, still we had been warm and merry indoors, with cords of seasoned wood just a step from the house, cranberry jam and stewed pumpkin with brown sugar and butter. I recalled pans of whole baked onions and apples in cider and pepper, with my sage and fennelseed pork sausage and light griddle cakes and our own maple syrup at breakfast, a pot of coffee with beaten cream, *Kaffee mit Schlag*.

And Bram. Always Bram pulling me onto his lap.

Perhaps if I were to show the German tailors I could cook the German way, they would hire me? Perhaps if I grew feathers, I'd have wings, and I could fly to California where there were gold nuggets in the streets. I had to face facts: New York City was not Newburgh, silver coins had flown from my purse, no one in this building could hire me, and we were going to starve if I did not find work, make work for myself, determine how to survive.

We had been a scant three months on our own, a mere moment in time, and here I was sniveling into my handkerchief in despair. This couldn't go on. I must find something to do. Thank heaven for Mrs. Scott.

I hemmed Mrs. Scott's plain black gown with a tiny running stitch, my fingers pressing the hem as I sewed, then on to the blue-black buttons made of mussel shells, two tiny holes in each, to be sewn firmly down the front. A row of well-knotted buttonholes, some hand-whipped picot trim around the stand-up collar-band, a knot of black ribbons to be pinned at the throat. It gave my pleasure to feel the slip of lace, of poplin, of woolen goods in my hand, but pleasure is fleeting. Hunger looms. My children must be fed, their appetites endless. This one gown kept us in Irish potatoes and porridge, in tea, and little else unless I could work against a rising tide. My head ached and I reached for my tea, stewed and bitter but strong with whatever energy powered my along. The sleeves must be set and then hemmed, pressed and hung to show Mrs. Scott in the morning.

"Look at these pretty flowers, Mama." Sarah was reading through the old *Godey's* again. "Like your paper flowers but made of feathers."

Homer cruised along the edge of the bed and toward my knees on the packing crate stool. "Ma ma, ma ma," he said, grinning his little toothy smile at me.

"There you are, young man." I nodded at Sarah, "Hmmm," my eyes on the last buttonhole in the bodice, pulling and teasing the last few stitches tight. "Feather flowers. How do you wash them?"

"I don't guess you could wash them, Mama. But maybe for hats? I think they would be sweet," she said, using her pet word, picked up from the Purdy girls downstairs. "Feathers for hats, or maybe for a boutonniere, for a gentleman?"

"Hats," I repeated, thinking of the last time I bought a hat in Beacon, on that ferry trip with Charlotte, in a mercantile that offered chapeaux for men and women as well as all manner of made clothing. Some bonnets sported a feather or a plume; others had those silk flowers like the paper ones I had crafted. If I could find a millinery, a mercantile, somewhere in the City, I could perhaps—?

"Will you read it to me?"

Sarah obliged, stepping closer to show me the drawing and reading the directions aloud. "First gather from your chicken yard or poulterer's copious feathers, enough to fill both hands, and place into a brown paper poke or bag made of coarse calico, tied closed. Shake the feathers vigorously in the poke or slip to dislodge any loose dirt or vermin. With care place into a moderate oven, where they should be kept for some hours, where the heat is enough to kill vermin but not discolor or burn the feathers. Oh, Mama, where would we get so many feathers?"

"If only we were still on the farm," I responded, then stopped. If only, if only. None of this would be necessary on the farm, where all things grew in abundance, in plentitude. Feathers simply floating around the barnyard. Trees full of apples. Ricks full of hay, fields of rye, bushels of Indian corn. My husband's arms at night.

"*Pick each feather out and cut off the little hard piece of quill at the top. Before your birds are plucked they should be gently washed in lukewarm water and soapsuds with a little whisky or gin in it*—Mama!" Sarah broke into a giggle. "We would have a drunken bird."

I couldn't help but laugh. "It seems rather complicated. First you have a bag full of loose feathers, but before you pluck the bird you have to wash the feathers. The quill is at the bottom, not the top! Never mind, Sarah. For half a moment I thought that might be something we could try, but there's one thing I shall not do, and that is wash my chickens in whisky or gin."

I wondered who were the ladies who had such time to

bathe their birds in drink. "Someday, my dear heart, we will have such riches—to bathe ourselves in asses' milk like Cleopatra and soak our chickens in whisky or gin."

"Well, for now it will have to be bathwater." Homer grinned his four-tooth smile at Sarah. "Isn't that so, Homey? Bathwater for you and me."

I took the last few stitches and hid the tail of the thread deep in a seam where it wouldn't easily come loose. "There, now." I shook the dress again and admired how easily the pleats dropped into place. *I did that well*, I marked myself. It was good. Why couldn't I sew a black dress every week? Who would be the next to pass, so I could step in and ask for the seams to sew? It was a vulturous business, waiting for someone to die. Ghoulish and un-Christian. I set the sadiron on the back of the stove to heat, so I could press and set the hems, and shoveled in the last of the wood scraps. Water was warmed already for Homer's bath, and George's afterward in the same water. Supper would be brown broth with a handful of barley and onion in it, and biscuits crumbled and softened in broth for Homer.

George and Ira came in, clattering up flights to our perch above, while the window showed purple sky, then black, with gas lights lit below, and the horsecar still clopping toward home, filled with tired workers. George made his cold sound, "Brrzshh!" his fingers almost blue with cold after an afternoon of following his brother around, his mittens lost, and not enough yarn to make another pair. Ira had a bundle of wood scraps under his arm, not enough for a long evening, just sufficient for breakfast tea and porridge. "I'll get more tomorrow, Mother," he promised. "And George will help me." He ruffled his brother's hair. "Right, Georgie? We'll get wood tomorrow." George nodded, ruffling his own hair, then reaching to ruffle Ira's.

"Come, Master George, it is time to wash for supper, then bed." I hung the black dress on a peg to press in the morning. Not enough wood to heat the stove and do a proper job tonight, anyway.

In the morning, tea and porridge made and consumed, hems pressed, I took the dress, covered with the spare muslin sheet, over my coat sleeve and walked down the stairs and around the corner to the Scotts' home on Twenty Sixth. Mr. Scott owned several buildings in the neighborhood and beyond but liked to stay nearby so he could keep his eye on his tenants, he said. Mrs. Scott greeted me at the door, took the dress and paid me three dollars, then casually mentioned that another tenant, Miss Scully, was making silk flowers and wondered if I wanted to join her.

"It pays as like as anything else," Mrs. Scott said in her English accent. "You might have a go. She's a spinster," she added. "A good worker but nary a beau. Irish." She clucked her tongue, disapproving.

"Ahh. Please tell her I will—or may I tell her myself?"

Mrs. Scott told me which apartment housed the flower woman. I went directly to the woman's door, top floor of the Scott's building. I knocked at the door, open like the doors in my own building, the worn floorboards the same, the dim gas lighting, the same grim stoves and coal soot dusting every surface. The same kind of sassy Irish children clattered up and down the stairs, playing with ragged dolls or shooting marbles in the halls; the same types of mothers called downstairs or up. Through open doors, small industries churned—another tailor, with a family sewing men's shirts, another mother and her children sewing buttons to cards; a woman filled her tray with pies to take out for sale. How many other buildings like this did Mr. Scott own? How many other buildings were there like this, owned by other men, on each and every block in this City, and beyond? The numbers must be uncountable—thousands, tens of thousands.

A woman's voice called from within, "Come, whoever 'tis, I can't get up."

I stepped cautiously into the room and found the owner of the voice, a Miss Eileen Scully, seated at a table, her fingers dark with mucilage, rapidly rolling pink silk flower petals into roses, a splay of white pistils at the center. As fast as she rolled the one together she was already reaching for the white cluster, dipping the ends, and pressing, rolling, twisting, and setting aside another while beginning again. "Are ye here 'bout the flow'rs?"

"Mrs. Scott said you knew where I could get such work. I'm a dressmaker, but—"

"But work is scarce, I'm thinking. But ye sew, she said. Ye can move yer fingers fast, I'm thinking. Would ye want such work? We're the *sweat* of the sweat shop ye've heard of." Her never-hesitant fingers continued to dip, twist, roll, press, grab, turn, twist and roll again. The table was covered in made flowers, the bed stacked with boxes of petals, the wire stems, the beaded pistils. The room looked like a fertile field of blossoms fallen from an orchard, this one-woman factory.

"Whatever you know of, whatever there is, I want to work," I said. My voice shook. As trivial and useless as were these flowers, if someone paid for them, I was willing. Every day my secret fund grew smaller and smaller, and winter was cold. And there was no going back to the farm.

"Wait, now. Let me wipe me hands. I'm sorry I can't ask ye to sit, but it's me last day for this order. That's what they mean by sweatshop—it's not the heat, it's the man breathing down yer neck! I'll write his name and the main shop; go down there as quick as e'er ye can and tell him I sent ye, and he'll give ye what ye need for the makin's." Miss Scully cocked her head. “And I don’t mind tellin’ ye that I get a bonus of fifty cent when I find a new sweater. It helps.”

“Can you pay the rent with what you earn?” I had to know.

“With this and that extra, I can. We don’t eat like kings, but we git enough. Stay warm enough.”

Enough is as good as a feast, they said.

“I thank you, Miss Scully.” I took the slip of paper and hurried home, the paper folded tight in my hand.

Chapter 8

February 1860

February began with Homer's birthday, a day we celebrated with many kisses, and scrambled eggs for supper. Homer loved eggs and could eat them by the fistful, but eggs were dear in winter, and I had none preserved like on the farm, as I had every winter before. But Homer's first birthday was special (his own father hadn't lived to see this day), so we marked the date with eggs. The baby shoved the curdled yolks into his happy mouth, and we all laughed to see how chubby his pink cheeks were. A child passing his first year unscathed was always something to celebrate. I thought of my lost two infant daughters in the churchyard in Newburgh, near their papa and grandpapa in the Lozier plot. We had not named them, but I thought of them often. Homer's eggs went down his red gullet, as fast as coins in the hand of the little monkey on the corner.

Life was different on the top floor now, with neighbors looking in to say good afternoon or trade a bit of food or handwork, but I was getting used to it. Lizzie Hearne still snipped at me on the stairs, but now I recognized the twinkle in her eye and snipped back. I started to understand the Irish way, Lizzie "just taking the piss," and abundant laughter, from a people who seemed steeped in tea and sorrow. Each one was a walking tragedy, when I heard their tales, and yet they laughed every single day. Between the dour German Seybolts and the staid Greenleafs of my youth, I had always kept a stiff upper lip and my feelings locked up tight. The Irish were vastly different in so many ways from me, and yet, they strode onward, their hearts on their sleeves, crying or laughing, a prayer and a swear on their lips. It was something to ponder as the winter days passed.

February was a short month, but a slow one, too, with slushy, dirty snow and sleet, icy fingers and toes, a cold bed that needed all of us together to stay warm. It was too small to keep us all in comfort. With George's occasional bedwetting, Sarah demanded the side of the bed away from the wall, necessitating that we climb over, with her indignant tsking. I don't remember being so tiresome to my elders as Sarah in her moods. Homer's sleepy kicks in my ribs or my gut were a rude awakening as well. Ira toughed it out on the floor. I had long since sold the last of our treasures. I paid the lower rent each week, and the grocery bill, bought more beans and Indian meal, the cheapest of tea leaves. We just needed to get to spring; it was like this at Newburgh, too—the cows stopped milking, the hens stopped laying, the root cellar started out full but emptied as the weeks and months passed. A few weeks more, if I could make the silk flowers pay, if I could eke by a little longer and not run out of money.

We had a system now with the silk flowers. I rose at five o'clock with Sarah, went to the table straight away; we both made flowers while the boys slept in, relishing our uninterrupted time to make a dent in the day's stint, if I were to make the week's quota of flowers. We rolled flowers for an hour and a half or two, if the little ones slept through til seven. We enjoyed the first pot of tea together, quietly, not talking, but working meditatively, pausing in the dim room to sip our hot drinks. Ira awoke at six and took care of the night soil and brought up fresh water; he helped box the first finished flowers with clean hands. The little boys were got up by seven, because I needed the bed to lay out boxes and flower parts.

We took breakfast at the table and washed up afterward; Ira supervised the boys' breakfast while we washed and dressed. Sarah and I replaited our sloppy night braids and put on our black dresses, by now patched and thin. By eight o'clock, when the children should be trekking out the snowy road to school, Ira took the hessian sack and put his own gloves on George's hands; they went out together to look for coal and wood and old newspaper to roll. They had leave to roam the streets until the noon hour, as long as Ira kept two eyes on George, but they came in once or twice with their findings: a bundle of newspapers, a bruised apple the costermonger had given them to share, a half-filled bag of rough board ends from the cabinet factory. They warmed themselves and I promised to bake the apple for their dinner.

I sent Sarah to the grocery for Irish potatoes, a penny's worth, and some bacon ends. I baked potatoes and the apple for the hour before dinner, my middle feeling pinched like my worn corset (oh, how I wanted a new one); I looked forward to the meal with an eagerness that surprised me. The scent of roasting potatoes and apple together made me swallow over and over with appetite. The boys' morning forage had brought in enough fuel for the afternoon, but Ira must go out again after eating to find more. He had a half-dime in his pocket in case he was unable to find enough scraps and bits for our supper and breakfast fires; he could go to the coal yard and buy what he hadn't found. It was no kind of life for a boy, this scavenging, and endless shame burned my face, the pride wiped off it like jam from a child's face.

Afternoons, we cleared the bed so Homer could nap. George played with his soldiers and his wooden men, talking quietly to himself in words we could only sometimes understand. I made fresh, strong tea and we girls made headway on the flowers, although by this time our backs were sore and the afternoon seemed to stretch before us like a Sunday. Dark still fell early, though there was the faint knowledge that March was near, that April would follow, the light would grow and we could put away candles. Homer awoke from his nap and Sarah played and sang with him while I sped onward, rolling, dipping, setting the roses just so in boxes on the bed again. George might play with the neighbor boys in the hallway, and we took a break of half an hour to walk up and down the hall with Homer to practice his steps, or to go to the grocer or deliver the completed flowers. I ran other errands for flower supplies or a few penny candles from the chandler, to check into the shops where my curling, fading card still hung, catch a breath of fading afternoon light, then home to trade places with Sarah, either to chop the cold baked potatoes and fry them with grease, or give that job to Sarah while I spun and dipped another hundred roses before supper. Ira returned by six o'clock, when the bells of St. Stephen's a short block away rang out the hour of evening service, with coal or wood in his bag and fingers and lips blue from cold.

Sometimes I made potato soup from the leftover potato water. Sometimes we ate the potatoes cold, when there wasn't fuel enough, and if there wasn't still a half-dime for coal; when there wasn't light enough to go on, it was early bedtime for all. We rolled into the bed together, stockings and nightshirts and gowns and caps, and said our prayers together under the quilt, with Ira mumbling "Amen" from his bedroll. Sarah might sing a song or tell a story in the dark. The days were long, but not long enough to make enough flowers, and each week, I took another fifty-cent piece, another half-dime or dime, for fuel or milk or potatoes, one day, one week, until rent was due again, until the next batch of flowers came through.

A job of sewing a mourning gown would make the difference (but when would I sew it? Or when would I sleep?). My thoughts turned ghoulish when I heard of a sickly neighbor, rumors that a new baby or an elder might not make it to spring. A set of mourning for an entire family would put us ahead for once, instead of behind.

In March, the snow disappeared, turning to icy rain and cutting winds, runny noses and earaches for all three boys. Ira blustered through his cold, wiping his nose with a handkerchief when he was indoors, his sleeve when he was out. He called his handkerchief a *muckender* and blew his nose with his fingers into the street when Sarah and I weren't about. George and Homer fretted and squalled and whined, perpetual green and yellow crusts in their nostrils, skin chapped pink where the drool or mucus ran down their faces. I asked the other mothers for chamomile leaves and flowers for tea; Lizzie suggested giving them hot water and vinegar and another insisted on hot moist towels against their faces or ears to steam out the sickness. Grandmother Seybolt had always fed an invalid from a silver sipping flagon, but no such help was at hand; I had only old wives, like myself, and their tales to rely upon. The vinegar cost five cents to fill my jug but neither boy would swallow it, not even if I pinched his nostrils and forced it down; they spat it out and screamed as if I were skinning them alive. A hot cloth against my baby's ear left him sobbing, but whether for relief or pain, I could not say. By the end of the evening, with two sickly boys fretful and damp, and Sarah weeping from exhaustion in the same bed, I lay back, my arm around Homer and my hand patting George's leg, as all their sobs and hiccups slowly turned to deeper breaths.

We should never have left the farm.

My children slept, Ira on the floor near the cold stove, Sarah still sniffling at the edge of the bedframe, George and Homer snoring slightly through their congestion. I couldn't close my eyes; they stayed open like embroidered eyes on a stitched-on face. I should have answered the newspaper notice. Tomorrow more flowers to make, rent due in two days, grocery bill due as well. No help was coming. Bram couldn't help me, and neither could Malcolm. Their bodies were worm-eaten now, too far away to weep over. Bram's brown face, his lush brown beard, sometimes slipped from my memory, his voice a hazy bit of music from a far-off tavern. I felt so alone.

I had sometimes wondered, as a girl in Newburgh, what I could have made of myself in a City like New York or Philadelphia or London, my needle threaded with silk, and my choice of fine ladies clamoring for my skills. Silken dresses of my own in a cabinet of cherrywood made just for my garments, City shoes of calfskin or kid with high heels, silver buckles at the instep, silk ribbons at my ankles, feet on a hassock and a cup of hot chocolate in a Dresden cup. What if I had not married Bram, not that anyone else had asked? What if I hadn't been sent like a load of dung from Otisville to Newburgh when my Grandmother Seybolt died and the cousins thought I was a hussy, sending me onward to the fashionable Greenleafs, who let me fall between the cracks? If my father hadn't died when I was a girl, and my mother hadn't left me behind when she went off to marry her cousin Mr. Tooker? If my protector-husband had not died and my father-in-law had kept his health, and the children's legal guardian not a wolf and a menace to young girls?

What if I had said yes to the haberdasher? Or—maybe not said no so quickly?

So many ifs. If I could only have a shop, and make more dresses, and send my daughter to school and get my boy off the street and the slang from his mouth, both of them, all of them in school with enough to eat. If I could sit for a cup of hot coffee somewhere that was warm enough, and my feet didn't hurt, and my eyes didn't stare at the darkness while the building creaked and settled and other people's footsteps sounded on the stair, in the hall, and the clop of horses on cobbles or a rowdy man singing off his drink, and a fight in the street. Nights should be silent, and restful, not full of noise and a roll of tasks ticking by in my mind.

How long could I keep going? One more hour. One more flat of flowers. One more week. One more day.

I couldn't sleep anyway, so I slipped out of bed, wrapped my shawl around myself, lit the candle and rolled silk flowers at the table until I was sapped of all vigor and dawn was breaking through the window, stuffed with rags where it leaked a bitter draft.

• • •

March dragged past and April hitched itself in with Easter and the clanging of Catholic bells nearby. I kept the Sabbath with my children at home, when I could, instead of the stiff wooden pews of church. I heard the new Dutch Marble church bell ringing far off, like a song I'd known since birth, from three long blocks away. I had walked to see it one Sunday but hadn't gone inside. The bronze bells chimed for the holiday in the steeple; black iron bars kept roving pigs and horses out, and there stood a minister in the same black suit, the same starched white lace at his neck, as ever I'd known. The remembered hymns and psalms ran through my mind as I rolled roses and dipped the little stamens, pinching and pleating for a penny, just a penny, another penny more.

I didn't feel like the virtuous wife who'd attended services, who had stood in the churchyard while dirt rained on my husband's coffin. I felt as if I'd lain my cloak on a chair somewhere and couldn't remember where I left it—the pious farm wife, the sanctimonious mother, the put-upon-daughter-in-law. I'd had grievances in my Newburgh days, that I hadn't left my small town, seen taller buildings and wide avenues; that my babies died in their beds and my husband went on sowing the rye, shucking the Indian corn; the year turned on a millwheel and I was with child, little William Homer growing in my womb, the sixth seed sown by this tall, sturdy Bram. I hadn't got around the newest bitterness, the wretched truth that Bram was gone. The bells rang, and I barely had time to go to the privy alone of a morning, much less the church, and so my soul suffered. Grandmother Seybolt would have been so disappointed.

"Read something for us, will you, Sarah?" I asked, and my daughter did, her elocution lesson wrapped into a Sunday school and a storytelling. The boys listened in, hearing the tale of Jonah in the belly of the great fish, the lure of the Tree of Knowledge, the lesson of Cain and Abel, brothers who fought instead of helped each other. Joseph and his high and mighty dreams got him sold into slavery by jealous brothers, but Ira chucked George under the chin and said, "No fear, Georgie-me-lad! We're kin!"

"I'm your kin, too," Sarah added for George's benefit. "It means family." George looked at his siblings but didn't say what he thought. Homer babbled and grinned. It pleased me to see such bonds between my children, remembering my sisters Ida and Aramantha, and how we'd all been scattered when Papa died. I'd written to my mother and sisters when Bram passed, but not since I'd come to the City. Not since Newburgh. I couldn't, now. Not until I could tell them I was well, I had prospered, my children were in school and becoming gentlemen, a young lady. Until then, my safety was my secrecy.

Easter Monday passed; Tuesday rolled around and it was my day to take in the flowers. I left Sarah with the little boys and the wash to boil, taking Ira to help ferry the many boxes of silk roses. We cinched them together with hemp twine and, though the boxes were light, they made a tall stack. I wrapped my shawl around my shoulders and pinned it closed, slipped my arm through my reticule and picked up my two stacks of boxes, the hairy twine already smarting my fingers. Ira's stacks were almost as tall as he was but he refused to trade stacks. "I'll do it, Mother. Never you mind." In Newburgh, I might have soaped his mouth for such high backchat, but now, he was my man, my eldest, and he said he would carry the boxes.

The walk to Mr. Meagher's wholesale workshop was better now, as the snow and slush had melted away, but mud and puddles and liquid horse dung slicked the cobbled street. Hogs ran in the street sometimes, loose from up island where there were still farmsteads and market gardens. I felt the hairy twine cutting my sore fingers, knew Ira's fingers felt the same, but he didn't complain. A rattle of drums turned his head.

"Mother, the 69th!" I turned to see a unit of the Irish regiment turn the corner on Second and head west on Twenty Sixth, back toward their garrison. Ira's eyes followed every row, his head bobbing a little in time to the drum. He put down his boxes and saluted as the last row of soldiers passed.

At the rear, on horse, a corporal winked at Ira. "That's a good boy you have there, ma'am." He trotted past.

I nodded my thanks, proud of my son.

"When I'm grown, I'm going to war," Ira vowed. "I'm going to march and ride in the cavalry and shoot cannons and carry a sword. I'll wear a blue coat with a line down my trousers, and gold braid on my shoulder. I'll march in parade and stand ever so still when we're at attention." He nattered on, describing the ranks of the military and all their duties to me with an intensity I found endearing, if somewhat tedious.

Someday, I had no doubt, he would do just those things, and do them well.

We rounded the last corner and entered the building where Mr. Meagher did his business. We waited our turn to give him our completed flowers, his cheerful voice giving good news and bad in the same tones.

"No, Mrs. Brown, these won't do. These won't do a-tall. Look at these—they're falling apart." He opened another box and looked into it. "These alike. Lady, that was your last chance. I haven't the time nor the money for a sweater who can't do the work. Here's all I owe you."

I heard a few thin coins clink, and the woman gasped.

"But I—"

"Mrs. Brown, please. This isn't an almshouse. I'm out of patience. Next!" Mrs. Brown took her coins and stepped away from the desk, weeping. "Go on—out!"

Ira and I shuffled to the desk. Mr. Meagher untied the hempen string and quickly flipped through the boxes. "Your work is fine, Mrs. Seabolt. Right fine."

I was relieved to hear.

"But this is it—the end of this line. Hatmaker wants something else now. Birds or fruit or maybe another kind of flower, whatever the fashion demands. Come along sometime next week and we'll get back to work. You're a fine worker, Missus. I don't want to lose you. But I've nothing for you now." He paused to count the layers in boxes and do a quick tally on a scrap of paper. "Three dollars," he said, handing me two bills and some coins. "Come back next week, if you would, lady."

"Good day, Mr. Meagher," my mouth making the polite and appropriate reply while my mind leapt ahead to the rent I could pay, or the grocer's bill, and whatever other expenses came our way. I still had some money in my reticule from the last week, but it wasn't spending money. It was all we had left for the next week's rent and groceries. I smiled my polite farewell, my hand on Ira's shoulder. "Next week."

"No more money until next week?" Ira's voice squeaked a little, his voice beginning to turn.

"So it seems." I was calculating in my head how much savings I still had—I wouldn't check my purse on the street, but on the bed, sorted into piles of coins for each bill, I could see exactly how much we had left, and for how long it would last. We walked briskly to the corner of Third and 27th and waited in a cluster of people for the horsecar to pass before crossing. I felt a tug at my arm and almost lost my footing in the mud. Ira and a gentleman bystander caught me and helped me to stand when I realized my reticule was gone, with only its pathetic frayed cords dangling from my arm.

Ira stared, shocked. "A cutpurse!" He looked around to espy the culprit.

"Are you hurt, ma'am?" The gentleman supported my arm still.

"No, but—" I held up my empty arm, didn't know what else to say then.

"Some rascal has robbed you, ma'am! Shall I whistle for the police?"

"No, I thank you. No policeman." Montgomery might have let my name be known, perhaps he was looking for me still. Ira stood on a box at the curb, looking around for the miscreant, but gave up, apologizing. The kind bystander made his farewell. There didn't seem to be any other thing to say.

Ira took my hand and we crossed the street together toward home. "It's cold coffee for us, then." He squeezed my hand. His paws were bigger than I recalled. "I don't mind. Sarah won't mind, neither. Don't worry, Mother. You'll make a dress or something good will happen soon. It has to, doesn't it?"

"Yes, son. Something is bound to happen soon. It always does."

Chapter 9

April 1960

In the room there were few treasures to be sold, and little reserve upon which to draw. I had my silver thimble and sewing shears and my gold-colored stork scissors with the red-painted eyes. I had three dresses; I could sell one. I had a ragbag. I still had my wedding band. I had that old *Godey's Lady's Book*. The children had their few toys and their clothing, and I couldn't sell those. There was a measure of beans and Indian meal, two onions, some bacon fat, a few potatoes. I had no money. Not a penny. Two dollars rent was due on Saturday, and my grocery credit was good until then as well. Four days to earn the two dollars, and then again the following week.

I sent Ira out to search for fuel. "Don't talk of it, son. Don't tell the neighbors. We'll tell Sarah, but no one else."

My face flamed at losing my money to a cutpurse on the street—all we had earned, with Sarah's help—all the silk roses for the past week, earnings gone, and my last five dollars rolled in Bram's monogrammed handkerchief besides. Plus my own cambric handkerchief, a stub of a pencil and a Sunday School card I had carried in my reticule since I had married, with the Twenty-Third Psalm on it and a tinted picture of The Good Shepherd on the other side. And yet—we were one week from destitution, so what mattered my best handkerchief?

I stirred the white clothes in the kettle, hoping to boil out the worst of the stains and sourness. I'll sell my stork scissors—those were extra. With my sewing shears I could cut a thread as well as fabric goods. I couldn't sell those; how would I ply my trade without a pair of shears? And the silver thimble—it could fetch a price, but how could I present myself a respectable dressmaker without a silver thimble on my finger? It was the badge of my skill. I could work without it, but a single poke would leave blood on a garment, and slow my pace; I could make myself a leather thimble from a piece of my shoe's tongue, but what it said about me, a dressmaker with a leather thimble? It was my inheritance. My family had lived here since New York was Dutch, and before then. The silver thimble was everything about my family, my place in this nation, in America, in the silversmiths of Boston, and the pride of the colonies. I could give that up, sell my inheritance from Grandmother Seybolt—and when we'd eaten the bacon and beans, I couldn't work. It was a short-sighted bargain. The thimble—not yet. My wedding band, neither—it made me respectable. It gave name to my children, proved my widowhood without uttering a word.

My spare dress could go to the Russian near the docks, and the ragbag, to the papermaker. I would send Ira to take a note. And if I was writing one note, I had a letter that would pain me to write, but at this moment seemed necessary.

> *My Dear Mother,*
>
> *It has been some months since I received your last missive, and being under extreme urgency to leave the farm after my Father-in-Law's death, we removed to New York City. With the Good Lord's blessing and the health of my four children, we have settled and I am obliged by*

my circumstances as widow to undertake dressmaking in my home. We are distressed just now due to a seasonal slowing but I anticipate with much regard a return to my busier state. However, in these reduced times, with all strictures measured to our economy, I must ask your kindness and indulgence of a gift of some ten dollars to see us through this rough weather.

Your granddaughter and grandsons, being in good health and spirits, send their dearest love, Mother. Please respond by soonest post. With loving thanks from

Your eldest daughter,
Martha Seybolt Lozier

I gave my address care of the grocery store at the corner, still reluctant to give up my location. It was a terrible letter to have to write, leaving me scraped bare with self-loathing, and having to use my married name at the grocer. A begging letter to my mother—who had not seen fit to offer us a home for even the shortest of sojourns after my husband's death. I expected nothing from my mother and step-father. I hadn't asked for Mr. Tooker's health and looked for a way to add it in, but that would only show I had forgotten him, and I didn't have another clean and unwrinkled sheet of writing paper. If Mother was going to deny me anyway, let it be without regard from my step-father/cousin.

I folded the letter and addressed it, with Homer hanging on my dress, steadying himself with handfuls of my fabric and his mouth open and soaking my skirts. I sealed it with a drop of wax from our penny candle, but I knew I did not have the three cents to frank it. I still had credit at the grocer's until it came due at the weekend. I wiped Homer's nose and mouth and pulled the shawl around myself and the boy, taking Sarah's shopping basket on my arm. "I'm taking my letter to post, George. Mind Sarah, now!"

Sarah gave a worried smile in farewell. "Please be careful!"

"They've already taken my reticule. I haven't another to lose." I laughed a little shrilly, startling Sarah. *I'm becoming like the Irish,* I realized, at last starting to comprehend. When things got bad, they could always get worse. No wonder they laughed at trouble. There was always more trouble at hand. In some backward way, that made sense to me. I could cry or laugh, and it was infinitely better to keep from crying, even if bleak laughter was the only escape.

"Don't worry, my dear. I'll be back soon." I waved the folded letter at my daughter and took myself and Homer out and down the stairs.

"Look at the horse, Homer," I said softly, as a horsecar clopped along Third. "The horsie says *neigh*!"

Homer made a sound somewhat like a neigh, more like a little cough than a horse's whinny, but he was a sharp little lad, already ahead of George at that age. Homer had never seen a cow, nor a sheep nor even a pig yet, living in the City. I pointed out a dog, a pigeon, and a donkey on the short walk, eliciting half-barks and attempted brays from my son. I heard there was a menagerie somewhere in the City and wondered what it would be like to see a real tiger in a cage, or a great ape from the jungle. Homer's brown curls tickled my face, and though I felt him go damp against my gown, I was glad to have a little time to cuddle him against me, after so many weeks of galloping through mountains of silk roses and seemingly acres of mourning wear.

Mr. Newman, the grocer, was pleased to frank my letter, adding the three cents to my bill, and promised to watch for a letter in return. He would send his errand boy if any correspondence came to me there. I asked for a pound of tea, a pint of molasses in the milk pail and two more pounds of Indian meal. I would make weak tea with molasses, and the sweetness would give us energy. George could drink it, too. We'd get along until I got more work. We'd make it. I was almost sure of it.

Mr. Newman added the groceries to my slate and said, as if he already knew my plight, "We'll see you Saturday to pay this down."

I forced a little laugh and answered, "Yes, of course," and we both knew I was lying.

I hitched Homer up my hip and nodded my farewell, knowing I wouldn't be back until I had coin in pocket or a letter had come. And perhaps I wouldn't get the letter without paying my bill. I felt myself melting like a candle too near the fireplace, how it softens and bends, its wick sagging as the wax fails.

Back toward my building, passing the haberdasher, pausing to look sideways toward the glass door from the sidewalk, not daring to step closer and see if Keeler was within. To offer up my services at whatever price. To take whatever pennies he said he was willing to pay. Whatever he might not pay afterward, regardless. I felt the familiarity of the slim gold band on my third finger, always there, marking me as a married woman—it hadn't stopped Mr. Keeler or Mr. Tavish from harassing me, but without it, I was laid bare. I was dropping my shield.

Feed the children or walk unguarded into the light—and let go the last link to my late husband. I couldn't choose. I couldn't act. I kept walking, turned into our building and climbed the steps with the baby on my hip.

• • •

The Russian from the docks agreed to buy my goods; he took my stork scissors and second dress, the indigo blue one.

I still had a very faded washday dress and my one good black dress, fading. I sold the bag of rags, the *Godey's* and my pen, as well, to save me the trouble of carrying the bag to the paper mill. I sold George's shoes and put Ira's outgrown pair on him, stuffing the ends with newspaper. Homer had outgrown his moccasins but with warmer weather coming, could go without shoes. Sarah's shoes still fit, and though she might fill out a corset, I doubted the girl would grow any taller on our short rations. I paid rent and the grocer, who seemed surprised to see me. I hoarded the remaining cash for the next week's rent and groceries, keeping it in a much-mended stocking since I had lost my reticule. Going through my sewing basket, I found a way to sew together strips of ribbon and lace, to make a somewhat gaudy little coin-purse, with a single shell button to fasten it closed. I crocheted a simple cord to help secure the opening. I wore it pinned in my bosom when I left the house, my shawl wrapped Sontag-style over my bodice to further secure it.

There were no more silk flowers yet, but Mr. Meagher said there might be something in the next week.

• • •

My dearest daughter:

Rec'ved your missive with joy that you are hale and living in good circumstances, that the children are also well despite such illnesses as accompany city living. It grieves me to return your letter with no reward. I do not have the pin money to spare at this time and your Step-father will not give it me.

I have just got the prettiest brown bonnet and I wish you were here to do it up for me; you are always so clever with your needle, I am astonished that you have insufficient employment.

When you have the time will you go down to the docks and look for some silk or lace for me for a petite fichu? I can repay you when I see you next or by post. You are my beloved daughter. May the Lord keep you in his Hand alway.

Your loving Mother,
Mary Greenleaf Tooker

Such a letter, from such a mother, must only remind me that I was a fool to have thought and a fool to have hoped. I crushed the note and threw it in the fire.

I took to keeping the soup pot at the back of the stove and scraping our plates back into it. Anything we hadn't finished—a crust of cornbread, a bone or gristle, an onion string, and more water—went back into the pot and thickened it for the next meal. Spring was hard upon us, and I felt the need for a tonic, some kind of fresh vegetable or green, and took the children with me to look for dandelions, for sheep sorrel, for Jack-by-the-hedge, and found that I was not alone. The places where there were grass or weeds creeping up through mud had been picked over. I saw several women scouring the margins of the roads for the same, and yet some had been successful and were selling bunches of dandelion greens for a penny in the street. I looked longingly but saw that it was bruised and mixed with green grass. Were I an unwitting City-born soul, I might be serving grass to my children this very evening. The thought made me wry, like my Irish cohorts. Move to the City just to eat grass, I'd say, if I'd felt easy enough to try a bit of badinage with Lizzie Hearne.

We scraped through another week, and into the next, eating of the neverending pot of soup, the porridge in the morning that thickened the broth later in the day. A little salt, a little water, and a pot of weak tea with molasses for all the children. I preferred it stronger, blacker, with sugar, but there was none else to sweeten. I soaked beans overnight and boiled them, saving the broth; baked some beans with molasses dribbled across the top, served it hot, then dished up cold the day after. The plate scrapings and the broth went into the pot, I stirred it, salted it, and we drank it at supper.

Homer became fretful, not his usual smiling self, and it was probably biliousness from the beans; we all knew how sulfurous the air was at night with the door closed and all of us suffering. George and Ira could not stop giggling some nights, and truth be told, it was black comedy, how we could gas away the evening, or hold it in and suffer the pains. Sarah pretended indignation at their low humor but I giggled all the same. A dash of *sal aeratus* in the beans, or in a glass of warm water, might alleviate some of the symptoms, but it was out of my budget now. I saved wood ash and some of the charcoal when I could, to use for a sour stomach, or scouring pots, and cleaning teeth with a damp finger.

Not Sarah, neither Ira nor George complained, but I knew they were hungry, or at least hungry for something else. I went around to Meagher's again, and still they told me there was no order yet. I twisted my wedding ring, cupped my thimble in my hand. One morning as I was brushing out my bed-braid, I wondered if I could sell my hair, while it was still ash-brown, and not gone over gray straw. My hair, my teeth, my daughter's hair, my children's labor, my wedding ring, my thimble, my scissors, my sex. These items tailed each other like a children's round song, chasing each other through my waking hours at the stove, at the mangle down at the standing pipe, at the slosh of night water and the sour scent of baby flannels and our scant monthly rags. I couldn't sell my ring,

I should sell my thimble. I could sell the thimble but not my shears. I could sell the shears but keep the thimble. I looked around the room to see what else I could peddle.

I could pay rent or pay the grocer that week. I paid rent and added more water to the soup. I made mush instead of baking cornbread; I fried it on the stovetop, but it stuck without grease and made an awful mess. I made patties from the cooked beans and fried those, too. I was out of sorts and my gut complained, without greens or meat or corn and potatoes, and the baby cried for my thin milk, though he didn't have the words to say so. Ira still went out twice a day with George, to bring back fuel; it took less time to find, since the snow had gone. They stayed out as long, however. At dinner, Ira came home with two apples he got for sweeping out the tavern for Mr. Tavish. "One for me, for sweeping, and the other for George, for holding the door for the barrel man." Ira insisted on giving his apple to Sarah and Homer at dinner.

I chivied George, "Share with your brother!"

"No, Mother, I don't mind. We had a glass of cider at the tavern and I'm not hungry."

Cider was healthful food but working in the tavern? Yet he had provided for the family. How could I say him nay? "Eat your soup, son, and I thank you for your generosity." I had to get work. But Ira said he wasn't hungry and left his bowl of soup for the others to greedily finish.

The next day, Ira and George were an hour late for dinner, coming in the door cheerfully, and there were unmistakable crumbs on George's blouse and a milk mustache on his dirty face. Sarah served the soup, taking Homer on her lap to share.

"Where have you been, boys?" I looked at the hessian bag that Ira set down and it was less full, but heavier than usual. "Did you not find scraps?" Inside the bag was coal, not a stick of wood.

George pulled off his shoes, his toes black from newspaper in the toes, and went to the bed. He lay his head on his pillowed coat, looking like an old man replete with the Sunday repast. He smiled and his eyelids sagged.

"Are you tired, Georgie?" Sarah asked, feeding Homer.

"Mmmm hmmm." He patted his middle and said, "Good."

I almost dropped my spoon. "He said *good!* Ira! What's this?"

"Oh, Mother—we ate like kings. It was so good," Ira exulted, and George mimicked him again, "Good."

"Ira, please."

"There's a kind of school where we ate, over Fourth Avenue," he said, a little sheepish after gloating. "I wanted to see the garrison and we were walking that way, before we went down to the cabinet factory for scraps."

"I don't understand."

"It's got a queer name, like Home for the Friends," Ira said. "It has a stone sign. The lettering is fancy. It's hard to read. They have school every day and they feed children. They asked us to come in and eat. They want us to go to school there. We can eat dinner there every day, but we have to go to school. They'll give us new clothes and teach us to work, too. And this lady made George talk."

"What on earth?" I puzzled over this description. It sounded altogether too much like the almshouse—teaching young children to work. But my children worked anyway. What was the difference, after all? "How did she make George talk?"

"There was a lesson going on, and she promised the children a cooky if they said their lesson. It was like Sunday School, 'God is great, God is good, Jesus wept,' words from the Bible. 'In the beginning God created the heavens and the earth—.'"

"I didn't know you knew that, Ira," Sarah broke in. "That's good!"

"Good." George repeated the word from his sleepy position on the bed, and curled a little tighter, pulling at the quilt.

I pulled it up over him. "Are you sleepy, son? You ate your dinner and you are tired?"

He smiled a little, something he rarely did, and then yawned. "Good."

I stroked his back, then turned back to the table. Sarah had finished feeding Homer. I changed the baby's flannel and tucked him in with George for a rest. I returned to my soup but it was cold. I poured it back into the pot and stirred a little, then ladled up a warmer serving.

"Are you sure you ate?"

"We ate a very good dinner, Mother. I'm sorry I boasted. We had ham and potatoes with gravy, boiled cabbage and carrots, bread and butter, milk and a big piece of pie. It was apple pie at our plates but they also had vinegar pie and raisin pie. You just got what you had at your plate. Mother, it was so wonderful. We didn't ask for anything. Honest, we weren't begging.

"They were outside talking to children and they invited us in, and they had a lesson and George was watching and he said 'Good,' when they asked him to speak. He got a cooky and then we had a prayer and dinner and came home. I'm sorry we were late, Mother. I just thought if we had our dinner, that you wouldn't have to feed us."

I felt that in my conscience. "No, son, it sounds wonderful. What kind people to give you dinner, and they got George to speak." The moment could not be underestimated. George *spoke,* he *responded* to a request. He *smiled.* He could talk, if he wanted, if he was led along in the right way, a way I had not yet discovered—had been too tired to find that way. My eyes filled, shame and relief together.

"I didn't mean to make you cry." Ira came over and took my hand, awkward as a balky calf. "I was thinking what would Papa have done."

"You did right, son." Ira had found a way, like his father. "I didn't think George could really speak. But maybe—perhaps they can help him at this school."

"Oh, wouldn't that be wonderful?" Sarah put my bowl in the dishpan and added boiling water. "If George could speak, could he read? Could the boys go to school?" She paused, looking at the floor. "Could I?"

"I don't know, Sarah. Perhaps I should go and visit the school and see what they want to teach children. If they will feed their students, that helps." The children could get one good meal per day, at least, while I worked. And the boys out of the house made it easier to work; but Sarah would have to mind the baby. Perhaps there was a way for Sarah to go to school, too, to get the meal. But if I had to mind Homer, who was too young for school, I couldn't really work; I might ask another mother to watch the baby while I worked, but then I'd have to pay the woman, and that wouldn't pay the rent. Sarah would have to stay home, perhaps with lessons she could do while Homer slept. It was a conundrum. What to do?

"Leave the dishes, Sarah. You and Ira go run about outside for a bit, and I'll watch the boys and clean up. You're a good boy for telling me, Ira. Go out and play for a while, and—Ira, did they give you coal, too?"

"Yes, ma'am. They said to take some of their coal so I could stay for the lesson and the dinner."

"We have enough for the evening and for breakfast, too. Go play, both, and be home by supper."

At the unexpected release from chores and baby brothers, my two eldest clattered down the stairs, and then the next flight, and I could hear when the big door banged shut behind them. With my window at the back, overlooking the Alley and the privies, I couldn't see them go out front to play, but whatever they did, watch for the horsecars and pet the horse's nose, or look for the organ grinder, or watch for soldiers, or however they might spend their free afternoon, I was glad they had a moment, a few hours, to be children again. Sarah was chained indoors, unable to explore the streets like her brothers, except for forays to the grocer's. It would be nice for her to get some sunshine on her pale skin.

The two little boys were asleep, breathing softly. It wasn't like George to nap, but he had been hungry. A full belly, especially after deprivation, will put anyone to sleep, I shouldn't wonder. I finished cleaning their bowls and spoons, scraped the thickening soup a bit and added more water. I wished we had some bread, but we were down to beans, tea and molasses, and Indian meal. The thought of a heaping plate of ham with potatoes dripping with gravy, thick slices of soft white bread smeared with butter, boiled cabbage and carrots with more butter and salt and black pepper, and a thick flaky slice of pie, apple or raisin or vinegar—such tastes I hadn't had for months. My Grandmother Seybolt had used to make a vinegar pie with beaten cream and a grating of nutmeg on top; it somehow tasted of lemonade. All of that and a cooky, too; no wonder the boy was sleepy.

I brewed another pot of tea and pulled the crate I usually sat on to the window. Out the back, from behind a brick wall, the tree had leafed out, small baby green leaves that would broaden into leaves the size of a man's hands, then crisp and fall that autumn. Home for the Friends sounded like a nice place, perhaps run by Quakers. I didn't know any Quakers, but they called themselves "Friends." A Quaker school that also fed the children their dinner: That sounded very likely, so I put away thoughts of the almshouse.

I kept my own counsel. In the morning, I would go with my sons to see the school. An education and a good meal were hard to decline.

Chapter 10

April 1860

"Won't you come in, Mrs. Lozier? And would you care for a cup of coffee?" The lady was some sort of forward woman, a so-called businesswoman, perhaps, the like of which I had never met. She was neither beautiful nor plain, tall nor short, old nor young, but, dressed in dark clothing, an indigo patterned dress with bell sleeves and well-pressed pleats to her cuffs and neck ruffle, and shiny small buttons of brass, the effect was smart and official, almost military. I felt my shyness return, but gratefully accepted a china cup with black coffee and two small shortbreads on the saucer. I gave Homer one of the cookies to smack upon; Sarah and the boys were being shown around the building and yard by a girl about Sarah's age, with a clean calico gown and a simple black hair-ribbon. Her stockings were black, and so were her shoes, polished boots with heels that looked new and soles that didn't squeak.

Mrs. Phillips called herself an Agent of the American Female Guardian Society and Home for the Friendless. She asked me some questions about myself and the children, taking notes with a pretty ivory and gold pen in a composition book at her desk. "I like to write things down so I don't forget, Mrs. Lozier. We see so many families here that one is apt to mix up the information if one doesn't keep notes."

"Please, Mrs. Phillips, I would like to hear about the school." I held my muslin handkerchief, a scrap from a petticoat, hemmed and utilitarian, tightly in case I teared up. I had foolishly given my real name, I was so flustered. "My younger son does not speak well—he is not dumb, but he does not often speak. But yesterday—." I choked up on my words.

"There, there, Mrs. Lozier. We were so pleased to welcome George and Ira into our classroom yesterday, and we hope to see them again. We hope you will consent to let them join us. We have the most modern, up-to-date methods of pedagogy and instruction for backward children, one that does not seek to punish for sloth and refusal to work, but rewards their efforts and their achievements. Although it is said that to 'spare the rod is to spoil the child,' we believe that the Rod is the Word of the Lord and to spare a child this reed of instruction is to lose him to other forces. Our school and our occupational programs are rooted in Scripture and rewarding a good effort. The Lord loves those who help themselves." She smiled after this little speech.

I sat in awe of the woman in blue, with the way she sat behind *her* desk and spoke so knowledgably about *achievement* and *pedagogy*, such newfangled words. Mrs. Phillips was so self-assured, so welcoming and confident in what they were doing. As she went on, it became apparent that the building was both a school and an orphanage; not all of the children were full orphans, but many had been brought by their parents to stay while the parents worked. An injured father, a mother who died in childbed, a parent's unemployment or a spouse's desertion were some of the reasons a child might come to the Home for the Friendless.

"You're a widow, Mrs. Lozier?"

"I lost my husband in the fall."

"And—please forgive me but I must ask for our records—were you unable to stay with family in your hometown?"

"It was not possible," I said evenly. I would not say more than that. I was already at risk by using my married name.

"Have you found work in the City?"

It felt as if I were undergoing an inquisition. "I have tried many things. I am a dressmaker. I make mourning clothes." I looked down at my fading black dress. "But it is not dependable income." I would be working right now, if only there was work I could do. "Death is a tragedy but—not everyone can afford special clothes."

"I understand. And you are forced to find—," Mrs. Phillips cleared her throat, "*other means* of earning your bread?"

I raised my chin. "I have been making silk flowers for a factor. I have tried some other methods of huckstering, but not what you suggest."

"Please do not take offense. We have many such mothers who come here to inquire about placing their children, for the short term or permanently. We are not here to cast judgment upon you." Mrs. Phillips leaned forward. "We want to make Christians of the suffering souls on our City streets. If those are the waifs that hunger in the darkest corners and sleep like dogs in filthy holes, or the proudest working man and woman, the lowly, the meek—whom has the Lord called? Blessed are they—come, you know the Sermon on the Mount, are you not a Christian yourself?"

"Blessed are the poor in spirit, for theirs is the kingdom of heaven." I had been raised on it.

"Blessed are they that mourn, for they shall be comforted," Mrs. Phillips returned. "It is these, the least of these, we wish to raise up. We feed the hungry, clothe the naked, teach children the Word, visit the sick and comfort the dying. If we can bring this mercy to you, we should love to."

I wanted to believe her. "Please, tell me more about the school?"

"Why don't you come and see for yourself?"

I set down my empty cup and, with Homer on my arm, followed Mrs. Phillips through a tour of the dormitories, the classrooms, the play-yard with rubber balls, skipping ropes and a swing; workrooms, the infirmary, the infants' ward, and the chapel. Boys and girls slept separately, of course, but learned in school together in the modern co-educational style. Each child received new clothing, a Bible, a toy, had their bodies and teeth looked after, took Christian instruction, and trained in an occupation when they were old enough. Older children were sent out to apprentice or work on farms, or into service to learn a skill or housekeeping; these children were paid for their labor and the moneys kept in savings until the children were of age: 18 for boys and 21 for girls. Railroad barons and their wives sat on their governing board, Mrs. Phillips said, so the agency's train tickets were free. Orphans and other waifs were sent out via the trains for adoption elsewhere in the state, or beyond.

It sounded like riches to me.

The beds were clean and neat, one child per bed, without sharing. The children's clothes were quality wool and cotton from the mills of the North, their stockings and hats of good wool, their shoes polished brown or black leather. Their faces were clean and the hallways smelled like lye soap, except near the kitchens, where the scent of freshly baked bread and a savory smell like stewed chicken wafted through, making my stomach growl with hunger. The fresh coffee teased my senses, as did the smell of toasted nuts—walnut cookies or cakes were also baking. The abundance was staggering, after our lean months.

"It is a kindness that we do for the City, and for these children," Mrs. Phillips concluded. "Our girls learn to clean, cook, preserve food, wash and iron clothing, sew, knit, and care for the younger students. They will make excellent wives and mothers! Our boys might learn farming, blacksmithing, printing—we have our own print shop on the premises. They learn logging, milling, fishing, or business principles. They will attend chapel and get a free education, with all their books paid for. Every slate pencil, every piece of foolscap, every cup of milk from our own dairy, every egg from our own flock of hens, is free to our children."

I saw a motto painted right onto the wall, in large block letters, so anyone could read them: "*Suffer the little children to come unto Me." —Luke 18:16.*

Were my children suffering? I must own it—they were. Would they thrive, given all of this? We caught up with the boys in a younger student classroom, George and Ira sitting on a bench together while the class recited the alphabet, and repeated the teacher's sounds:

Ma, pa, ba, ta, la, fa.
Mat, fat, pat, bat, cat, hat, sat.
Hit, mitt, lit, sit, pit, bit.
Let, set, wet, get, bet, pet.
Hot, pot, lot, rot, cot, got, not.

George watched, his eyes on pretty Teacher with a kind of love-gaze, his mouth moving but no sound coming out. He was learning something, I could tell, just watching his little mouth move. And Ira, reading silently ahead, his finger running along under the words in the *First Reader*—he would be through that and onto *McGuffy's Second Reader*—which we didn't have, couldn't afford—instead of walking the streets gathering scraps of wood from the factory, looking for leftover bits of coal, or sweeping out the tavern in exchange for an apple.

Sarah stood at the back of the room, watching, listening, her hands behind her back as if ready to recite, her mouth pinched to keep from crying aloud.

Ira, my young man, so full of potential—and George, my little fae star, so lovable but missing the spark of his brothers, the common sense of his sister. Whatever world was locked into his head—could these people—these Agents at the Home for the Friendless (*but we had friends! They weren't waifs!*)—could these Agents open George's mind, give him a life beyond a corner near the stove and a broom in a tavern?

At home, we had no food. We had the soup pot and nothing more. How could I say no to an opportunity for my sons, especially for my George?

Back in the receiving office, a gentleman joined us—Mr. Portland, an Agent and member of the governing board, he said. He wore dark trousers and a well-cut coat, showing his stock and a muted tartan waistcoat underneath. Mrs. Phillips opened a bound book with a clean certificate page for me to sign.

Signing the page meant the boys would stay at the Home and

This may certify that I,____________________, being unable to provide for my child, __________, do hereby commit and surrender ________ to the care and management of THE AMERICAN FEMALE GUARDIAN SOCIETY, with the powers and subject to the provisions contained in the Act incorporating said Society.

Dated New York, ___________________,18____

Witness:_______________________________________

I consent to and approve the above surrender.

Dated New York, ___________________,18____

I would leave with Sarah and Homer. Just the three of us, while Ira and George remained behind, my family broken up, what I swore I would never allow. I hesitated while I fought back tears.

"It is just a formality, Mrs. Lozier. It signifies nothing, only makes our records complete," he urged.

"I understand," I said, though I burned with shame. *I don't wish to* commit and surrender—*just to leave them here a while. Just so I can catch my breath.*

The boys would be fed. Ira was reading. George had spoken. And they looked happy. Meat and milk at each meal. Warm beds of their own. "I must get their things from home first."

"No need, madam. We have everything they need right here. Sign here, please." He placed the pen in my hand, dipped and ready.

• • •

Sarah was silent on the way home, barely speaking to Homer in her arms and not to me at all. At first I thought she was as sad as I at leaving her brothers there, then I realized she was angry with me. I tried to take her arm for the walk or rub her shoulder and she slid away from me. I walked along next to her, my heart already breaking, at a loss what to say. Finally, when we were passing the carved stone front of St. Stephen's, I broke the silence.

"I know you're angry at me for leaving the boys there," I began, but she turned on me with a rage I had never seen.

"I don't care that you took them there. I care about *me*! Why do *they* get to go to school, and have food and *new clothes*, and *everything*, and I have to go home with you and *starve*?" She screamed this last word.

"We're going to work and work and work, and sleep on a hard bed, and have nothing to eat but potatoes, and no school for me, not now, not *ever*! I'm going to wear this dress to rags, and my fingers down to blisters! I didn't care when it was *all* of us, when we were all in it together. But you gave them something I want, I have wanted forever, more school! And you're keeping me to mind the baby or do the work because *you* can't do both. You've made me your slave! A sacrificial lamb! Why can't I have those things? Why?" She sobbed bitterly into Homer's hair. "It's just not fair."

I took Homer on my hip and pulled her into my shoulder. She had said all the words I couldn't say aloud to myself—all my maternal failings, laid bare by a daughter's appraising eye. Never had I felt so deficient as I did then. "Sarah, my love. Let's go home and have something to eat. A good cup of tea and a bite to eat will help, won't it?"

"Yes, of course." She wiped her eyes. She wouldn't look at me. "I'm sorry I made a fuss. Let's go home." She reached for Homer and he leaned toward her, saying, "Bah-bah," his name for her. "That's right, come to Bah-bah!" She walked on, sniffling, talking softly to Homer, not to me, all the way up the four flights of stairs.

Homer looked for his wooden men, formerly George's toys, and a pair of clothes pegs he liked to bang together. Sarah sat on the bed and played patty-cake with him as I raked up the coals to boil water, make tea. I took my time, thinking about what to say next. Our potatoes sat in a bowl of water from earlier, waiting to be mashed and fried. It wasn't roast beef and gravy, and there was no pie, and we were wearing rags, and yesterday we had been happy. I made two tin mugs of tea and set them on the table, one near Sarah, and, instead of saying what the doting mother in *Godey's Lady's Book* might say, I spoke from my heart. I didn't know how else, by then.

"Sarah, it breaks my heart to put the boys away. I have done everything I could since your father died to keep you all safe. If we had stayed in Newburgh, Mr. Montgomery—he would have ruined you. He tried to do that to me when I was your age, and he almost destroyed me. Your father saved me," I choked. *Bram, my heart.*

"Bram pulled him off me and took me under his protection, so that Montgomery could never hurt me again. But here we are. You are that man's ward, and I am—I don't know what to call myself, a fugitive from the law? If Montgomery finds you, he will take you from me. I have no legal right to roam about the state with my own children. We came here to get away, to keep you all safe. Not ravished. Not broken. *Safe!*"

She tried to speak, but I held up my hand. "Hear my piece. I am trying so hard, but I can't keep us going. You see how we've sunk. We're eating pig slop and glad to have it, and we could have been in the townhouse in Newburgh eating roast beef and pie like the boys are. We could all have stayed there, if you—and I—were both willing to become that man's playthings. Or maybe just you." I bowed my head. "I did what I thought was best for you, though perhaps I was wrong."

"I don't think you are. I'm so glad we left there." Sarah played with Homer's hand while he chewed on his spoon. She drew a shuddering breath. "That would have been horrid."

"Who knew it would be so difficult, the five of us trying to get along here? I didn't realize how hard we would work to buy our bread, or how tired I would be. I'm thirty-two now and I feel like I'm eighty." I had seen my face in Sarah's tiny looking glass. I knew what the months had done to me already.

"Mama, you look pretty. You always look pretty."

I let it pass. "This school for the boys—that takes them off our hands for a while. For how long? Just a couple of months, I hope. I need to earn enough to rent a home somewhere, maybe up the island, where there are cottages and some open space, nearer Harlem. Then I can get the boys back and we will put you into school."

"I want to go to school so much," she said again. "I just *need* to learn. I want to learn scientific facts about insects and flowers, and memorize the rivers of South America, and study Latin and ancient Rome. I want books! I want it so much, Mama. And it hurts me in my heart to see the boys have it and not me." Her tears flowed but she wasn't angry any longer. "And they don't even want to go to school. They just get it for free!"

"I need you to help me, Sarah, for a little while longer. If you will help me take care of Homer, I can work harder than ever. Our expenses are lower now, less food to buy. And we can bring in another woman, a single woman to share living expenses? Let's keep going, and I'll try to save some money. Let's give it a try, please?"

"I want to go to school, Mama." She covered her face. "I know girls don't need school like boys do. But it hurts me inside not to be able to study and learn."

"I want that for you, too. Let's try it for a few weeks. A month. Will you let me try one more time? And if I can't get good work by the end of May, I'll take you to the school and you can stay there with the boys, until I get us a better home."

"Mama, for heaven's sake. What about Homer?" She blew kisses to her baby brother. He made a kiss smack back to her. "You can't work much with a baby. We both know that."

"I can't think about that, Sarah. I can't give up all of my children. You don't know what you are asking me to do." Horror swept through me, like fainting, like falling. I had lain two babies in the graveyard. This felt infinitely worse. "I said we would give it a month, so let's try and see. Don't ask me to give up my baby, Sarah. Please."

"Mama, I would never. I don't know what to do. How do we do what we want and what we *need* to do at the same time, 'specially when they are the opposite thing?"

"My dear love, I have been asking myself for years. I don't know. Let's try. That's all I'm asking. Please."

Chapter 11

May 1860

My Dear Mother,

Missrs Filips says I can rite a leter to you if I want to. I want to.

Mister Portland says boys like me shod study hard so I kin go to work. I want to be a soldier. I am pratising how to march and stand in line with the other boys. We play war and there is so many boys here its fun. George is eating so much he has a fat

Wen kin you come visit us and bring my marbels. Kiss Homer for me. I missed Sarahs birthday and tell her I said many happy reterns.

Your Loving Son,
Ira Seabolt Lozier

Though the ink was blotted and the handwriting poor, Sarah and I read the letter aloud to each other so many times that the paper almost fell to pieces. We each kissed Homer for Ira and made sure to put Ira's marbles in a place where we wouldn't forget when we went to visit. Visiting day was every three months, on the quarter day. We could visit June 30. Although the letter was a comfort, it was also a worry to me. It was just a temporary situation; of course I would earn enough to take care of my children before long. The hat decorations had begun again, with little wax fruits on wire stems, twisted together to make a bunch. Though Sarah and I worked day and night to finish, spelling each other to care for Homer or step outside for a breath of spring air, the work wasn't enough to pay the rent. I sold the rest of the boys' clothes and George's threadbare winter coat.

We took in a mother about my age, Julia Pendleton, and her daughter Amelia, seventeen, who were in much the same straits as we, minus the baby. In our one room with one bed, we strung a curtain of sheets between the bed and the table and stove for a semblance of privacy. Each of us took turns at the stove, and at sleeping in the bed with a daughter; Sarah and I took the early-evening sleep shift, then arose early so the others could sleep. We worked for several hours of making fruit picks, then fell back into bed when the two left early in the afternoon. We awoke to the mess left in the wake of when Mrs. Pendleton and her daughter left the house to sell their wares. Homer went to sleep at his usual time but could now wake himself and get out of bed. He crawled between and on top of me and his sister and babbled at us, sometimes pulled our hair, or snuggled between us until we rose again for our day.

Mrs. Pendleton and her daughter were home midday for a rest in the bed, and to restock from their cheap trinkets in a wooden box in one corner of the room, then out again in the evening hours to sell what they could while businessmen and workers were out. Some days the Pendletons didn't sell enough and other days they sold out. They split up to double their efforts. They sold prettily colored pictures of flowers or animals; they sold rubber combs for a little girl's hair or toy birchbark canoes, bright red- and yellow-painted lead pencils, and felt needlebooks tied with ribbons. The more frivolous the item, the better they sold, it seemed to me. A pencil was sensible, and anyone could use it, but those gaily colored printed pictures of lions and elephants, or the rubber hair combs that lost teeth when pushed into thick hair—there must be children who got whatever they wanted and teased their parents into buying such trash.

I supposed I should be concerned that our tenant was selling worthless gewgaws on the street, but I didn't care, so long as the rent was met. Perhaps my morals were gone. We had to earn enough each week to pay our two-dollar rent, a dollar per family, and anything over that went to pay the grocer. It frustrated me beyond belief to be scrimping for every penny, to pay for what I had used to own, to pay for what had grown in abundance on our own farm. I repeated these same old gripes to myself every time I had to pay for an egg or an herb. I sighed over our country quiet, our simpler days, the seasonal rhythm of our early lives. I used to care so much—about what people thought, about everything—but what did it signify, now that I was rubbing my fingers into blisters, twisting wax fruit stems for fashionable ladies' hats I'd never put on my head, even if I could afford to buy one. And life in a crowded apartment, although there were still five beings, was far different now from when it was my own kith and kin underfoot. I felt broken without my boys at hand, but relieved that at least they were eating and learning.

Amelia spent much of her time arraying her hair and curling it in night rags. The resultant corkscrew curls, what Lizzie Hearne called "follow-me-lads," and some very red lips made grown men stop on the staircase and in the streets; Amelia's wares sold out very quickly indeed. She was home before her mother and put herself to bed in curling rags, taking the comfortable center of the bed and using her own dainty pillow with her name embroidered on it. Her mother came in and looked into the soup pot, ate a hunk of Indian bread right from the pan and went to her daughter behind the curtain.

"Give over, gel," Mrs. Pendleton, tugging at the quilt. "You'd better ain't be playing in dark corners with them delivery boys 'n such. Where's the money? Give it over."

"It's in the can," Amelia snipped, meaning the tin can in the corner where their funds were stashed. "Count it if you don't trust me."

"I trust you, all right. Trust you to buy yourself something with my coin. You work for me, gel, not for yourself."

"I could if I wanted!"

"You're mine until you're twenty-one or married, and I aim to get my share of work out of you before you skedaddle," Mrs. Pendleton wound up, and the nightly argument began.

We kept twisting fruit picks, trying to ignore the hugger-mugger right behind us. Homer looked unhappy, walking shakily to the table, then began to fret and fuss at my skirt.

Mrs. Pendleton called out. "Why's that kid crying? Hasn't he had his tit yet?"

"Mrs. Pendleton, please." I already regretted taking in this harpy. "He's tired. He wants his supper and to go to bed."

"That kid's spoiled," Amelia announced from the bed. "He pisses and moans all day long."

Sarah opened her mouth to defend her brother but I shook my head, rolling my eyes vulgarly.

"He should still be on the tit." Julia Pendleton poked her head out of the curtain. "Why ain't you nursing him? Is he really your baby, or it is hers?" Mrs. Pendleton thumbed at Sarah. "I had mine awful young. I was thirteen when I had my first one. Younger than you, little mama."

We sat in appalled silence.

The other woman burst out in her grating laugh. "I know you're trying to count my age now. Well, Amelia ain't my first and she won't be my last, I'm sure. My big boy Albert is on the farm with his pap in New Jersey state, and I don't expect we'll see him any time soon. Pappy's got a loaded gut-buster and said me not to come home. So we lit out here, seeing Amelia ain't his anyway."

"Please, no more of this talk." I got up and stirred the soup. "Would you care for some soup, Julia, or shall I push it off the fire?" I picked up Homer and jiggled him on my hip while I stirred. Such impertinence, such manners! It had been a gross mistake to invite them in, but the Pendletons paid half the rent. A dollar made a big difference. Disgusted, I turned the subject when I could, but we loathed the Pendletons before the first week was out.

Gossip on the stairs said that war with the South was coming, that prices in the City were rising, but wages were still low, and many of our neighbors were struggling. Some familiar faces disappeared, new faces came in, and word at the standpipe was that Mr. Leeman and clan had moved out without paying the week's rent, nor the taverner nor grocer. The effect of one family's perfidy rippled through the building. The washerwoman had not been paid, so she couldn't pay her grocery bill; Mrs. Tavish was shorted by three young men who scarpered on the rent and tavern slate, so she couldn't pay the washerwoman, either. She and the corner grocer toughened up on those who remained, still struggling, and when those folks hadn't enough to eat, they also skipped on their bills.

As May was rolling toward June and the promise I had made to Sarah, an early heat wave made all our skin glisten with perspiration and our many layers damp with sweat. We had not had proper baths since leaving the farm, just sponging ourselves before the stove in the evenings, and the heat made me miss our Saturday night ritual more than ever.

I saw Amelia one afternoon on a street corner with her tray, showing her wares to a dandy who leaned into her, breathing at her neck, twirling a finger in Amelia's brown ringlets. Sarah should not be sharing a bed with the likes of Amelia.

The making of wax fruit bunches did not last as long as the popularity of silk roses on hats, and when Mr. Meagher had had his fill, the orders stopped, each party bumping against another like a string of horses stopping too quickly. I had enough for the week's rent and no more, and the liquid in the soup pot would not last the week, if there was nothing more to put into it.

I broached our situation with Mrs. Pendleton.

"You're into the sinkhole, if you're asking my opinion," she snorted. "No pennies, no peas. Whatever shall you do?" There was a jeer in her voice. I changed my mind; I had been going to ask if Mrs. Pendleton could buy us some beans or an onion, seeing how I had given them half my own bed. It wouldn't have been a question with any other woman. Lizzie Hearne would have lent the food or given it freely. But the sneer in Julia's voice was unpleasant in the extreme. I would rather literally starve than be under Mrs. Pendleton's thumb.

We were at the end of the rope.

Little Homer, playing patty-cake with Sarah, could not starve. Sarah could not go hungry anymore, either. I would cook and carve my own arm for my children before letting them feel any more of a pinch in their thin cheeks, in their empty bellies. There were no more safety nets below us. I put the water on for tea and asked Sarah to watch it for me. There was a pinch of tea leaves yet, although we had been pressing them twice or three times until there was no color left.

The weather was so warm that I did not need a shawl, but I put on my bonnet and walked out the door to the hall. I heard

Sarah sing nursery rhymes to Homer, and his little voice starting to mimic her sounds, the words changed for Homer's sake.

Bye, baby bunting, Mother's gone a hunting,
Sarah's got a rabbit skin to wrap the baby Homer in!

I went down the flights of stairs, out the heavy door and down the iron steps, steeling myself to the interview. To the *reckoning*. Took a deep breath. Buttoned down my despair. Went down the three steps into Keeler's Haberdashery.

The bell rang as I opened the door. He was waiting, his black coat correct, his beard and mustache neatly trimmed, his *pince nez* on his nose as he looked over a new order for shirts. He smiled.

"I knew you'd be back."

"I need work, Mr. Keeler."

"I could find some sewing for you to do. Some seams and hems, perhaps. Buttons and bows."

"I need money to feed my children."

"Of course you do. How many did you say you had?"

"I can start tomorrow." I swallowed. I would have one more night with my family before stepping down another rung. "At noon. I have to take my children to—away. I will be back and able to work. Able to—" I faltered. "Whatever you want me for. But I need money now."

"An advance?"

"A week's wage, in advance. I will work it off, I promise."

"You will, my girl. You will."

I held out my hand for the money.

• • •

I went first to Mr. Newman to pay my week's bill, and bought new foodstuffs—a bit of sugar, a half-pound of tea, a chunk of salt pork, potatoes, a piece of yellow cheese and apples. It wasn't a feast, but it was better than we had eaten in several weeks. I asked for milk on my account, and would send Sarah down for it presently. I crossed the street to the baker and bought a loaf of white bread and a small cake. I wished I didn't have to cook with the Pendletons there, but they were usually out in the evenings. Still, I would make it festive at whatever cost.

"Sarah, take the molasses pail down for a pint of milk—please, Mr. Newman is holding it for us."

"Mama, how in the world? Did you rob the bank?"

"Don't ask, my darling; just know that I have work, I will be sewing. Now quickly! I am cooking a feast for us tonight!"

Sarah handed Homer to me and clattered down the stairs; the boy babbled at me. I handed him Bram's carved maple man. He looked at it and gave it a kiss.

"Homer," I said. "Say *Mama*."

"Mama mama."

"Good boy! Say *Sarah*?"

"Bah-bah."

"Good boy! Can you say *George*?"

"Dosh!"

"Can you say *Ira*?"

"Wah-wah!"

I laughed and kissed his cheek. "Such a smart boy. Can you say *Homer*?"

"Mama."

"HO-mer!"

"Mo-ma!"

"That's right, HO-mer! Such a good boy!" I held him close to my chest, smelling his sweet baby scent, his becoming-a-toddler-scent, less damp flannel and milk, more salty and boy-ish. George and Ira had both smelled this way. I wanted to dig my fingers into his very flesh, inhale the essence of him, this beautiful boy, this precious being, until I was drunk, I was drowning in it. My boy. My boys. My girl. I cradled him in the hollow of my neck, my elbow, loving him with my whole heart. I was still holding him, my baby, when Sarah came in with the milk.

"Look, dearest, milk for Homer!"

"Mo-ma!"

"Homer!" I kissed him again, then set him on the floor and got his mug, pouring a smidge of milk so he could practice drinking as he had with the sweetened tea for so many weeks. "Sarah, I'm all behind in my work; I was playing with Homer. Will you help me with the potatoes?"

Sarah took the potatoes to the table and washed three in the dishwater. I sliced the salt pork and laid it in strips in the pan. I sliced a piece of cheese for Sarah to nibble on while she pared potatoes.

"Thank you, Mama." Sarah tasted the cheese. "Mmm, it's been so long," she said, but stopped herself. "I'm not complaining!"

"I know you aren't. It has been too long. You children have suffered. I've been selfish. There is too much here to—to lead you all astray, that you shouldn't see."

"No, Mama, it's all right."

"Sarah, you're almost a woman now. You're like my sister in more ways than you're like my daughter." I watched my daughter pare the Irish potatoes with one long, curling peel. "You know how hard it has been. And look at you—you're worn down with worry and woe. You should be in school. You should be in the *Third Reader*, or *Fourth,* and learning history, and learning mathematics or German or reciting the *Declaration of Independence*, something other than making fruit picks while waiting for a turn to sleep in our own bed. 'You are my shield, my glory and the lifter of my head.'" The psalm choked me. "My lovely girl. I want so much for you." *No matter what it costs me.*

"Mama, this is—" Sarah started to declare, but she stopped. "Well, it's not so bad. At the least, we're together." The absence of Ira and George was palpable. "You and me and Homey."

"Daughter, listen to me. I cannot work enough to keep us. It is all uphill, and I don't like—" I eyed the Pendletons' corner, where their satchel and box of gewgaws were stacked. "I want better things for you. An education. I thought I could do this my way, but I am afraid for what lies ahead. I want you to go to school, and Homer to have milk every day. Warm beds of your own! And to be with your brothers, while I work. Tomorrow we are going back to the Home so you can be with your brothers and get an education, and I can work and save money for our own house."

"Mama." Sarah put down the knife and placed her hand over her mouth. Tears rolled down her cheeks. "I'm sorry, Mama," she struggled. "I'm trying not to cry, but I wonder— How long will we be there?"

"Six months or a year, at the most. I can work harder and longer if I don't have to worry about Homer falling down the stairs or getting burned on the stove, and I will feel better knowing you are getting a good education and keeping an eye on your brothers. I can come every visiting day and see you all. I'll bring a cake, and we will have a picnic right there—if it's nice out, or a tea party if it's snowing or what have you."

Sarah left her seat and leaned into me. "Tell me everything will be fine. I'm afraid of how hard you will work without us. I'm afraid you will miss us too much!"

My arms went around her slim waist. "So much. Every day and night, every minute, I will miss you. But you may write to me, will you not? Ira wrote."

"I shall, I shall write every week. Whenever they give me paper and leave to write home, I shall."

"You watch out for your brothers and see that they don't become great brutes. See that they act like gentlemen in school." Homer had finished his mug of milk and banged it on the floor. "This one in particular!"

"Of course! They're Loziers! They have to be gentlemen. Right, Homey?"

I rose and turned toward the stove, pretending cheer. "My goodness, this pork is going to burn. Have you finished the potatoes?"

"No, Mama. Come, Homey, want to taste this cheese?"

"Bah-bah!"

"He's saying your name," I said, laughing, my eyes full. "Say Sarah," she coaxed. "Say Mama."

"Mama mama mama. Bah-bah."

• • •

I think I will remember forever every step I took, like a prisoner going to the scaffold, that morning. I had failed my children, failed my husband, failed in my role as wife and mother, and why had I not just given them over to Montgomery when it was clear they would be schooled and fed? But I had to shield them from his harm, and from the harm of too much too soon—Amelia offering her neck to the wolf at the corner, Julia Pendleton criticizing, drawing down to the last penny until I was now at Keeler's call. I must return to his shop that very afternoon to take on my role as an underling in his shop, for the foregone price he would exact.

It was one or the other—I could mother these children but not feed them, or I could feed and clothe them but not mother them. If the children could wait for me a little while at the Home, watch for me in their own Gethsemane—I would be with them as soon as ever I could. As soon as I had money and means to support them, I would be back. I had not given up, by any means.

In the office at the Home, Mrs. Phillips praised Ira and George. "They have already come so far—Ira is an intelligent boy and very clever. George is painfully slow, as you know, but he has learned to answer when we speak to him, and not be so much in his own little cloud. He needed some discipline and a little more—" the woman paused and forged ahead, "*attention,* I expect, from a man. It is so hard, Mrs. Lozier, when there is no father to take a firm hand."

I bit hard on a number of unsaid retorts. "May I see the boys and say good morning to them?"

"Oh, no, that would be quite impossible. They are at lessons now, and then they have dinner, and chores to do, and chapel this evening—it is quite a busy day here for the children. You may come at the quarter day, as we agreed." Mrs. Phillips smiled and nodded, although I had not strictly agreed. "They will know quite well when they see their sister and brother that you have been here today."

"Yes, of course, but I would like to explain to them—"

"Oh, no, Mrs. Lozier. *Never* explain. Not to a child. They will see their sister and I will tell them anything they need to know." Mrs. Phillips turned to Sarah. "Of course, you must not upset them. They must know that Mother is working very hard, but they are to stay here for the present. No sentimental carry-ings-on, please. They don't need to worry about Mother now."

"No, ma'am." But I saw a glint of determination in my daughter's eye.

"What will my daughter be studying?"

"Oh, such a lot of things. In school, Sarah will have reading, mathematics, history, geography, and penmanship, of course. She might have a chance to learn the piano or singing, depending on where she is placed. Some of our children have an excellent musical education. But all of the girls of Sarah's age will learn housekeeping and practical management of the household, including childcare and cooking."

"She already sews and crochets, and her cooking skills are very good," I said.

"That will come in very handy," Mrs. Phillips said. "Now, just to be clear, Mrs. Lozier, some of our older girls and boys are sent out to other homes, you understand, private homes where they are raised as part of the family. If they are fourteen years old, they receive a wage for their work. Sarah is—" Mrs. Phillips looked at Sarah. "You are fourteen?"

"Yes, ma'am."

"Such a grown-up girl. I'll bet you have been a great help to Mother."

I hated that false cheer.

"And this little lamb?" She held out her hands to Homer, but, shy, he turned toward me and hid his face in my neck. "Oh, I hope he's not spoiled."

"He just awoke," I lied. But he wasn't spoiled. He was a baby. My baby.

"The little ones go into a nursery and the older girls help care for them," Mrs. Phillips explained. "This little one, William?"

"William Homer, but we call him Homer." I chucked his little cheek. "Homer, that's you, isn't it?"

"Mo-ma." He said his word like a grumpy old man. Sarah smiled at him and held her arms out.

"Come to Sarah, Homey!" Homer leant into Sarah's open hands. My hands, quite empty, went to my heart.

"Let us take him down to the nursery, shall we, Sarah? It will help if you carry him there, his first time away from Mother." Mrs. Phillips tugged a needlepointed pull on the wall and far off, a bell rang. "Say your goodbyes, Mrs. Lozier, and then we can finish the arrangements."

Sarah came over to me, pressed into my neck as closely as she could with Homer between us. "Mama."

"My darling girl. Write to me. At Mr. Newman's?" The ground was dropping beneath me.

"I will, Mama. Say bye-bye, Homey."

"Bah bah." He opened and closed his hand, a toddler's wave. "Mama."

"Take care of your brothers," I whispered into Sarah's hair. Kissed my daughter and my baby boy. Watched them walk through the door, Sarah's blonde head bent over her little brother's brown curls, the white part between Sarah's braids so pale it shone like moonlight.

• • •

I walked as if dreaming, out the double doors and down the steps, turning not toward home, or the haberdasher to whom I had just given my promise, but to the west, walking without thought. I had become the woman who abandoned my children, the wicked mother in Hansel and Gretel who left my children in the woods. I could not go back to my empty room, or the Pendletons—unbearable.

I turned toward Fourth, crossing the street without care, heading toward the steeple rising already above me, reaching toward a heaven I no longer believed in. The old farmhouse at the corner smelled of pig dung and old hay. A rooster, unseen, shrilled the morning hour, over and over, rasping from his efforts. A dusty brown mare tied loosely to the new iron fence at Marble Collegiate rolled a liquid eye at me and twitched her ears, stamped a foot, switched her dry brown tail at pig-dung flies.

The church bells tolled the midday, just as the saloon across Fifth Avenue began to serve its first meal; I had promised to return to work by noon but I couldn't yet. The taverner came out ringing a dinner bell, calling for patrons who might like baked oysters in cream for luncheon. I walked up the church steps, into the doorway of the vestibule, my shawl folded like a newborn in my arms. Clear diamond panes let in sunlight, showed the blue and white sky and green leaves of the farmhouse tree. Everything about the church shone: its ornate doorknobs and locks, its whitewashed walls, the magnificence of the organ pipes clinging to the walls. I stepped quietly onto the red, yellow and black tile patterned like a child's bed quilt and stood in the doorway. Rows of pews, their crimson cushions, gates closed against winter drafts, polished brass plates on each pew.

But I could not pray. I couldn't think.

A closing door startled me. I turned to see the minister, in his black parson's robes, his white starched collars flat against his chest, the very strands of linen bright in the churchy gloom.

"Are you quite well, madam?"

I had only my muslin handkerchief made from a patch of petticoat, my black dress, my wedding band; my silver thimble and German shears, my hair and my teeth. But I had given my soul away, pushing my children onto the raft, lest they all be lost. They had life; mine no longer mattered.

"Thank you, Parson. I felt—faint."

"Please, do seat yourself until you feel well again. Our doors are open to you."

I did not believe him, awaiting fire and sulfur and smoke in the end. I would die for the children. I had sold myself into bondage. It was both too much, and not enough, to save them. Speechless, I nodded.

He bowed a little, his hand to his heart, a gesture of humility and spirit, though I did not feel like one of the chosen. My children, gone from my grasp. This church was no place for me.

I walked toward home, the sun overhead now, my posture erect, my gut in rebellion. My body felt feverish, as if illness approached. I passed Keeler's doorway, knowing I was already late to begin work that very day. Let him refuse me now; I was ruined anyway. I stumbled up the flights of stairs like a woman in strong spirits, drunkenly taking the turn at the top and colliding with Lizzie Hearne.

"What devil is in ye today?" she snipped.

I stared at the wiry red hair alight like an orange halo in the dim hallway light, her freckled skin, the bright blue eyes, the battered hands holding a basket of clothes at her hip, the cock of Lizzie's head, mesmerized.

"What is it? Ye seen a ghoul? Come now!"

"My baby." I choked up the word. "I've taken them to the Home just now." I blinked. "I gave my children away."

I crumpled there at the top of the stairs, my hands over my face, a howl inside my mouth that I'd held in when Bram left me, when Malcolm left us, when my mother failed me, when my own wits failed me, when the children hungered, when my two boys went willingly to where the food was aplenty, and my daughter and baby as well, without me, and I alone in the City, my hands and body and soul now allied with that man, the manacles of work and industry.

Lizzie's arms went around me, crooning, "There, my girl, there ye go, it's all out now. Let it out."

Doors opened and heads peeked out up or down the stairs, to see what racket, what woe, and silently the women crept near, gathered, German, Jew, Irish, Pole, native-born, rocking babies on their hips, crooning soft foreign words under their breaths, witnessing my pain, holding me in the silent cocoon of our sex, as we always do.

Part II

Chapter 12

New York City
June 1860

I wore my new widow's weeds every day. Mr. James Keeler, Haberdasher, had immediately told me to make up a new gown, to look respectable, and gave me money for the materials. He made me work behind the screen, hidden from view, until the dress was complete, so I wouldn't shame him in my worn-out weeds.

"You cannot have purchased more black, Martha!" He gestured around the room. "Your gown is to show off your needle skills, to illustrate to the customer we can provide any garment they desire! What is this black?"

"I am a widow."

"But surely you no longer mourn. At least half-mourning, woman—indigo, or gray, or lilac. Forest green. Anything but black."

"I shall never stop mourning my husband." Nor my children, until they were back in my own home again, something Keeler would never know or understand. Then, with my nestlings beside me, perhaps some gray or lilac or forest green. Mayhap a topaz or wine, with a little fringe, then. No lace. Someday, if I had cause to celebrate, I would even dress in cherry red. Until then, my bombazine was as bereaved as I.

Nonetheless, it was also the finest dress I had ever owned, nearly 20 yards of cloth with cartridge pleats fanned perfectly at the waist, room for the crinoline hoops now in fashion, which he had ordered me to wear beneath. I buckled the hoops as narrowly as I could; widows in mourning ought not take up as much room as debutantes. I added pintucks across the bosom, rows of narrow ruffles on my bell sleeves and midway to the floor, with black picot ribbon tied at the collarbone, and a matching cap. I would advertise my skills as well as my grief.

"The devoted widow," he mocked. "Penelope, weaving a burial shroud. You look like a spider in that corner. Get on with it, then."

I am not an educated woman, but if I were a spider, with my silken thread, so be it. There were worse things to be called. At least spiders made webs to catch flies for their children. My black dress made me feel connected to my past, my losses, instead of lost in the debasement of my current role. And I was grateful my children would not see me at it. But might there be a letter today? I always ate my small dinner quickly behind the screen, so I was allowed to step away from my corner table in Keeler's shop for ten minutes, to check the post at Mr. Newman's grocery in the early afternoons, to stretch my shoulders from their perpetual hunch, feel the sunshine on my face.

"A letter for me?" I had learned not to expect, to anticipate the bitterness of no mail. It was easier not to expect than to live in crushed hope day after day. Sarah and Homer had been away for just a few weeks.

"Yes, Mrs. Seabolt—today you have a letter!" Mr. Newman seemed genuinely glad for me and handed over the note without delay.

I gazed at Mr. Newman, my hand to my heart. "Oh, a letter! Gracious! Bless you, Mr. Newman!"

He chuckled and went back to dusting his shelves.

I walked along the side of the building to a shady spot where I could lean, yes, lean like a schoolboy against the brick wall and read my missive. It was Sarah's round hand, I recognized at once. The letter was encased in one of those newfangled envelopes, with a pretty green postage stamp in the corner. Four cents to mail a letter six blocks, why, the very idea of such an expense! I slit the paper flap open beneath the blue wax seal with a hairpin.

There were two pages, written on both sides of a fine linen paper, with the name *Sylvanus Ferris, Esq.* engraved in black at its head.

June 16, '60

Dearest Mama:

I hope this finds you keeping well. I have been unable to write until now. I am in Galesburg, Illinoise, in a town with a family called Ferris. I rode on "the Iron Horse" with Ira and so many other children. I was heartbroken to leave Homey and George, I had hardly seen George even a minute before they were pulling us apart and Homer was crying. At least they are together.

We left New York the day after you brought us to the Home. I sat with Ira on the first day until we got to Lockport. We all got off and a farmer came to take Ira. He did not want to go but he did not cry. He said he will write to you. I was distrait, Mama, I had no thought that they would separate us two. We had to leave Georgie and Homey behind at the Home and I don't know what will happen.

After Ira left the train I had to watch over the other children, but we looked out the window and I told them stories and sang songs. It was a long journey. It took four days to get here after Ira. We stopped many times for children to get off and taken to new families. We stayed in boarding houses all the way. Galesburg was the last stop and we were only a few children left by then.

The Ferrises are very kind and comforting to me. They are Christians. I believe they are Abalitionists as well. They tell me not to worry about Ira or George or Homer, the Society is very good to children. I have a bedroom of my own and a pretty, soft bed. I am to go to summer term at the Galesburg school. They have grown daughters and sons. The Ferris' grown daughter Mae is giving me lessons until summer term. The family came here to start the town and church and a college, they say. They have prayer meetings at their home, which is a large plank house as big as Grandpapa's.

Please don't worry about me, Mama, although I know you will. There is plenty to eat from their farm and although the weather has turned dreadfully humid, inside the Ferris house is cool with a lovely breezeway down the middle. They have gas lights and a porch swing where I can read poetry. It is very elegant! I have crochet thread again and am starting a new reticule for you. They also have a collie dog named Brutus, although he is very sweet and not a brute at all.

I miss you and my brothers so much I could cry, but I am trying to be brave. I say my prayers every night and wish we could all be together in Christ again soon.

Your loving daughter,
Sarah Delaphina Lozier

I read my letter outside the grocer, my private business in public on the corner. I read it again, shocked. *Galesburg! On the train. Ira in Lockport! The little ones left alone!* I folded the letter into my hand and strode up the streets to the Home for the Friendless, disregarding the unfinished shirt I'd left on the worktable. How could they send my children away, cross-country, to strangers? But when I burst through the double doors of the building, Mrs. Phillips came out to greet me with an air as calm as a farmer's wife applying linen to a wound.

"I explained to you, did I not, Mrs. Lozier, that our older children might be sent to other homes, where they would be treated as one of the family? Did I not tell you that older children would earn their bread? Sarah will, and Ira, when he reaches his fourteenth year, will begin a savings on account with their foster parents, and when they are of age, they will receive this money in return for their labors."

"I wanted my children near, where I could see them—"

Mrs. Phillips did not care. "They attend school and church, Mrs. Lozier. They have warm beds, good shoes, a roof over their heads. They don't breathe the fumes of this pestilent City. Your son is with a respectable Lockport farmer. He will grow into a fine young man. He's at home in a churchgoing family. How on earth could you possibly complain about that?"

"Yes, but my daughter—"

"—is in the bosom of a renown family of good name. Mr. Sylvanus Ferris—don't you know who he is? They founded the town of Galesburg—they founded Knox County! And Knox College! They asked for a good girl and I sent them Sarah. You should be proud! She will be brought up to womanhood with these kind people as a lamb of their own flock. Do you begrudge your daughter that opportunity? When you have nothing to offer them but poverty and degradation?"

The words felt like blows to my body. Each one hit, solid

contact, on a bruised place already welted by my own doubts and recriminations. "But Illinois is so far away. I had no inkling."

"No one expects you to know, Mrs. Lozier. The important thing is that your children are safe, they are fed and warm and cared for, and you are able to go to your work without worry. That is why you came here. That is what you asked for. You signed your name and we took care of the remainder."

"May I see my little boys? George and Homer? Please—while I'm here, I have only a short time before I must return to my work."

"William is in his nursery and George is in his classroom. They cannot be disrupted now; it would upset them and the teachers and the other children, as well. Do come at Quarter Day and you will see them then."

I gave up my last bit of fight. "Very well, then. I shall be back on Quarter Day. In ten days." At least my little boys were here, six blocks away. Close enough to see the same stars, to feel the same breeze, as if they noticed such things. I needed to hold them again, remember why I lived.

"We shall see you then. Good afternoon, Mrs. Lozier."

• • •

I bore the bedlam in my home as long as I could, then changed rooms with a cousin of Julia Pendleton. They would all three be miserable together. I shifted downstairs to share a room on the third floor with Patrick and Bridget Dunn, who wanted a quiet boarder to help pay their rent. I paid a dollar per week, but I no longer cooked, and I shared a bed with 11-year-old Maggie and 14-year-old Bridey. I let the Pendletons have my kitchen gear and bedding, except for my quilts, in exchange for my walking away from that week's rent; they fussed and struggled, but I presumed they would find a way to make up the difference quickly enough. And nothing else mattered without the children.

At Keeler's, I worked like a millwheel, nonstop, mechanically, my arm sweeping stitches all day at the white linen or cotton shirts, the silky cravats, and the broadcloth waistcoats that James Keeler offered for his merchant clientele. He had expanded his line of work from just shirts into tailoring, and now took measurements of any and all comers who wanted suits of clothing. The full-belly waistlines of the German butcher and the Irish taverner who wanted a clean suit for Sunday Mass or Saturday stroll with the wife, or the dapper young man seeking a striped waistcoat and tan trousers, to show off his dance steps at the pavilion in the nearest park. Sunday afternoons in the City were much more festive than the old Martha, at my staid Dutch church in Newburgh, could have imagined. The haberdashery provided suitable attire for the merchant class and an occasional social climber trying to crawl upward to the clerical level. I was on hand to measure their wives, discreetly, behind the screen.

A newly arrived Scotch cousin of Keeler's sat cross-legged, tailor-fashion, on a low table and sewed the woolens, while I basted, lined and finished for him, and sewed shirt upon shirt. Angus Keeler came in at sun-up to tailor in peace and finished by three o'clock. Angus played fiddle in a Scotch Masonic orchestra and wanted his evenings free. A Presbyterian, he refused to work on the Sabbath, which suited me. Mr. James Keeler bade me work just six days and left me alone on the seventh.

In late afternoon, after Angus left and the shop was still, Keeler pulled down the shades. I lay back on the cutting table, my skirts hiked up, a folded cotton beneath me, and Keeler took his quick pleasure, for the extra 25 cents. I closed my eyes, unwilling to see his red face grunting above me, imagining a thread following a needle, pulling a dashed line in its wake. I smelled his brand of shaving soap, his tobacco, his hair oil, nothing like Bram's clean sweat, Bram's hayfield and dark earth scent. I might get caught with a baby, but Keeler was afraid of that as well, unwilling to risk the ire of his wife or cousin, or the reputation of the shop. He pulled out at the end, splattering my thigh like a sick child's snotty mess. I took myself away in those moments, far away to golden fields of Newburgh rye and red leaves in autumn, to bluestone houses with deep windowsills and hazy winter smoke, anywhere but Keeler's sewing table. I couldn't think about Bram like this, unfaithful wife, staining his memory. He wouldn't know me anymore. I didn't know myself most days.

And no one in my building could know I was Keeler's jezebel. I let it be known I had daywork sewing in the haberdashery but I would lose my place in my small society if they thought I were an adventuress with a married man. No one would share my room but another such as Julia Pendleton. Secrecy, sin, and lies weighed upon me like a sodden cloak.

I had not heard from Ira. I knew nothing more than the town where he stayed, not how to reach him. But to Sarah I could write. I took my pennies to the stationer's down at Union Square to purchase sheets of writing paper and envelopes which kept a letter safer than one merely folded shut. I could seal it with my candle. I purchased two postage stamps and a lead pencil and took my paper package home in my arms. The June evening was warm, cooler than the sticky afternoon, a perfect summer day coming to its grand closure. I made myself notice the soft breeze, the feeling of walking after a day of cramped sewing, smell the scent of other people's suppers cooking, see the bright gas lights springing up in the gloaming. I had but one more day until Quarter Day and looked forward to seeing my little lads with sudden rushes of emotion, the like which I hadn't felt since Bram came calling before we wed. I debated writing to Sarah before my visit or afterward. I decided to wait, to give good news of the little boys and help to cheer my daughter.

I dressed with especial care in the morning, brushing up my brownish hair with an extra curl at my temples, and tucking Homer's wooden men and George's toy soldiers into the former milk pail, now my dinner pail, to play with the boys. I planned to stop at the bakery next block on my way and buy some small cakes with nutmeg and whole raisins for a treat. My stomach tickled with butterflies as the day rose and I walked down to Keeler's. I had left the shop in perfect array the night before, but when he arrived at eight, Keeler unfurled a bolt of brown and cream herringbone wool suiting across the cutting table and upset my tin of straight pins and creels of thread.

"Look at this jumble—it's a disgrace!" He kicked the spools away like a stubborn child and I could not help but eye him as an exasperated mother. "Stevenson, the stonecutter—he's no common mason! Importers of stone and marble, he's an *industrialist*, for pity's sake! He's coming to be measured at nine sharp and this place is topsy-turvy!"

Angus on his stool marked out buttonholes on a waistcoat with chalk, porcupine pincushion on his wrist and tape measure around his neck like a dashing scarf. "No more'n usual, cousin, if ye'd stop this twaddle."

"I'll sweep this up," I soothed him, cursing silently. "Never mind—have you had your cake this morning?" I had long ago learned the benefit of distraction. Men are such children.

Keeler perked up at the mention of his midmorning cake. "It's too early. We must get ready! The pins, the floor—look at the window shades, they aren't even drawn yet, Angus!"

"That's all right, Mr. Keeler. I'll lay this out and we'll be ready for Mr. Stevenson in no time." I had the pin can in my hand already and was using a little magnet to gather sharps and straights from the floor. "See, it's better already. Let me just draw the shades up."

He ignored me as he measured lengths of woolen with his arm, folding the cloth back and forth in heavy layers, murmuring, "Can't leave this shop in the hands…ruin my chances…depending on this business…a golden opportunity!" He muttered like an old woman, but I managed to get the pins swept and spools sorted, then tucked back at my corner table to resume stitching shirts.

Keeler fretted and fussed with his bolts of cloth and his window display of caps and gloves until the grand man arrived at nine o'clock with his grown son alongside to take notes and hold his top hat and walking stick.

"I have in mind a grand scheme," Stevenson announced, unbuttoning his coat and lifting his trouser legs before sitting in the comfortable chair near the long looking glass. His still-dark side whiskers were shiny with beard oil, though his chin was naked as a newborn pup; his somewhat bushy gray hair was a bit crushed by his top hat. "I should like all of my salesmen to dress in similar fashion—the same cut of coat, or some other reasonable similarity, so that it's clear they are *company* men. *Stevenson* men." He nodded sharply at his son, a younger version of himself including the side whiskers, who remained otherwise silent until called upon to agree or speak.

"The same cut of trousers, the same white shirts, same coats," Keeler enlarged upon the idea, no doubt seeing dollars and cents instead of clerks in matched attire. "Excellent. They might wear the selfsame cravats or ties—all of them should look as though they are company men." He echoed Stevenson's terminology.

"Not a uniform, mind you," Stevenson shook a thick finger that had been battered by hammer and chisel in its day, but now wielded the power of pen and of gold. "I don't want an army of wax dolls, I want something distinctive. I want to stand out at the warehouses, at the docks, the merchant exchange. What can you do that I can't get from Cohen or Lundberg or any other two-bit tailor?"

Keeler fawned, "Of course, sir, of course."

Angus cut in. "Tailors are tailors, sir. But *we're* Scotch," he gestured with his head at Keeler, while waxing a thread for the waistcoat buttons. "As good as kin."

"You hit that on the head, my friend. I may be an old hammer hand from the stone pit, but I know what I like and I know what I want, fancified duds or a slab of marble. Scotch cousins! Show me what to do here, lads."

Keeler sketched some angles and curved lines in his master-book, showing Stevensons Senior and Junior what style he could present for their higher-level employees. I listened while I seamed and hemmed, considering the directions Mr. Stevenson gave.

"I want them to look efficient and grand, not foppish. Not dandies—*businessmen!* Something distinctive!" Mr. Stevenson knew what he wanted but seemed unable to articulate it.

I couldn't help myself. I leaned and whispered to Angus.

"Say it," he nodded. "Tell them."

Keeler cut his eyes over like poison to silence me. Angus repeated my whisper. "Perhaps a double row of the topstitching down the front, on all the coats. Grey wool, black stitching. And different buttons, depending on the employee's position?" Angus glanced back at me. I nodded slightly, and continued with my stitches, eyes downward.

"There's a thought." Stevenson tugged on his chin.

"Black buttons for the salesmen, nickel buttons for the board," Keeler suggested, as if it were his idea. "I have several styles to choose from—Angus, just draw the lines while I get these buttons here—."

An hour later the gentlemen bowed each other away, Keeler promising the first suit—for Stevenson Junior—in the new week with the rest to follow, gentlemen's measurements notwithstanding. At last they left the little shop, Keeler unctuous, all but kissing their rings like a Papist.

He rounded on me after the clientele left the front of the store, doorbells still jangling. "How dare you speak up? Impertinence!"

"I whispered." I knew my ideas were good. But I was anxious to see my sons, and sick of the demon-bargain I'd made.

"A silly schoolgirl, lisping behind your hand?" He stood over me, jeering.

I flared. "I'm a needlewoman. I know what works."

"You're a *seamstress*, and you do what I give you to do, no more."

"But he liked it." I couldn't help the sauce in my voice.

Keeler stepped in close and I wondered if he might strike me. "You forget yourself, Martha."

"I like her idea, as well," Angus said. He totted up his measurements on his slate and calculated the materials. "And so did His Majesty Lord Stevenson. We'll need the notions—buttons and the like. Don't have it at hand, but fetch it from the warehouse Monday. I've got Monsieur Gaspin the music teacher back for his order at two o'clock and no time to spare." He held up the suit's coat, half-sewn buttons and his waxed thread.

Keeler chewed on his mustache for a moment, then agreed. "They did like it, cousin. We might have something, with that double line of stitching. Contrasting stitching. The buttons—I have to order more cloth, and the colored thread, and—Monday I'll get the notions from the warehouses." He muttered to himself, then turned back to me. "The shirts. That order. Get it done. We need a clean sweep before we start this order Monday. Those shirts, today!"

"It's my half-day—I am to visit my children today," I ventured to object. "This afternoon."

"I think not. There's far too much to do." He wanted to punish me for speaking up, for talking back. "Get to it, and if you finish, you are free to go. If the shirts are not finished—." He did not complete his sentence, but his intention was clear. "Or just go. I'll fill your place next week. Women like you can be got cheap."

I bent my head, my hand jabbing the needle faster, shaking, the burn of rage in my throat. I took but a moment midday to use the privy back of the building and to eat my apple at two o'clock when he left me. Angus had long gone, off to play at some Masonic outing in the Madison Park square, and Keeler was taking his wife and three children to listen. I didn't waste time feeling sorry for myself, only sewing faster than I wanted in my anger, having to stop and redo the collar and cuffs of one particularly troublesome shirt twice. The blouse was limp with perspiration and needed a wash and to be pressed before it could face its new owner. I washed it out with a little soap and cold water in the basin back of the workroom, and hung it to drip dry on a little line above some old newspapers on the floor, behind the screen. But Keeler's orders or no, I couldn't make the shirt dry faster.

The clock was showing half past five, and I left the last shirt unironed, I forewent the dusting and sweeping. I drew the vexing shades down and pulled the door locked behind me, then scurried as fast as I could on tired feet and legs that had sat cramped all day, knowing that visiting day was almost over. I despaired of seeing my boys, knowing I couldn't explain it to them even if they saw me—that Mama has been working, Mama has been doing unspeakable things to earn money to wrap my baby buntings safely in my arms again. George in his fae world and Homer too young to understand,

and it had been almost three months since I had seen George, almost three weeks without Homer, and now it would be three months more. Would they remember their mama after so long away?

I forgot about stopping for cakes or having a picnic together. I only wanted to see them, to touch and smell my boys. I hurried through the midsummer evening still humid, sticky as jam on fingers. Moist with perspiration under my heat-damp dress, my face beaded, I rushed up the stairs to the closed double doors of the Home for the Friendless. The press-printed sign on the door, "Visiting Day, 1 to 6 o'clock afternoon," warned me, and knowing full well I couldn't see them, I knocked anyway. Silence. I knocked again, frantic.

A big girl, sixteen or seventeen, hair combed into a black hairband, wearing the telltale dress of a Home for the Friendless inmate, answered the door. She opened it enough to say, "The Home is closed now. Please come back Monday in the morning."

"But I want to see my boys, please—the Lozier boys? George and Homer—no, I mean William?"

"Ma'am, I can't open the door. Please come back Monday. Visiting hours are over and the children are at supper." Apologetically she closed the heavy portal.

I knocked again, harder, bruising my knuckles. The door remained closed. "Please!" I called, my lips against the door, my voice a whimper, angry tears pooling.

"It's no use," a woman's voice said. I turned to see a woman of unsavory character, a soiled dove of the street, as they were called, sitting on the curb. She was no different from me except in owning her status as a plaything for men, while I hid mine. "Them cussed bitches won't let you in after hours. Even if yer hair's afire."

I gave up. I only wanted to see my children. I shrugged a

little at the woman, not willing to make conversation.

"Me babe's in there, too." The woman cleared her throat coarsely and spat. "I put her in a month ago and was all aflutter to see her today, but they wouldna let me in." She looked down at her gown, stained and mended, her bonnet's plume and limp ribbons sadly drooping. "I tried wheedling, coaxing, and threatening, and they said they'd call the officer. I don't want to be spending the night on the island, so I let off. Me babe's in there. They'll have her on a train to some rich folk, before I see her again." She put her fist to her mouth to hold back a sob. "The mothers don't matter here. It's the babies they want."

I hadn't considered the children on trains beyond Sarah and Ira. She must be lying. "How do you know?" The woman was constructing fairy tales, perhaps, but the moment I heard it, I knew it for truth.

"Han't you seen them parading out of here on a Tuesday? Every Tuesday week they take out with a string of children down to Central Station, and off they go. Dressed in bonnet and waistcoat, with new shoes and a satchel each. All aboard for the great far West. Oregon, California, I shouldn't wonder."

"California! That can't be." Now she was lying for certain. I turned to go.

"I'm only guessing. Haw far west can ye go til ye fall in the ocean? Them settlers need help, they need arms and legs to drive a plow and turn sod. This place has got children, big boys and girls, willing hands. What is this but a baby factory? You sign their paper. Put two and two together, missus, and see what's before yer own eyes. They're taking our babies and making them into slave workers."

"They're not slaves. We don't sell children in New York state." But Sarah's words came back to me. In trying to save them, had I put them in worse danger?

"It's worse'n slavery. It's adoption. A slave might be freed someday. But you put a little baby in a new family and they'll never know different. She'll never remember her mama now." The street woman began to cry in earnest now. "My little Alice. I want my baby," wailing into her hand.

I put my hands over my ears and ran down the steps. It can't be true—but what if it was? I wanted my babies, too. Hadn't they asked me to sign a paper? I had signed it. *Surrendering*. My babies, in someone else's arms. I had get them back. And yet, even if I could walk out with them right now, no money, no place to stay, impossible, all of it. I walked along East 29th Street toward the river and crossed the tracks, passed the quiet brassworks and the iron foundries awaiting their Monday crews, turned down Second Avenue and came back around to our corner again. I hadn't the will to go on. Where there's a will, there's a way, Grandmother Seybolt had said. With no hope in sight—was there a way to get them back, out of this tangle I'd made of their lives?

Chapter 13

Summer 1860

At the bottom of my milk pail after the failed visit, I found the little soldiers and and sticks decided they should stay in my bucket, I should carry them with me, at least these little things that my sons had played with, to keep them near to my hand and heart. I wished I had snipped a curl from their heads, and promised myself I would do so the next time, September Quarter Day, and from that morning through the humid, sultry summer, when my fingers reached into my pail for my breakfast or dinner, or to search for a forgotten crumb, I bumped against the musket or plumed hat of the little tin soldiers, their paint licked away by a babyish George, my little monkey I had brought to the City so many months ago—and I could feel the boys' embraces, almost smell their salty necks, see their tender pink ears.

Summer passed in a dreadful fever, my sweating hands marking the white silks and cottons despite my best efforts, and adding an additional step of washing, drying and pressing each shirt again before it could be considered complete. At least the light fabrics were cool to work with, while the itchy wool suiting lay across me like a blanket of briars. The heat was merciless over cobblestones and in rooms without a cross-breeze. At seven in the morning, I descended the stairs and went in the front door of Keeler's, grateful for the anticipated cool of the shop inside, Angus already in his cross-legged position seaming trousers. A wave of heat broke over me, dampening my forehead, my underarms with first sweat. My toes blistered inside my boots and a steady stream of perspiration flowed down the channel of my back. It was hard on my friends the Irish, who had never seen a day this hot, a sun this bright, on the foggy banks of their home country. Now they were melting like butter in a hot pan. The humidity ruined their bread and their fruit, wilted their dresses and their hair frizzed like sheep's wool in moist air. Only a blessed rain shower in the afternoon seemed to relieve them, even a little.

I took my quick break up to Newman's to ask for a letter, then quickly came back to my sewing, the lightning stitches I needed to finish before day's end. By late afternoon, I was dull and unable to see a thing except a running stitch, another buttonhole to be whipped; my finger was sore under my thimble, my neck cramped, my body damp and ripe from sweat. I must sponge out the neckband of my black dress, change out the dress shields I had tacked in place when first I sewed this gown, knowing even then how much I would need them in summer.

Through the livelong week, I sewed so many seams that I still saw needle and thread in my mind's eye when I closed my lids. At night, in the iron bedframe with the two Irish girls softly breathing, I went to sleep, weak from exhaustion by the time I slid off my corsets and lay my head on the flat straw-filled pillow. My eyes closed, the endless lines of endless stitching blurred into spots, then dreams, until about two in the morning. Then my eyes popped open as if the rooster was at my ear, and my breasts tingled as if my milk were rising. Some nights I found myself standing or already crossing the room to a cradle that no longer existed, to nurse a baby no longer mine, my gown unbuttoned to quiet the phantom child. I put myself back to bed, but lay there in the dark room, warm Sarah-like bodies breathing behind me in bed, in the same room where three other such Sarahs slept, and none of them mine. I had the perpetual sensation of needing to hurry, to be somewhere or do something, and knowing in my rational mind that there was no such task, no such mouth opening for the feeding spoon.

The millwheel turns when the water is there, whether we're thirsting or not; I had birthed six children, buried two, and given four away—and yet here I was, two o'clock, my arms empty, three o'clock, a lullaby stuck in my throat, four o'clock, a cradle I couldn't rock, five o'clock and the birds starting to chirp in the gloom, a potato I needn't mash for a baby's meal. The sensation was vertiginous, leaving me feeling always amiss; I'd taken the wrong turning in the trail, I'd lost the path, I'd never be able to make up this lost time, and no one understood that I'd had no more rope. Feed the children or house them—but not both. Work for money and leave them alone, or stay with them and starve. Those aren't choices a mother should have to make, but I'd made it, day after day, until I ran out of road.

I tried to slow my breathing, I tried counting sheep, or stitches, mentally sewing together a sleeve or a hem; I counted my blessings at the most minimal level—*I saw a blackbird. Someone fried some ham in the tenement, and it smelled so good, even if I didn't taste it. I like those new buttons we have in the shop*. I trickled off at least three blessings, if I could find so many, and finally fell into exhausted slumber, deep as a fever dream, waking at the slim edge of enough time to get to work. Quickly, then, hair combed through, dress shaken out, corsets tightened, shoes given a quick polish with a piece of crumpled newsprint, and a fingerful of charcoal from the stove to clean my teeth before I left at a quarter hour before seven, a biscuit spread with bacon fat, an apple and slice of cheese for my breakfast and dinner, packed into my pail.

It seemed an age until I had a letter from Ira. His birthday passed in early August with no word and no acknowledgement from anyone except myself, his mother. I prayed for him, asking health and safety for him from an unsympathetic Creator, and worked through the day as any other, as if I hadn't birthed my first son thirteen years before. When his first letter came, it was like a gift, a beautiful treasure, until I opened it and read his message.

August the 28, '60

Dear Mother,

How are you keeping? I am keeping well.

I have leave to write a letter to you and Sarah but I havent her direction and I don't know where she went. We rode the train and they put me off with a farmer in Lackport. I coudent help it. Mr. Alberty is stern. I am the same age as Charly one of his boys and we share the bed. I milk two cows every day. I remembered how to milk from Papa. I am going to the Lackport school with Charly and I ahead of him in the Second Reader; he is taller but I am stronger. We Indian rassle and I win. I am game to fight the other boys but fighting is not allowed. Mr. Alberty gave me a licken for fighting and he might have to lick me again because I hate it here. I no hate is a sin, Mama, but that is the Gospel truth. I don't no about George and Homey and where is Sarah, and when can you come and bring me home? I want to go home.

Sincerely Your SON,
IRA Seabolt LOZIER

His letter, folded the old-fashioned way and sealed with a stranger's wax seal, ignited my rage. The boy must have been told what to write in a letter; his form was so stilted, blotted and scratched, but when he turned the pen to his own words, his heart poured through and I wanted to whisk him home. Instead, I counted to ten, to stop the trilling of my heart that made me faint with anger and emotion, and went back to work. I kept sewing until I had finished for the day. I rolled up the shirts outside-in to keep them clean, swept the floor, and straightened the shop. A flick with the feather duster, and I was allowed to close up after six o'clock, when Keeler had gone home to his family.

At last, I knew where Ira was and could send him a letter. Lockport was not so far away from Newburgh by water—just two days by wagon, though the train would be faster now—a day's journey from New York City on the train. At least he was in the same state; he was still within my reach. Illinois was so far away, it would take me a week to get to Sarah. I wrote to Ira, unable to express all that I felt, but enough to keep hope alive.

August 31, 1860

My dear son:

I am joyful to hear from you after these months. I am keeping well and trust your health is also well. You're a good boy, son, and Papa would be proud to know you still know how to milk. I beseech you not to fight, Son, but to use your wits in school and get a good education while it is offered.

Your sister is with a family in the state of Illinois, and you might send a letter to Miss Sarah D. Lozier, care of Mr. Sylvanus H. Ferris, Post Office Galesburg, Knox County, Illinois.

Your brothers are in the Home and I remain in my self-same location, sewing for a nearby tailor. I maintain hope of seeing the boys, and of bringing you home to me soonest possible. Pray for me and your sister and brothers and be a good boy, Son.

With affection from
Your loving mother

• • •

By August's end, the leaves were beginning to curl in a tired manner, the City streets were thick with dust, and I had money in my corset that I carried on my person every day for fear of its being stolen while I was at work or asleep. I had no reticule, no coin-purse, anymore. Easier without it, to watch my money.

Keeler had found his niche, after Stevenson's grand order, as a maker of uniform suits for the locals who were stepping up the ladder. In the country, a man had his place: He was a farmer or a townsman, a son of the soil or a slave to the clink of coins. There was no moving up, only success or failure. Here in the City, everyone shifted up or down a notch together. As the merchants noticed each other's garments, they came to Keeler, and he raised his rates; I frequently found myself sewing Keeler a new waistcoat or cravat to keep him looking his best for customers.

On half-day Saturday, he liked to take his wife and daughter to the park to hear Cousin Angus's band perform. I had been Keeler's fancy woman, as it were, since June, and though I had earned a handful of dollars as his plaything, it was money I hated, a corner I'd mopped myself into. This particular Saturday, Mrs. Keeler and their three young daughters met him at the shop, bustling through the door with a jangle of bells and a light chatter of voices. The little brunettes wore square-necked gowns in rose sateen, blue serge, and an amber and brown stripe that complemented the youngest daughter's green eyes. Mrs. Keeler herself was no fashion plate, wearing a gown of silk, but the cut was not made for her stout figure. Her mantuamaker had done her no favors. I noted this from my back table; I would not place myself forward.

The youngest girl, about four years of age, came directly to me while her parents spoke near the front window. "Who are you?" She spoke with the unabashed frankness of the very young.

"I am Mrs. Seabolt. I work for your papa." I smiled at her, pleased at the pretty picture she made, despite her loathsome father.

"How do you do?" She dropped a curtsey, holding the pleats of her gown to each side like a princess.

"Very well, I thank you." I continued sewing the last button on the coat as she watched, my eyes flicking to the adults. I missed my children dreadfully. "What is your name?"

"Priscilla Aurelia Keeler," she said, lisping on the Ss and Rs. Her green eyes watched the needle poke up through the button. "I want to do that!"

I parked my needle in a fold of fabric and reached for a wooden button and a scrap of wool. I threaded a larger needle and made the knot, showing her, "I lick my finger, roll the thread and pull with my fingernail, and it makes a little knot, see?" Then I showed her how to poke through the button and the fabric and pull from the back, crisscross to make an X, and she had made two such stitches when her mother bustled back to us.

"I hope she isn't making a nuisance of herself," Mrs. Keeler made apology. "My Prisca is a forward girl. Curiosity killed the cat!" she scolded her daughter.

"Not at all. Your daughter is a keen student of the art." I looked up at Mrs. Keeler, nervous that she might see my guilt;

behind her, Mr. Keeler glared at me over his daughters' heads, a look of murder in his eyes. My black dress shielded my sins, though; I looked a respectable widow. No one would guess at our congress. And at that moment, I realized it was terror, not rage, that he was afraid his wife might find him out.

I seized the moment.

"Mrs. Keeler, pardon *my* forwardness, but may I show you something?" I stood and met her, eye to eye.

"Why, I—yes, of course." She shooed her youngest daughter back to her sisters and followed me.

I led her to the screen and pulled it around us. I brushed my hands down my gown while I spoke, indicating the narrow waist, the wide hips. "Do you see this new style of pintucks and pleats?" I showed her my sleeves, my bodice. "These would complement your figure, here and here. I made this gown as mourning, but in the right color for you—" I looked at her pale blue eyes and mousy hair. "This color we call teal, in silk, with a reticule and black gloves, would be the very picture. And we could try it in russet, I saw a likely tartan at the dry goods the other day. An ostrich plume on a straw hat with a russet ribbon for summer. Will you let me dress you? The latest London style, as befits your role as his wife?"

I cannot describe the pleasure that lit her face, unless I call it relief, or gratitude. She had thought to dress her daughters well but hadn't managed herself. I took the measure of her figure, and she promised to send the materials to the store, on her husband's account. When we withdrew the screen, she looked a happier, more confident woman. Mr. Keeler was pink in the face, flustered by his daughters frolicking up in the shop and his two women conspiring before his very eyes.

"We'll be late for the concert, dear heart," he blustered, cutting his eyes at me. He stepped to the back table where I had sat to work again. "What did you say to her?" With pins in my mouth, I could not speak but I looked at him in the eye, then returned to my seam.

The girls called farewell to me, and Mr. Keeler urged them toward the door. "Wait for me outside a moment, my dears. I forgot my hat," I heard him say.

I spat the pins in my hand, rose and found his straw hat on the back shelf. When he reached me, I held it firmly against my chest. No one else could hear us.

"Listen, you cat—don't go filling my wife's head full of tales. You stay away from her and tend to your work or I'll bounce you out the door, you!" His tone menaced—but he was impotent. I saw that now.

He tried to take the hat but I held it tighter, my fingers bending the brim. "No, you listen to me."

He drew back.

"I will make her gowns and she'll look like a duchess, and you'll pay for it. You owe her that," I said. "I'll not lie on my back for you again. If you even suggest it, I'll tell your wife. And if you think you'll cast me out? I'll tell her anyway. I will be her dressmaker and whatever else suits me in this shop, for—" I calculated fast. "—two dollars a week, and that's how it will be. I'm a dressmaker and nothing more." I handed him the misshapen hat. "I shall finish this seam and take my half-day. Good day."

"You little—" he sputtered — "nobody!" He snatched his straw hat and swept from the shop in impotent fury.

I almost pitied him. What a bully boy he was, ready to torment and bruise until someone got the better of him. Count me now as a blackmailer as a jezebel, but I may as well be hanged for mutton as for lamb. I am perhaps a nobody, but I was his victim no longer.

Chapter 14

September 1860

I opened a small package from Galesburg, with a hand unfamiliar on the label, but it was Sarah's own letter inside, and a lovely crocheted black reticule wrapped in thin white tissue paper as fine as lace. Sarah had lined inside the reticule with pale blue silk, and the article was so beautifully made, it was too pretty to use. I was touched by the thoughtfulness of Sarah's choice of black, and the care with which she had sewn the lining. Such an item would last a lifetime. But the letter was disquieting.

September 10, 1860

My dearest Mother,

How do you like your new reticule? Mrs. Ferris gave me the cotton to crochet with, and at first she gave me white, and I started it but thinking you might prefer black, I chanced to mention that you were yet in mourning. She immediately brought me some black thread and bid me start anew. I finished yours and went to work on the white one again as a gift to Miss Mae Ferris, who tutored me until school began and helped me with my elocution and I am learning to speak French from her.

Miss Mae calls me Delaphine in French, and Mr. and Mrs. Ferris call me Della. I don't mind it, it's nice to have a grown-up name and I do feel so grown up speaking French words. My new Sunday dress has a long hem and my new shoes have a heel to them. They also gave me a parasol for walking out so that this Western sun and wind don't burn my complexion. I am in the Fourth Reader in my class and am doing well except in geography. I don't have a head for it.

I got a letter from Ira and he says he is going to run away. His foster-father thrashed him and he wants to come home. Mr. Ferris says he might come here, there is no thrashing here but only the welcome love of Jesus. I am going to write Ira and tell him. I am crocheting for him a warm hat for winter with red yarn. How are my brothers? I miss George and did you see him for his birthday? I have a warm hat almost finished and will send it as soon as I do, so you can take it to him. I miss Homey. Is he yet learning to speak much?

From your loving Daughter—
Delaphina Lozier

This letter vexed me greatly. I am *Mother* now, no longer her mama. At least the siblings were corresponding; I counted that as a blessing at night when I could not sleep. But it sounded as if Sarah were becoming a cream puff, concerned about her complexion, fashionable clothing and using her middle name—that impulsive random choice I had thought so much prettier, instead of naming her for my mother-in-law Charlotte. Now I reached for my familiar daughter, the sensible helpmeet who had steadfastly rolled silk flowers alongside me, and found this almost-stranger, getting a fine education and living in a style I couldn't match. Was that what I had desired for this daughter? It was all as I had imagined—except without me, *in spite of me*, in utter disregard for even my daughter's own given name. And Ira's news confounded me further. If he ran away, how would I find him? Where would he go? His foster father had whipped him, and I couldn't bear it. Surely he was not so misbehaved. How was a mother to bear her son's punishment and her daughter's social elevation, neither one of them in my reach?

• • •

"The presidential election is coming," Keeler told us. "We must hope for a war. Can you imagine the benefit of providing uniforms to the regiments?" His enthusiasm did not touch me, as the thought of war was far from my present state of mind.

Newspaper headlines roared about the Lincoln-Douglas debates, and just by hearing headlines shouted in the streets, I knew a little about the coming fall election. New Yorkers were supporting their senator, candidate William Seward, but there were so many gentlemen in the running that I found it hard to remember their names. Slavery was a sinful practice, a position the Greenleafs had long held. But the vice had gone on so long, with so many compromises. Calling a sudden halt to the long-held practice was bound to bring protest, if not cataclysm. I heard rumors of secession from South Carolina and Georgia, tobacco and cotton and rice states, and murmurings of war if the Democrats did not win the presidency. Headlines and scrubby newsboys dizzied me with callouts, with black letters shouting terrible news.

I felt compassion for the slaves of the South, if my own existence was anything to compare with theirs—the endlessness, the hopelessness of my path. But I was no longer manacled by

Keeler, and I wasn't branded by my skin, hampered only by my gender and my lack of means. What would happen to the nation if we went to war one half against the other, and would it affect me? Would I have shirts to sew, and when could I retrieve my children, keep them safe from the troubles? I tried to listen more carefully when the topic arose among Keeler's customers, and at corner gatherings on the street.

"I'd rather see women in trousers with *the vote*, than see the Negro go free," I heard on my way to the corner grocer. A white man selling watermelon slices from his cart in the afternoon heat of Indian summer seemed to hold the crowd in his hand. "It will be the end of civilization as we know it. Food prices will rise like Jacob's Ladder, and the stock market will crumble like the walls of Jericho. Good working farmers shall lose their lands when we have to give it away to the freedman. I'd sooner see a cat on a velocipede or a fish with a telescope! Ants shall inherit the earth and elephants shall wear trousers and mince on Wall Street. No, the natural order of things is cattywampus if the Negro goes free."

A free Negro and his hoop-skirted wife stood and listened to him rant, and then the Negro man asked, "And what of my wife? Should she wear trousers and vote, or no, sir? Should she drive the buggy and I pull it? Or should we not take valid employment from a donkey? I await your logic."

His streetwise audience burst into laughter and the watermelon vendor turned as crimson as his melon-flesh. "Verily, I say—" he began, but street b'hoys—those intrepid scamps—spat watermelon seeds at him. A street rat of indeterminate gender pushed at the pyramid of melons and they fell, splattering red flesh and green rinds in the dirt. The Negro man tipped his stovepipe hat to the vendor and took his elegant wife away from the hurly-burly.

September turned the streets golden and I knew the harvest was beginning in Newburgh, the oats and rye were cut and shocked, the hay had long been stacked, that potato greens and cowpeas were drying in the field. Soon, not Bram nor Malcolm, but Jesse and his own hired farmhands would dig a furrow to upend the brown-skinned tubers from their summer rest, and the beans were slated to pull and stack for threshing. Sacks of beans and bins of potatoes, turnips, carrots, beetroots and rutabagas, winter squashes and pie pumpkins, with apples and cider to come soon enough—I missed the earthy smell of my root cellar and spicy pickles, the yeasty scent of beer and cider fermenting, dripping chunks of perfumed honeycomb sliced from the hives behind the chicken coop, that made up the inventory of my winter pantry.

Uprooted from my seasonal farm work, I sometimes forgot the month or the day, detached from having to remember daily chores with a mnemonic or a rhyme, from making jam, crocking pickles and potting meat, what begged to be done to keep these summer fruits for winter. In the City, the September sun beat down on still-dry streets, coal dust settled thickly on every ledge and table, and my hands couldn't help but smudge the white, white shirts I sewed as fast as I could. But slowly, a day at a time, the last day of the month grew closer, and I looked forward, after three long months, to seeing my little boys again.

Quarter Day was conveniently on a Sunday that September, and I hoped to take the boys to stroll together away from the grounds like any respectable family. I made my hair sleek with the brush and cool water, parted in the middle and brushed tight plaits from my loose tresses, coiled them in the back. I covered the mass of hair with a black snood I had purchased from Amanda Pendleton for a penny, pinning it snugly. I had pressed and sponged my steadfast widow's weeds

Saturday night, and pressed my new handkerchief, from muslin scraps at Keeler's, into crisp white folds. To look at me, one wouldn't think I was anything more or less than a genteel widow. I was, though, more shabby than genteel.

The weather had finally turned and lent a crisp edge to the fall morning air. I shook out my shawl and wrapped it Sontag-style, with my new reticule proudly on my arm—holding just my handkerchief and some pennies for sweets with the boys. My coin stocking was pinned tightly into my corset where it could neither be seen nor stolen. I tied my boots firmly over new black stockings, knitted for 10 cents by my room-fellows; I shook out my petticoats. Stylish crinoline hoops filled out my skirts, though they filled the rooms and made passing down the stairways a ridiculous chore, and I could but perch on a chair's edge, not sit back.

At quarter to one in the afternoon I walked down the three flights of stairs to the street level and through the heavy front door of the tenement, uncommonly fevered with anticipation at seeing my boys. Three months—Homer must be walking well by now, talking, too. Fifteen words by fifteen months was the rule, for all except our Georgie. But George—might he be talking after almost six months in school? Really conversing like any other child? Meeting my eyes, greeting me? I felt foolish tears rising, excitement mounting, my arms already curling to encircle them, and forced myself to be calm, to be still, to prepare for the inevitable petty bureaucracy that the Mrs. Phillipses of the world seemed to throw in the way.

The cross-town wind blew chill against me all the way up East 29th but I warmed to the walk, my cheeks pinked from the brisk air. The white-columned Home for the Friendless rose before me like a wedding cake. I was not the only mother entering the iron fence, climbing the marble stairs with gifts or treats. The front door stood open, Mrs. Phillips and other Agents of the Society on hand in their dark blue coats or cloaks and bonnets, a neat stack of the society's newsletter on the front table, in the hands of well-scrubbed children, offering the paper like programs at a theatre.

Mrs. Phillips caught my eye and nodded, saying again and again, "Good afternoon, visitors, good afternoon."

"Good day, Mrs. Phillips. I am here to visit my sons."

"Oh, how wonderful for them. You are—?" It was clear Mrs. Phillips could not recall me.

"Martha Lozier, their mother. I have come to see George and Homer—William Lozier."

"Ah, yes. Madam, forgive me, we see such a number of parents and guardians, I could not place you. If you will go with—" she looked behind me at one of her sister-agents, "Mrs. Hartt, there, into the private parlor? That would be good of you. Good afternoon, visitors! Good afternoon."

I followed young Mrs. Hartt into the parlor and was seated on the brocade settee as invited, awaiting my boys. Mrs. Hartt, a fresh-faced girl who could not have been married more than a few months, excused herself, closing the door behind me. I waited. My heart sped up each time I heard a footstep in the hall. One time someone opened the door and started in, saying, "Pray wait in here for Mrs. Phillips—oh, my, pardon me." I kept my place on the settee, arranged to look the proper matriarch, the farm widow in City clothes, waiting to greet my sons.

The minutes turned into quarter hours, marked by the ornate wood and brass clock on the mantel, and then an hour had passed. I paced the floor now, hardly daring to leave the room, awaiting my boys. But, of course, they must be changing their clothes, tidying up. With this thought, I calmed myself and sat again, wishing after another quarter hour passed that I had a cup of tea, or could find my way to the privy. My excitement dimmed as my need became more urgent, and at last I stood and made my way to the parlor's hallway door and out through the hallway to a door that led to the back quarters of the building, where servants and kitchen might be located. Passing through that door, I found a girl, perhaps fifteen years old, and asked for the necessary.

The girl directed me down another hall and down the back stairs to an enclosed yard that seemed separate from the children's areas; I hurried to attend to my needs, and then made my way back. When I got to the hallway again, Mrs. Phillips was standing with some children, listening to one reciting his letters. Mrs. Phillips saw me with surprise, and, patting the little lad's head, came to me.

"Oh dear, are you still here?"

"I have not seen my children yet. I was told to wait—I have been waiting close on two hours."

Mrs. Phillips gestured me back to the parlor. "My apologies for your long wait. You ought to have been told and sent home."

"Told what?" The same old rage welled inside me. "Mayn't I see my children today?"

"My dear lady—"

"Where are my children? My boys?" I turned sharply toward her. My hands clenched, ears throbbing with pulse. Other visitors were looking, heads turning.

"If you would please wait and—" Mrs. Phillips shushed me. "Please keep your voice down. You're making quite a scene!" She looked at someone behind me.

I spun to see who it was, what was happening. "I want my boys. Bring them to me. I need to see them."

"That is quite impossible," Mrs. Phillips said.

I turned back, unbelieving. "What excuse this time?"

Was it my imagination, or did the moment slow into an eternal pause, awaiting what came next: Calumny and doom.

"They are no longer here."

I sucked in a breath I'd need to scream. I leapt toward Mrs. Phillips, feral with rage, and grabbed her shoulders. "Where are they? Where have you sent them?"

Mrs. Phillips tried to step back, fighting me off. "Mr. Rogers! Help me!" and the parlor doors flew open. Mrs. Hartt and another woman in dark blue habit rushed into the foyer, a gentleman in a top hat and cape sweeping in afterward. They pulled me backward from Mrs. Phillips, shushing and chattering, while I tried to shake them off.

"No, no, where are they? What have you done with them? I want my babies! Homer! George!" I was shrieking, sounded utterly lunatic to my own ears; they would call the guard and have me taken to the madhouse at Bellevue, but what did it matter if my boys were dead?

"Madam, please," the man said, speaking calmly into my ear. "Cease your hysterics at once, and I will be glad to tell you." He swept his hand back toward the parlor where I had waited so long. "Won't you come in?"

I stopped fighting, wanted to collapse on the floor. "Please tell me. Where are my sons? George doesn't speak and Homer is just a baby."

"Let me introduce myself—Joseph Rogers, an Agent for the Society. Now then, Mrs. Phillips, Mrs. Hartt, Mrs. Fitzhugh—ladies, will you please give me leave to converse with Mrs.—"

"—Lozier," Mrs. Phillips supplied.

"Won't you come chat with me, Mrs. Lozier? Would you like some tea? Mrs. Hartt? Some tea, please!"

"No, I don't want tea. I want my boys. Where are they—if not here—what have you done? Where have you sent them?"

Mr. Rogers made a whisking motion to the ladies, shooing them from the room, and guided me into the parlor again.

"Very well," Mrs. Phillips said. Mrs. Hartt put her arm

around Mrs. Phillips' waist and the three women left me alone with Mr. Rogers. He was tall and thin, and his dark clothes made him seem thinner yet.

"I apologize for whatever misunderstanding there was this afternoon, madam; will you please sit down? Allow me to look into the books a moment and get an understanding of the circumstances? I will be in this next room, which is an office—I shall leave the doors open. One moment, please."

I sat stiffly, my hands clenched, shaking, my mind racing. The same question spiraled through my mind, where were they? O Lord, where? Where?

Mr. Rogers, true to his word, left the double doors open between the parlor and office, set his top hat on the corner of the table, and flipped through a large ledger book. He opened another such and paged through it as well. I sat in silence, rocking slightly, trying to keep my panic at bay. Where were my little ones? I could not bear it.

At last he looked up and saw me watching him. "I found them," he said. "Won't you come in?"

Shakily I stood and walked into the office, toward the desk where he held the two books open before him. "What is that? Where are my boys?"

"These are the surrender records. It shows here when you brought in your children for surrender to the Home, and where they are now."

"I did not surrender them forever. I brought them here temporarily—for a little while. Not for the rest of their lives. They are my children."

"Mrs. Lozier, even if for just one day, one hour, we require that the child be 'surrendered' to us." He emphasized the word. "He—or she—is then in our care, to take care of them as the Lord sees fit. That is the very reason we founded the American Female Guardian Society—to help women such as yourself who could not properly care for their children. Many women have fallen on hard times, very sad situations, and cannot protect their children from the vice and sin of the world." He recited this as if reading the Epistle at a church service.

"It is understood, Mrs. Phillips always makes it plain, that we may send the children out to other homes, out to be indentured, as a bound boy or girl, or as an adoptee. It is understood from the first, Mrs. Lozier. Did you not understand that?"

I faltered. "I did understand that *some* children, orphans and waifs, were sent out, but I did not think *mine* would be sent away from here. Their father is dead, but I am their mother! They are but half-orphans. My daughter was sent to Illinois, for mercy's sake!" I choked. "Where are my babies now?"

Mr. Rogers sighed. "It is not in our practice to tell you where the children are, for the good of the placement and the new family setting." He smiled gently at me. "I would not ordinarily be able to tell you a word more—except that I was on the train with the boys; I escorted them to their new homes. I feel I can tell you from my experience, if not strictly by the book, as it were."

"My boys are not *in this City*?"

He looked at the book again. "Allow me to narrate from the ledger, and you will see that this is for the best. No, please," he said, raising a thin hand. "I want to help you, but if you're going to fuss, I shall close the books and escort you out. Will you be a good girl and listen?"

I pinched my lips together and nodded, forced into silence.

He turned to the page. "In April of 1860, the Home received Ira Seabolt Lozier and George Frederick Lozier on the same day, and bathed, clothed, and fed them. The boys were summarily schooled daily, taken to chapel on Wednesdays and church on Sundays; Ira was given some initial occupational training in the print shop." He glanced at me. "*Surrendered*, the book says.

"Your son, George Frederick, was surrendered with Ira on the same day, yes, but as he is a bit slow, not to say idiotic, but somewhat stupid and dumb, he was seen by our excellent physician, Dr. Phillips—yes, Mrs. Phillips' husband, the very man. Dr. Phillips declared George physically fit in his physical body but deficient in his mental capacity. The boy's hearing and eyesight are fine, but he presented as mute."

I held my tongue, desperate to hear more, but I seethed. How dare he speak this way of my middle son, the quiet one with eyes that took in the world and a small voice that spoke up when he was ready to speak?

"Naturally, no Christian family wanted to take on such a burden, so we placed him with younger children. It says he played along well enough and seemed to follow the alphabets and early Reader lessons. However, our primary teacher found that George was capable of speech when he desired to speak, so under doctor's recommendation, the boy was thrashed a number of times, and soon enough he began to speak. His speech is affected and not normal, but it is a beginning."

Mr. Rogers wagged his head with sympathy. "He will never be a scholar, Mrs. Lozier, but your middle son has a sturdy physique and should grow up in good health. He will make a strong worker someday." He smiled at me.

"Surely he didn't need a thrashing."

"But it had its effect, madam, so surely he did. Now," he said, "your daughter, Sarah Delaphina. You brought your daughter and your infant son William Homer Lozier to the Home and surrendered them in June, it says here," he read aloud. "Sarah was deemed a credit to her family, and, being of a good age to be indentured for work, was sent immediately to the Ferris family—a most upstanding family, one of the first in Galesburg, as you are aware? It says here they are calling her Della, her middle name, much less *common* than

Sarah. Della has quickly caught up in school and is a great help to her foster mother, Mrs. Ferris. She is already beloved by her foster sister and is attending the Methodist church. That is a very good placement, and I expect we shall have no further trouble about Sarah."

"Certainly no trouble, but when will she be back?"

"Patience, Mrs. Lozier. Unfortunately your eldest boy Ira did not settle in well, and it says, 'he boasts about his father's farm.' He was sent north to a farmer named Alberty in Lockport."

"Yes, I have written to him there."

"He does not get on well with the Alberty children, and Mr. Alberty says, 'Ira is very immodest.' I suspect he is a bit of a braggart and a show-off," Mr. Rogers commented. "He has been fighting, it says."

"How do you know all that?" His commentary offended me deeply. Ira was not a show-off; he was desperate and angry at being taken from his brothers and sister. No wonder the boy fought with his new family.

"We send and receive letters from the families once a month, and we correspond with the children as well. Ira has not been writing to us, but his foster father has."

"My son is a good boy."

"Of course, he is at heart—but without a father, or a mother who could feed or discipline him, he has gotten out of hand and, might I say, incorrigible. Mr. Alberty will make him toe the mark, I dare say." He turned a page.

"He's not incorrigible. He was always well-behaved. I have always been proud of him." I gave up trying to defend my son to someone who wouldn't listen. "I want my children back." How I could make that work, I didn't know. But this separation, this distance—it could not stand.

Mr. Rogers, sere and gaunt in his dark suit, strands of dark hair touched with gray falling across his broad forehead, looked at me with pity and some condescension. "I'm afraid they have been indentured—that is a contract, Mrs. Lozier, a legally binding contract for a set period of time. We cannot—"

"George? Homer? Sent out to *work*?"

"No, of course, not the little boys. I cannot give you every detail, but I can assure you this, my dear lady." He nodded at me. "They are settled with good families, and you have nothing to fear for their well-being."

"What happened to Homer? *Where is my baby*?" I half-rose from my chair, as if to go search for him.

"Mrs. Lozier, please. I am giving you all the information I can," he said with asperity. "I can stop this meeting right now, or you can let me finish. Which would you prefer?"

I stood motionless for another eternal second, then slowly perched again on the edge of the chair.

He cleared his throat. "As I say, your son George is not a very desirable child. Some parents, you know, think idiocy is contagious and they won't have it around. But we have treated George with the discipline he needed, and while we were gathering a group of children to take West early this month, we decided to send George and his brother together."

"To California." Three thousand miles away. I felt lost in a nightmare. Perhaps the soiled dove had been correct after all.

"I cannot give you the particulars just now, but believe me, the group of children went together, and your sons were together the entire journey. They have been placed in homes in a western state, both of them in the same town, and they have both been indentured for adoption, not for work. So you can rest your weary soul on that account; both boys will be part of a family and treated like one of the children by birth. They will be able to stay in contact and be as friends growing up. They are together, and that in itself is unusual in the annals of the Home for the Friendless. So there, you see that your children are all in safe, clean, Christian homes, and you have nothing further to worry about."

I felt a wave of horror so strong I might vomit, and gripped the desk. "Mr. Rogers. I must have them back. My family—their own family, the Loziers. A respected name upstate. I must have my children. Please tell me their information and I will get them myself."

Mr. Rogers quietly closed the two ledgers and stacked them neatly, squaring their edges and firmly pushing the books to the far end of the desk.

"My good woman, you cannot have been listening. The children are indentured out, each for a period of seven years. Della will be of age and able to marry when she completes her indenture. Your eldest boy won't be of age but he may seek work or return to you at that time, if you are able. Your two youngest will live as children of the families into which they have been adopted until the seventh year, and at that time the families can renew the indenture or legally adopt them or send them back here. At that time, if they so desire, and if you are financially able to take them in, due to the generosity of your family or perhaps remarriage? At that time—in seven years, mind you—it is possible you may have back your children. But until then, they are no longer yours. You understand that, don't you? The document is legally binding."

"That can't be," I said wildly. "I never meant—I want them back!"

"I'm afraid that's impossible." He stood, placing his top hat on his head and now towering above me, the desk between us.

"Please understand me, Mrs. Lozier, in the plainest language I possess: *We do not choose* to cancel the indentures of your children. They are better off where they are. They have an education, a safe and clean home, enough to eat, and Christian families that will cherish and adore them."

"I cherish and adore them," I whispered.

"Then why on earth would you give them up? What loving mother would do such a thing?" He pressed his thin hands into the desk. "I believe our discussion is concluded, good lady. I will see you out."

"But—I—my—" I stuttered, tumbling over my words as he came around the desk and took my elbow firmly in his hand. "Their things? May I have their—"

"They had no things. They came here with nothing, and what they took, we provided. You brought them here with nothing. We gave them a better life. It's time you understood that. Move along, now."

He guided me with a firm step not through the front hall where other visitors, donors perhaps, and children still prattled together, but down the back hall toward the side entrance.

"I do not expect we shall have the pleasure of seeing one another again. Good day, Mrs. Lozier," he said, and closed the door.

Chapter 15

Autumn 1860

The boys were gone, possibly forever. For seven years, at least. I had to tell Sarah; the girl was waiting to hear about her young brothers. And then Ira. But how could I explain myself? How careless did one have to be to misplace trust, to misread the cues? I wasn't much educated, despite the books I had read with Grandmother Seybolt; I didn't know the full consequences of leaving my children in a stranger's kindly care. I had thought of the table laden with food, the warm beds, the free education—but not years-long separation. Such words, like *surrender*, the vice-grip of *indenture,* held my family apart as surely as a barricade or a prison. What solace was there for a mother who had lost her children? And how might my children judge me?

The night fell upon me like a sifting of snow, a dank fog. I could lay myself down by the river and let the night, the creatures that roamed there, do what they would to me. I could fill my pockets with stones, sew them into my hem. I had needle and thread. I could find the stones. I could step into the current. With the tide pressing inland, and then returning, and with night bearing down, I would be lost in the dark water and no one would save me. The children were safe somewhere now. They would hardly miss me. I longed for an end to pain, for the silence of deep water. The rocks and the sand and the fish. Just the river and I, forever.

Somehow, I held on. Days, weeks later, going through the motions of my day, dreaming of dark water as I sewed, as I lay awake at night, as I climbed the stairs, I kept the possibility of the river as a secret, ultimate choice. Maybe tonight, maybe tomorrow. Not just now, but maybe.

It depended on Sarah—I couldn't keep the news from my daughter, nor Ira, though I was loath to do it. They would hate me, blame me. How could I say it? Would they despise me, or disregard me as irreparably foolish, as I did my own mama? After several days of stewing, at last I wrote to Sarah, explaining in the simplest terms, but dreading my daughter's response, her likely rebuke:

> *The Society counts its books as legal documents and says it will hold the four of you for seven years. I grieve at the outcome of all my endeavors. I am uncertain as to where the little boys were sent. I know where you and Ira stay, and know you are safe, and that comforts me. In the meanwhile I attend to my job of work and strive to determine what next to do. I shall save all I can toward our eventual reunion. Let us continue as we are until we can do the next certain thing. May the Lord bless you and keep you, my beloved…*

Here I paused and forced myself to acquiesce to what had already come to pass—

> *…my beloved Della.*
> *From your loving mother.*

—and sent my letter before I could change my mind.

To Ira, I wrote as if he were a man already.

...When such time comes as we may be together again, I trust that you and I shall determine which next step is best. I look forward your guidance when you write to me next. Please do not judge your mother too harshly, for I only did what I thought wise at the time. Say your prayers for yourself and your brothers, my son.

I remain
Your loving mother.

But it was three quarters of a year before I heard from Ira again.

• • •

Missing my daughter and the closeness we had enjoyed in those months before Sarah left, I took a short respite from the sewing table and walked to the corner grocer to buy apples for my bed-fellows, Maggie and Bridey. The girls had been quietly kind to me, not knowing why their boarder was so sad, but they had traded and given me a better pillow and made sure to leave me enough room at night. My nightdress was always folded beautifully when I went to change. Little attentions that made me feel cared for—it mattered. It helped. I longed for feminine companionship. In the grocery I asked for a pound of apples from the fresh crop appearing in the City now from orchards in New Jersey and upstate.

"Post for you, Mrs. Seabolt." Mr. Newman handed me a letter, as his clerk filled a paper poke with several red- and green-striped apples, plump with juice. He weighed them at the scale and I paid in coin, having done with my tab since my children had gone. I felt better not owing anyone; *cash on the barrelhead*—a lesson I wished I had known before I started on this journey.

The letter was from Sarah. I was afraid—what must she think of her mother—and for a brief moment considered waiting until evening to read the missive, but my nerves got the best of me. I slit the envelope with one of my valued hairpins, then tucked my pin back into place, unfolded the letter, and read.

November 19, 1860

My dearest Mother:

I was so glad to have heard from you. I have some news of the boys, all!

Mrs. Penfield from the Home visited me (She says she will come twice a year) and then she visited with Mrs. Ferris in the parlor. The Ferrises are members of the American Female Guardian Society. They were speaking of Society business, and then Ira and George and Homer, and I was meant to be ironing but I listened. I know it's rude to eavesdrop, but I didn't know I was doing wrong until I found I had moved to the door and was listening at the keyhole.

But I had to know, so I ask you to forgive me, Mother, for my faults.

Mrs. P. said George and Homer were both put into good families up north. I don't know where except that it's in a free state and not down South. She said Ira has run away two times. The agent said Mr. Alberty has thrashed Ira but he (Ira) is unrepentant.

I wish we could all be together again. I wish we could go back to Newburgh and I wish dear Papa was alive and

Grandpapa, too. Galesburg is a nice town and I am to sing in the church on Sunday. Do you like my hand? Mrs. Ferris says it's the mark of a lady to write beautifully.

I miss you, Mother dear, and send you all of my love. My friend Brutus also wags his greetings.

Your loving daughter,
Delaphina Lozier

What was to be done? My sons needed somewhere safe, where no one would beat them, where I could hold them and await the things they would say, whenever they were ready to say them. My daughter was in that peculiar age between silly and sensible, and I found it difficult to determine what was utmost in Sarah's mind—dog Brutus and church, or her brothers' welfare. I went back to my work, helpless as always, crushed as corn in the gristmill, powdered into submission, with no will to take the next step, nor enough money. I could live one day to the next, if that was living—clothe myself, eat a cold breakfast, drink scalding tea, sew the many hours of daylight until lamps were lit, sew a while longer, trudge back up the stairs, undress, lie sleepless until I dreamed of my children, my many losses. If that was living, I lived.

Abraham Lincoln—another Abram but not such a one as mine—won the presidential election, and now talk of a war with the South was very real. I knew it was coming. Every day grubby newsboys shouted from the street corners, each with a differing headline, but all noise and bluster. A better class of men, those who sought to become officers, came in to be fitted for coats and trousers in Union blue. Soon Angus and I tailored blue coats with epaulets, sewed brass buttons in precision rows down double and single breasts, and narrow collars that stood just so, black or gold stripes on trousers, piping and fringe.

"Angus, are we down on brass buttons again? Coat and cuffs—and where is the braid and piping I ordered from London?" Keeler, in high-hand fashion, had the shop closed but was working us through inventory. "Button shanks low as well? I know, but we used the lot last week. We must—Martha, where are the brass cuff buttons? And the—oh, here they are. You have got to put them in the correct box after—drat all, is that the door? Go away, we're at dinner!"

A street arab rattled the door a second time. Mindful of Keeler's pettishness, I opened the door a crack. "What is it, child?"

"Message from the pier. Box come in from London, England. Come git it." The boy squirmed as if he had to use the privy.

"Do you need the necessary?" I asked. He nodded. "Quick, around the back in the alley, but I need to know which pier, so come right back."

"What maguffery is that?" Keeler roared behind me. He was such a bully-child, a tired or hungry tyrant in knee breeches—and all possessed-like if he didn't get his way. I'd known children to be thrashed for such displays of temper.

I turned. "Messenger boy—your order at the pier?"

"Where's the cursed fool?"

I nodded my head toward the back of the building where the privy was. "He'll be back soon."

My employer let out a string of curse words that would make a cabin boy blush. I smoothed my brow, hoping to forestall a headache.

"Don't just stand there, look for those buttons!" He kicked at the tailor's dummy, sending it into the table, and hurting his foot. "Son of a seacook!"

The young messenger came back to the door, knocking again. I whisked it open, bell jangling. The boy stood at the lintel, fingering his cap, shivering a little in the cold wind. "I come back."

"So you did," I answered. "Now which pier did the boat come to?"

"Pier Six." The boy looked cold. His hands were filthy, with black moons under his nails.

I heard Keeler approaching behind me. I turned, my body between him and the child. "The box is at Pier Six—I shall go fetch it, if that helps?"

"What kind of lickspittle is this? Where are my buttons?"

"Down at the wharf," I snapped. "Shall I go get them or would you rather?" I could bear him roaring at me, but I couldn't abide him abusing a child.

"You go. Go on, and get back again, quickly." He turned to Angus. "How many more trousers can you finish today? We're behind, man, we're losing gold and daylight while you stand there twiddling your fingers!"

I told the child, "Wait a moment, I'll be out directly." I got my reticule and coat, pulled on my wool mitts and hood. I noticed the boy had no stockings inside his battered boots, nor mittens and but a thin coat, not how I'd have dressed my little ones. "I'll be going then," I said to Keeler and Angus. "Pier Six. Might I have the fare for the streetcar?"

Keeler groused under his breath but gave my two five-cent pieces from his coin-purse. He could hardly evade the cost, as I was doing his service. I nodded to acknowledge the coins but didn't allow myself to thank him. I was doing him a favor, not the other way around.

The door of the shop closed behind me, and then I realized I hadn't had my dinner. It was all the same—I'd find a wagon selling nuts or cheese and get some for the boy as well. He stood at the street edge, his flat cap pulled down on his head, his pink ears bright red with cold.

"Come on," I told him. He turned and walked with me. "We're going to take the streetcar. I can't walk so far as you can."

"I dinna pull foot. I hitched a wagon." He scratched himself.

"What's your name, son?" I walked at a good pace, keeping up with him.

"Billy."

"Are you William?"

"Dunno. Allus been Billy."

We got to the downtown streetcar line at the corner of Fourth and Twenty-Sixth. "How old are you, child?"

"I'm twelve."

"Can't be! Are you all of twelve?" He was embroidering the truth. He was just a babe. He couldn't be as old as my Ira.

"Am so. I'm the biggest in me whole gang." He had dirt on his nose and gap teeth like a picket fence in his round face.

The streetcar, pulled by a muscular red horse with dinner-plate hooves, came clopping along while we chatted. I found myself drawn into the boy's prattle, missing my sons, remember our first day's trek with Ira up the horse-car line to find a place to live. I paid my fare and Billy rode with me, no charge.

"Tell me about your family," I asked Billy, just to hear him speak, and listened to him, soaking in his rough cadences and cheerful boyishness.

He told me he lived with a "bruvver" and they were both messenger boys; they stayed downtown, though he wouldn't say where. He earned a few cents a day for messages and got to keep his service pennies himself. The faster he worked, the more he earned. "I git a half-dime for goin' up to Keeler." The fare for one-way travel uptown—he could spend it getting there or improvise and keep it all for food. I admired his wily ways.

The streetcar rolled slowly along, the conductor ringing the bell when they stopped and started, dozens of times, all down through the Bowery and around Chatham to the end of the line.

"You're a bright boy, Billy," I told him. "I haven't had my dinner yet. Have you?"

"No, ma'am. I han't et nothin' today."

"We'll find a barrow or a cart when we get downtown, shall we?" It felt good to feed a child, to be with a child like this again. When at last the horsecar pulled up to the depot down at the Broad Way, Billy leaped out and I stepped after. "Which way to the wharf?" I was momentarily disoriented but followed his pointing finger toward the masts bobbing down in the harbor. I asked him which street but he couldn't read, so I read the signs to him as we walked. When we got to Liberty, I saw a cluster of barrows, one with the inevitable oysters, another roasting goobers. A pair of young men in striped black aprons sold small brown bottles from a wooden crate, with that seductive, exotic elixir, syrup of vanilla. Beyond them I saw what I wanted, a stout white man with red hands and a butcher's apron, selling meat pies steaming in the cold.

"Could you eat a beef pie by yourself?" I thought I could eat half and share with him, if he couldn't eat a whole one.

"Yes, ma'am. If I caint eat it all, my bruvver will eat 'em."

That settled it. I bought two meat pies and gave them both to the boy. "Take one to your brother, will you, son?" I gave him two pennies for his services and said I'd walk the rest of the way by myself. "I thank you for accompanying me, Billy. You've been a gentleman." He grinned and ran off with his meat pies held warm and close to his chest.

Still hungry, I looked around, the spire of Trinity Church looming like a solid old friend, the brackish smell of the harbor tinged with sea-fresh salt, the crush of sailors, merchants and pickpockets mingling; I kept my little coin-purse inside Sarah's gifted reticule tight in my hand clutched against my bosom. I made my way down to an agreeable coffeehouse on Greenwich. When I had arrived nearly a year before, the crowds and the speed of commerce had alarmed me, a country mouse; now I was used to people and impudent street boys, as well as rising merchants and their wives. Although it wasn't a holiday, leaving the haberdashery early, with a horsecar ride to a different part of the City and a child to accompany me, made the day feel something like it.

I found the coffeehouse, and, given a table and bench near the front, where the windows lent daylight to the room, asked for a cup of coffee and a plate of bread and butter. The coffee was the first I had tasted in months, despite smelling it in the air from other homes and doorways. My gift of the meat pies and this little meal put me a little behind in my expenses, but I counted the day as a treat. My back was straight and my wrists were free of cramps from close needlework, just for today. I needn't squint at my work. A cup of strong black coffee in a china cup, the fresh white bread and sweet butter tasted a genuine feast. The crust of the bread was hard to chew on one side of my mouth; I had noticed my teeth feeling loose, achy, and I wondered if I was going to lose one, or all of them. I hadn't eaten truly well for months now—mostly potatoes, beans, thin soups and starchy stews, tea—whatever my Irish family were eating, I shared in, yet they all had their teeth. I missed eating crisp apples and fresh cheese, drinking milk from the dairy, and potherbs from my garden, especially in autumn. A dish of stewed greens and smokehouse ham would set me right up, I shouldn't wonder.

Still, the clock was moving, and I must retrieve the box of buttons and hie back to the shop. I put on my coat and settled my hood and mitts in place, nodding my thanks to the coffee houseman. I walked the last few blocks to Pier Six, and though there was a flurry of activity, I was able to find a man who looked authoritative, and he sent me to the storefront of the warehouse back of the pier. I explained my errand and soon found myself holding a wooden casket tied and stamped, with a British export seal and a written label on its top.

Jas. Keeler—Haberdashery Et Clothier
City—New York,
United States

I quickly made my way from the docks toward the horse-cars, several blocks up, now carrying the box on one arm, now the other, and tried carrying it on my hip like a child to see if that were any better. The box wasn't large, but it was heavy with its England-made brass and nickel buttons, and made a thick rattle as I carried it, in time to my footsteps. I shifted it back to the front, both arms, at a street corner, half-way to the horsecar, when I felt someone seize my elbow. The box slipped from my grasp and hit the cobbles, denting the wood, but still intact and sealed.

"My hat! What are you doing here, Martha?"

The voice chilled me like a plunge through ice into a winter lake. I crouched to look over the box, praying I was wrong, that someone else had bumped me, that I was still on my way back to the haberdashery, that my silly mind was playing tricks.

"Well, if that don't beat all! I come here to mind some new business, and I find—some *old* business." Lawyer Montgomery loomed over me. His pointed shoes gleamed like polished metal. "Allow me to assist you." He bent to take my elbow again.

I pulled back. I did not want to speak to him, nor feel his hand on my flesh.

"Have it your way, my fine lady. Are we a messenger now, or a stevedore, hauling cargo?" The box shifted in my arms, the buttons jingling like so many coins. "What ho—are you a pirate, with a treasure chest? Speak up, Widow Lozier. Cat got your tongue?"

"I am on an errand for my employer, and I'll thank you to let me go on my way." I spoke firmly.

"I think not." He slid his hand along my coat sleeve to grip my arm tighter. "I believe we have some business to discuss." He pulled me beside him away from my course, away from the horsecars. The heavy box continued to torment me, slipping as I tried to hold it upright, not drop it, while walking faster than usual on damp cobbles, one arm held tight in the lawyer's grip.

"Let me go, I must get back to work."

"Quiet, you," he squeezed my arm hard. "I've had enough of your carryings on. First, you slip away like a thief in the night with the heirs presumptive. You stole possessions from the Lozier family, while they were in the throes of despair over Abram and Malcolm, and you ignored a legal summons to court. You haven't the slightest idea how much trouble you've made, confound you!"

My knees were weak as water. O Lord, let him not find out I hadn't the children. What would he do to me? What could he do?

Montgomery reached a certain varnished oaken door and pulled it open. It was a grog-house, the inside of which I was not keen to see, but he hustled me alongside him, calling to the Negro barman, "I'll take the private parlor, Orville!" He must be a habitue of the place.

We pushed through a green-painted swing door with a small window set in it, covered by a darkish velvet curtain on its inner side. The door swished closed, and I found myself in a small receiving room with a black horsehair sofa and armchairs, an oval table in the center, all set upon a blue and red Turkish carpet with a thick white fringe at its ends. A colored glass lamp with whale-oil in its base stood on a beaded mat upon the table, and lamps hung on the walls around, plumbed for gas. A flowered china ewer and basin stood on a corner stand. It was an elegant room, unexpected in a grogshop, to my mind.

"Well, put down your box and sit, Mrs. Lozier. *Please*." He drawled the word, insultingly, snidely, readying me for attack, it seemed. I had a chance to look at him, see that he was dressed more elegantly than when last I'd seen him a year before: his fine polished shoes, his top hat, a long charcoal woolen coat, posh striped trousers and waistcoat. His blouse was cream-colored silk, and there was a pearl stud in his tie. His face was neither younger nor older, just the same, clear skin cleanly shaven, his hair oiled and smoothly combed across, his eyes gray and inscrutable. I wondered at the pearl stud, how much of Malcolm's money had gone into his fine pockets, or how much of my own children's funds, if there were any to be had.

"I have no time to spare. I am on an errand—"

"For your employer. I heard." He looked at the label. "Is Keeler the Haberdasher and Clothier? So saith the label. What's in the box?"

"Buttons. Brass and nickel buttons from London."

"Are you an errand girl again?" He smiled at the thought. "And you were so aloof when you were married. Now we're sewing buttons for some townie merchant, are we?"

I stiffened, and against my will, reddened. He had seen the address. I couldn't go back to Keeler's now. Not five minutes, and my security was all gone. "We are suiting gentlemen for the Union Army and these buttons are needed—."

"I'm certain they are. But they'll have to wait. The North will win; the war will not stand or fall on a few buttons."

Wildly, I thought, *For want of a nail, the kingdom was lost,* but it was out of my control. I folded my hands and tried not to shake. I was trapped.

A young barman wearing a long apron, Negro as well, opened the parlor door and asked, "You be wantin' anything, sir?" He glanced at me. "Somethin' for the lady?"

"Mrs. Lozier, would you care for a cup of tea? Or perhaps you drink something stronger—you like sherry wine, as I recall." He told the man, "A glass of cider for me. And the lady? Bring her coffee. She needs to look alive!"

Two cups of coffee in one day—I wondered at Providence sometimes—famine or feast. I said nothing. That would be my strategy. Give nothing away, and escape when I could. I looked at my hands, grubby from carrying the box, and moved toward the ewer and basin in the corner.

"You still keep so nice and tidy, I see. So *pure.*"

I took off my coat and poured cold water into the basin, rubbing the soft-soap into my skin, washing my hands slowly. I hated having my back to him. I felt as if his fingers were on my shoulders, his breath at the nape of my neck; I shuddered at once with a ghostly chill. I wiped my fingers on the huck towel by the basin and smoothed my black skirts.

"Have you been here in the City all this time? We've been looking for months. Your mother said you never arrived. We posted announcements in all the papers. A year ago, was it just a year? You're a country cousin. What on earth are you doing down here with *children*?"

I turned around and came to seat myself. I still wore my wedding ring. My dress was still black. My long hair was still pinned up and I had all my teeth. He could not know from just looking that I was any other than who I used to be. What could he see?

"How are the children, anyway?"

"Very well." Well enough.

"Healthy, alive, in school?"

"Yes." Not a lie.

"And you are working? At a respectable establishment—in *trade,* of course, but it is respectable nonetheless?"

"I am." I was standing on the edge of the truth, but he knew it not.

"You never contacted me. You never wrote to me. You knew I was their guardian, and that I would want to decide for them, where to send the boys to school. Whether to send young Sarah to school or to keep her—at home," he said, pausing enough on his words that I knew he had the darkest of plans in his mind. "You're a widow now, Martha. You could remarry. It would make things so much easier."

The barman tapped, then came into the room with a tray of drinks, cider in a pewter tankard, boiled coffee in a tin cup. Golden sugar chunks in a wooden bowl next to it, a steel spoon on the tray. I looked up at him, my eyes seeking aid, succor, anything. The barman met my glance and raised an eyebrow, pursed his lips and left the room.

"Why did you run from me, Martha? Why didn't you come back to me, when you were free?" Montgomery lifted his tankard and sipped, licking foam from his lips. "There is money to be had. Malcolm left money for all of you—well, not for *you,* but your four darlings. You only need to come to me—that is, come back to Newburgh with me to act as your *friend,* to help guide the children. To keep a steady hand on the tiller. To keep you all under my care. Why do you tremble, my dear? What are you afraid of?"

He reached across, rested his hand on my knee. "I've missed you, my dear. It's been a long time. Too long."

I froze as he stroked my knee. I had always frozen, hoped he would go away, not bother me. I couldn't move, a rabbit, while his voice charmed me like a snake. "You're older now, softer, ready for the attentions of someone above you, someone who can show you the good things in life, take you by the hand," and he paused, as if appreciating his own words. He took my hand, held it like a dead thing. "When I see something in life that I want, I take it. And at last, here again, I have what I want. At last, I have what's mine."

I was afraid of everything. I tasted sick in my throat, wanted only to run from him. I had dared only to keep my children safe, risked everything to make it so, and had lost them, *but*—I felt as if my heart would pop from my corseted chest as I came to my senses. I could not believe it myself. *My children were safe*—they were far outside of Montgomery's grasp, and I would never tell him where they were, no matter what he did to me. He could look for a hundred years and never find them, spread out as they were.

I was glad, in that moment, that the Society had farmed out my babies. He'd never get his filthy hands on Sarah, never soil her as he'd ruined me. And that was pulling success from the depths of my failures.

I wanted to smile, almost, at the irony.

What, really, was the worst he could do to me now? Jail me? Commit me to Bellevue? How could that be any worse than the daily prison of life without my children, and lying on my back for money in Keeler's basement shop? Or even life in the daily terror as Montgomery's plaything? He couldn't force me to marry him. I was angry, suddenly, full of wrath. I took my hand away and reached for my cup of coffee, casually, as if agreeing to his proposition. I slowly stirred one after another lump of sugar into it, edging away from Montgomery as I did so. How could anything else in the future be worse than where I'd already been, no thanks to that man?

The tin cup was hot, the coffee so very hot it all but burned my hand. I made as if to sip from it, then, without warning, threw the scalding sugary contents into his face. The hot sugary liquid splashed across him, scalding, dripping, and he shouted in pain, scrambling for a napkin or handkerchief, screaming. "My eyes! You worthless slit! My eyes!"

I grabbed my coat and reticule and ran through the door with the velvet curtain. Montgomery was shouting and cursing in the parlor, and I heard other voices behind me as I headed through the building, looking for a door to the street.

The Negro barman came toward me. "Are you all right, miss?"

"I must get away from him!"

"Come this way," and he showed me a back door. "Go up that away and you can cut over to the Broad Way. Go up or down as you likes. I'll point him the other way."

Out the door, I grabbed the back wall, retched a minute against the wall, but rallied, running in my flat boots, so much better for cobbles than shiny pointed shoes. I hurried away from the tavern, and then turning, walked with City briskness, not as a woman escaping a devil, toward the horse-car on the Broad Way. I caught the first one rolling northward, asking the conductor if it would take me to Twenty-Sixth. It would, and it did, turning on Canal, Varick, and finally rolling up Sixth until I could step down at my cross-street.

What could I do, with Montgomery all but guaranteed to chase me down, with Keeler's box in his hands? How could I present myself at the shop without it? I was worse than sacked. Keeler knew where I lived and would give me up in a trice. The wind cut across me as I turned up Twenty-Sixth and slipped toward my tenement through the Alley behind the building.

Broad Way Alley, the tiny mud lane behind the tenement, was the butt of a joke made by our landlord, Mr. Scott: "It's not broad, and it's not your way, so stay outta there." Wet soil was packed underfoot. A short man sat on an overturned bucket behind a restaurant, smoking a pipe and playing with a knife, tossing it up and watching it land, blade into the mud. Laundry lines crisscrossed overhead. A bleak leafless tree overhung a brick wall, from someone else's yard. Gas streetlights, as yet unlit, stood at either end. I had heard that a traveling circus-man used to keep his elephant back here.

The Alley smelled, a malodor rising from the damp soil that I imagined could smell like a chained elephant: sour like rot, not sweet like the dairy yard in Newburgh.

I went through the gate and paused at the privy. It was too early in the day to go up to my shared bed, and nowhere else to hide. I couldn't bring Montgomery and his trouble upon my Irish friends—they deserved better for their kindness than that. As I stood wondering, my heart still stuttering from my escape from downtown, I heard the tenement door creak and Lizzie Hearne appeared on the top step, the eternal basket of clothes in her arms. I yelped when I saw my friend.

"Mother of God, ye frighted me," she said. "Whatever are ye doing down here, skulking in the gloom?" She came down the stairs, watching me, stumping with the heavy basket on her hip. "Ye look ill. Are ye sickening again?"

"I hardly know—I'm at a sixes and sevens."

"What, ye lose yer place at work?"

"No—not yet. But I will. There's a man—from my home, the countryside, come after me. He's a lawyer. He wants me and my children—"

"Cain't take what you don't have to give."

That black Irish humor, always a laugh and a cry in one breath. "I know, but he doesn't know I don't have them. He—used to—bother me." I looked at Lizzie.

She cocked her head. "Eh, one of them. They're everywhere, like dirty socks."

"He bothered me when I was young. Before my marriage. It was—terrible. That's why we left there after Bram died—so he wouldn't get to Sarah. And now he's here. He saw me, grabbed me—down at the piers." I pulled a shaky breath. "And he knows where I work now, he'll find where I live. He'll make me tell him. He'll throw me in prison or—I don't know, worse than that."

"Would that Keeler man be of any use to you? Tellin' that lawyer-man to feck off and leave ye alone?"

I looked at the mucky ground, then into my friend's eyes. "He bothers me, too."

"I wondered. He has an air about him, the kind where you keep yer skirts out of reach, and don't stay when the door closes. And ye worked for him all these months. Is it real bad?"

I could feel my tender arm-flesh pimpling into the nervous rash as we stood talking. "I had to work. I must earn some money to get my children back." I rubbed my arms as if cold, wanting to scratch the layer of skin away. "I must have my children."

"What a bags ye made of yer life." Lizzie said it without judgment, just stating the fact. "Whatever will ye do now?"

"I can't go back home."

"Ye never can. Look, girlie. You've spent your past year higher and mightier than anyone here. Ye've lost just about all but yer health. Don't ye think ye ought to stop lookin' back and start looking ahead? How will ye move on if yer brain is still back in the countryside like an old woman, and how're ye gonna outwit the grand folk of the world without a bit of takin'? Stop playin' fancy games, stop playin' at bein' one of em. Ye're here. Ye're one of us now."

"Take what's mine." Montgomery's words, echoed in Lizzie's, rose up like a bit of smoke in the cold privy yard.

"Yes, by all means, take what's yers. Find a way to get them children and hang onto 'em. Go west. Everyone does that who wants to start fresh. Lose yerselfs out there."

Lizzie looked for a dry space for her basket. The standing pipe dripped and the ground was hopelessly mucky. "We've got to get you out of here—them dogs will be sniffing 'round here soon enough. I've a cousin 'round the next block. You could stay with her a bit. She's banjaxed, husband's gone off and left 'er and she with an apron of babies. You could be a help, give her the dollar and help rock the cradle?"

"I must find work—but I can't—Keeler is just—they'll find me." I could hardly finish a thought. Still the rabbit, frozen in place. Still waiting for the snake to seize me.

"*Stop thinkin'* so much. You're banjaxed yerself—I'll take this back up and run ye around the corner. Wait here, will ye?"

"Lizzie—will you please tell the Whites I am moving on? I have a few things there—would you get them for me, please? My quilts, my letters, the children's toys?"

"They'll be sore to miss you but you'd better stay down out of view. Hide in the 'Irish shanty' if anyone comes down," she nodded at the privy. "I'll be back."

"I'm grateful to you, my friend." My only friend.

"Eh, Mart'a. Water under the bridge. It's all downriver now."

Chapter 16

New York 1861

The winter came on, and the new year rang in, in a different shared bed on a different third floor, and with it the strangest of ironies. I had no children of my own, but plenty of work. I shared a bed with three little ones, two wee girls and a toddler boy, and helped with the dressing and care of them, then set myself in the corner to sew or piecework, when I could get it. I had enough sewing to fill my every day, six days a week, with extra sometimes on the Sabbath. I made up the Hearnes' white sewing—drawers and shimmies and corset-covers—and I made their black mourning. I sewed bodies into shrouds, I rehemmed a Papist girl's white gown, much used by this family's daughters, for Confirmation or some such ceremony. I had more work than I knew I could do and hid every penny and dollar I made. I gave the little girls, Fanny and Peg, nine squares to sew together with a needle and thread to start them on their first patchworks, talking to them whilst I sewed.

And still I worked, with numb fingers and icy feet in my boots—new flat boots now, as my old ones had finally fallen apart, and I had to have something on my feet—but only what I needed, and barely that. Every dollar, every dime, into my corset, filling the woolen stocking I kept in a locked box I had bought off another tenant, in dribs and drabs while the snow blew and the wind screamed at the eaves of our top floor windows.

The spring was slow to arrive in 1861, and it was an angry year, a frightening year—with talk of secession and war, of the rights of the Southern states and the might of the nation. I listened with half an ear, thinking that the South was arable and made for planting and the North was stony and cold, made for the machines of the coming age—why must these two sides fight, dragging us all into the fray? Could they not free the slaves and give them land to tend, keep the fields planted by both black and white, and keep the Union together? But the problems of the world were beyond me; the rest of my mind drifted, thinking about the boys, and if George was speaking much now, if Homer had as many words himself, and how I wanted to send Ira a folding knife, now that he was going on fourteen and almost a proper man. Sarah asked for nothing, but I sent her a handkerchief, dainty with embroidery in the corners, SDL, a reminder of her rightful name.

Della, they called her, and the girl signed all letters that way now.

I had not ventured back to the Home for the Friendless again, fearing they would arrest me or cause me to be put away at Bellevue; I barely trusted myself to speak to them anyway. Rather, I had thrice written pleading letters, asking for my children's whereabouts. Mrs. Phillips answered once, saying it was not in her power to return the children to my care, without further elaboration. The second time, Mr. Rogers replied, reminding me that the children were indentured for seven years and that none would be free to my care until that indenture was up—in 1867, and only if the foster parents chose to end the situation. The third time, no one responded, and I knew they had done with me. By then, I had lost hope in trying to succeed by means of the Society.

There had to be another way.

I kept sewing in my corner, and sometimes in the corners of other tenants' homes, waiting for the weather to turn, for the snow to melt and the mud to dry up, saving my wages, gathering my courage, thinking of a plan. If I could just learn where the little ones were, which town held my smallest sons hostage. Could I get both boys at once, or could I get Ira, then the little ones, and go to Illinois for Sarah? We could head West from there, perhaps to Oregon. I turned my plans over and around to make sense, to make it work. *I am their mother. They belong to me. I am taking them home. I take what's mine.*

But in April, the Confederate navy fired on Fort Sumpter.

Life at the tenements took a turn for all involved. Young men were reluctant to volunteer until Lincoln's government began to offer a cash incentive; then the tide turned and recruits signed on the line, knowing they'd get thirteen dollars a month for their services, and a bounty of ninety dollars just for volunteering, plus clothing and food. Lizzie Hearne's charming younger brother joined up, and so did many of the residents of each tenement. The bonus cash came home and some tenement dwellers had enough funds to move elsewhere. Others stashed it under mattress or in strongbox or in their corsets, wherever folks like us kept our money hidden. The influx of funds was noticeable in new shoes on the children and the scent of meat roasting or stewing, through the hallways and on the street.

New York City offered up some thirty thousand young men to the Union Army by summertime, before any real skirmishes had begun. The New York Fire Zoaves and the New

York Fighting 69th, those neighborhood favorites of Ira's, marched up the Broad Way to grand acclaim when they went off to war in June. For me, the war felt like an alien thing, outside of myself, like the folktale about the North Wind and the sun bickering over who was stronger. The war might as well have been on the moon as in my privy yard; I registered the sights and the sounds that were changing, but it mattered not to me. A woman deprived of her children cannot care for much else in this world. Let the cannonballs fly, let the bayonets gore.

Ira, who had his birthday in August, would have been so envious of the young men decked in war uniforms, I imagined, missing him painfully. He had not written back to me, though I wrote to him every month and sent a paper dollar folded inside on his birthday. The residents of Fourth Avenue who worked in factories took on longer hours, sewing to meet the government order for soldiers' clothing and hats and flags, pounding metal for munitions and weapons; printing leaflets, pamphlets and other war materiel. Every corner post and wall was papered in recruitment posters, some offering to pay a substitute to take his place, others pleading patriotism of all City residents to take up arms in factories or to give generously to the war effort. Street musicians played "Rally Round the Flag." The corner monkey man changed to a Union-blue coat instead of his Old World-striped coat, and so did his monkey. The Stars and Stripes, once flying only at federal buildings, were suddenly everywhere, in tenement windows, as bunting across shop fronts, and in lapel ribbons on a pin. I had a short-term piecework making such ribbon-pins for Mr. Meagher over the summer. I could only hope for more such sweat-labor.

I used another corner grocer for my mail now, walking a different route to get there, always with a watchful an eye for Keeler or Montgomery, or any skulking shadow who might stop me. I was much more streetwise than I'd been in Newburgh-town. The year was slipping into autumn again and I noticed the change in the trees: elms and window-ledge chrysanthemums browned at the edges, like dirty silk ribbon. Green leaves looked tired, faded, beginning to curl dry at the edges. The sun was sinking earlier each night, and I felt the return of fall's crisp evenings.

The grocer had a letter for me that evening, no envelope, just a folded letter with an unfamiliar seal, forwarded from Newman's grocery to this one. But, praise Heaven, the rough hand was Ira's.

September 21, 1861

Dear Mother:

Please don't be disappointed but I have ran away, and jined the Army to fight for the UNION! I enlisted at Lockport as a private, and at first they tried me as a drummer boy but I was not good and I don't want to play drum; then they had me as runner, finally settled on private. They placed me with a New York regiment under Col. George Cothran. He is a fine man, they say, and he said 'good afternoon soldier' to me yesterday—

I waited till after my birthday, and I told them I was 17. I might only fetch and carry for the officers for now, but I am a soldier at last! We are marching in lines and practicing drills. I am not the youngest Union soldier and I'm not the shortest, neither. We are mustering through New York State and will get our orders before long, I'll wager. I could use some stockings, a warm shirt and woolens, and a mess kit if you are able; a knife and tin cup if nothing else. Send to me at the Lockport station until further notice.

We're going to whip Johnny Reb.

I will write you as soon as ever I can. I pray you collect Homer and George soon, and take them home with you. You are in my thoughts always, Mother, and I pray for your well-being even as I pray for my own. A soldier's life is dangerous, but I will make you proud.

I am enclosing my bounty for jining up. Save it for our future, dear Mother. I remain lovingly yours—

Ira Seabolt Lozier, Private,
New York Regimentals~~Federal Army

For the Grand Union and the Flag!

The war became suddenly quite real. The letter brought a rush of fear for my son, my *child*, really—how he had managed to enlist at just fourteen, how my young man could carry a pack and fight with the men in the fields, I did not know. He had enclosed a postal money order for ninty dollars, his signing bonus. I would save it until I knew where the boys were, and then would do whatever it took to pay Ira back, if I spent it at all.

Then pride overtook me, and I stood a little straighter, knowing my son was a Union soldier, fighting to preserve the great nation, recalling my Great Uncles Greenleaf and Grandfather Seybolt, who had fought as young men in the War for Independence and again, my late father-in-law Malcolm, who had fought the British and the Indians in the War of '12. A new generation of men fighting for the nation's honor gave me a proper feeling of status and pride again.

It took a war to do that, I noted, another small irony.

I sent thick stockings and a mess kit, an extra blanket and warm underflannels to Ira. I embroidered his initials and a red heart into the neck of his shirts and prayed his safety into each stitch of the stockings I knitted in Union blue. By the time I had gathered his items together, his Battery had moved east to Rochester, so I sent his goods there. That job of work complete, I pieced a new quilt for him, a four-patch in Union blue and tones of brown, when I had time, if the little children were sleeping, or I was restless at night.

I received his letter almost every week once Ira got to Rochester; without any fighting, there was nothing else to do but write letters, it seemed. Some of his brethren were unlettered and he wrote their letters for them as well, he boasted. He also complained of the food.

"There's scarce enough to go round us all in this town," he complained at Utica.

> *Officers eat at the hotel but we get fed by a steward so cheap, he keeps the oxen to ride and feeds us horse. Mother, I say so in jest, but mark my word, the meat is so tough I could saddle horse with it.*

At every town, he wrote in his stilted hand, they were greeted with cheers and bells, and when the regiment left, they were sent onward with huzzahs and handkerchiefs waving like leaves in a strong wind. He was seeing the state and the countryside as he went, and I felt he would return to me a seasoned traveler.

In November, I turned thirty-three, unremarked by anyone but myself. The soldiers were ordered onward to Albany, thence to Washington D.C. where they were joined into the First New York Light Artillery, becoming Company M of the regiment. I asked my fellow boarders to explain what the light artillery was, and from them, I understood that Ira would be loading small cannon, carrying ammunition, and helping care for and harness the horses, jobs I knew my strong farm lad was utterly able to do.

His letters helped Ira come alive to me, and I drank them in, reading each sheet over and over until it wore through at the folding lines. My chief joy was to hear from Sarah and Ira and writing back to them; the tenor of my entire day changed if a letter should come. Meanwhile, I sewed and fitted and pinned and marked with chalk. I basted and hemmed and saved a little more each week, the extra clothes I sewed for the other tenants of the building, the occasional mourning wear or baby dress. My little charges, Fanny and Peg, produced creditable patchwork tops that I helped them quilt into baby blankets, and I taught them to embroider a little heart into the backing of the quilt as a sign of their love. I worked at Ira's four-patch alongside, quilting a heart in each block, a mother's prayer.

A piece of silver or folding money at a time, our savings grew. And in this way the year turned.

Chapter 17

New York 1862

January 18, 1862

Dear Mother,

We have finally left Camp Barry at District of Columbia for Frederick City. We got our horses & equipments & six Parrott guns; our squad has our own horses and cannon—it taken six horses to pull one caisson & gun, which give us much to do. We have not faught no Rebs yet but that time is drawn near, says Sergeant. Weather is cold but we been eating good pone & bacon & look to keeping well as we can because Doctor's a terror.

I heard from sister Sarah and she is becoming a fine young lady, sounds like them Ferris folk are good to her. She send me a blue woolen for my neck & said she croshayed it herself. I wish to high Heaven I new where those boys went I would go fetch them home to you my dear Mother as soon as ever I could.

We are heading to Point of Rocks & to engage in battle soon—though I fear the Lord and all his ways, I do

> *not fear in this shadow for my battle is Righteous, said the Parson, & he is right. Well pray for me—my dear Mother & we shall meet on the other side of the river Jordan.*
>
> *Your everloving son,*
> *~Pvt Ira Seabolt Lozier*
> *God Bless the Union and President Lincoln!*

Ira sounded years older already than his scant young fifteen and seemed taken with a religious fervor. Perhaps war would do that, even to a young one. Glad he was receiving some catechism even in the army, I imagined that a little book of Psalms that fit slim into his pack would serve him in his weary hours. I found these booklets for sale at the stationer's and sent one to Ira at Frederick City care of the regiment. I kept another for myself.

Homer's birthday came at the first of February, and I counted three years since his birth, and what a world of changes, but I didn't dwell on them; Lizzie had been right. The less I dwelt and compared with the past, the better off I was today.

Nevertheless, I also counted on our savings, and when I had saved enough, to where I could travel to get my boys and go to retrieve Sarah, too, I would go. I was going. It was only a matter of months now, I was certain. When I learned where they were, there would be nothing to hold me back. Somehow, I must force the Society to tell me the truth.

But still I didn't hear.

Though I had been away from church for years now—since we'd lost Malcolm—I returned to my Psalms, to meet Ira in prayer, at our own River Jordan. We agreed to start at the first Psalm and read through to the last, one per day, and thinking on each other at candlelighting hour. I told Sarah in my next letter, and Sarah agreed with alacrity to join us. I felt the three of us uniting in prayer, in Psalm, as the daylight faded and the moon came up. It was the closest I had felt to my scattered brood in all the time we'd been apart.

After candles were lit and the gaslight came on in the hallways, I supped with my hosting family and then retreated to a corner of the room, where I read my psalm in silence. Sometimes my Irish family asked me to read to them, but mostly I kept to myself, inside my inmost heart.

A song of mighty David, he who slew the giant, might be the prayer that would keep Ira safe from slings and arrows. *Blessed be the Lord*, keeping the children safe. I repeated this verse, keeping them warm, *my shield,* as I rocked my Irish toddler to sleep for his tired mother, as I helped wipe the tin plates and cups after a colcannon supper. *My high tower,* as I nursed the pain in my tooth with oil of clove and a ginger poultice, *my goodness,* as I knitted another pair of blue stockings for my Union soldier.

I had received Sarah's missive already that week, and only incidentally visited my grocer for more ginger, with no expectation of further news, but luck was with me. The grocer waved a letter at me, a fine linen envelope from the engraved Ferris stationery. I picked it open, my mind ajumble—I hoped all was well with my daughter but hearing again so soon could mean only trouble. The letter was penned in all-fire haste and not the neatness of hand I'd come to expect from my young lady.

February 28, 1862

My dearest Mother:

I hope this finds you well, and &c. I write in haste to post this before the train comes. We have good news:

George is coming here! An Agent from the AFGS passed through to visit yesterday. Mr. and Mrs. Ferris have become benefactors to the Home, so we often see Agents here, as the trains seem all to pass through Galesburg.

Mr. Rogers said the farmer and wife, they who had George in Ohio, no longer want him. They said "he was slow and stupid, and they haven't the patience." They are moving back East to New England to work for Abolition, and leaving their farm. They wished to take him back to the Home in New York, unless we would take him.

My heart was in my throat waiting to hear what she said. Mrs. Ferris said yes right away. Then they asked me how I would like to see my little brother. I said, "I have missed him so much. Might you also bring Homer?" They shook their heads and said my brother (they call him William, not Homer) is growing up very happily in a family in Oberlin. They said his father is the fire chief and Homer has been adopted. They said he will grow up with them. I didn't know what to say, Mother, I was so shocked. If I cried or became angry, they might not let me have George.

If I can get George here, then you can go to Oberlin and get Homer back. I don't know the family name but there cannot be more than one fire chief to the town—with an adopted son named William!

I must dash to beat the post-train, but please, Mother, if ever you can, go to Ohio and get our little brother! And bring him here—Mrs. Ferris says you may come as well. I know you will, ~~Mama~~ Mother. I miss you so terribly. I must fly!

—Lovingly, Della.

So here it was at last—the key to my mystery. I walked home to my tenement stairs, my mind some five hundred miles away across the country, a little brown-haired boy with bright blue eyes, a sweet smile, fat dimpled hands and knees awaiting my kisses. And with my little one in my arms, I would head south to Illinois, following the railroad to that central point where all trains met, Galesburg. Beautiful Sarah, Della no more, and George, now nearly ten and perhaps talking—my children would come with me. We would wait out the war for Ira, together. No one, indenture or no, could have a greater claim on them than their mother.

The time was nigh.

Chapter 18

OBERLIN, OHIO JULY 1862

I SAT ON THE WOODEN BENCH inside the train station, my old carpetbag packed with my clothes and a woolen shawl, my dinner in the old milk pail, the letters I had received from Sarah and Ira, my savings sewn into a muslin bag stashed in the depth of my corset, my ticket, already punched by the conductor, in my black reticule. I had taken the steam ferry *Tappan* north up Hudson's River, spooked lest I see old acquaintance onboard, hiding behind a scoop bonnet that hid most of my face; thirstily gulping down the sights of the water and the villages at its banks, desperate to preserve in memory anything that looked familiar, that felt like my own. My black dress was also new, stylish with tiered ruffles and a black picot edging that Sarah—*Della*—had crocheted for me far away in Illinois; I had sewn the gown a little at a time between jobs of work. I wanted to show myself as Mrs. Lozier, respectable widow, and brook no questions about that status. My hands, thank heaven, were white and unspotted, and not as battered as they would have been had I stayed on the farm making cheese, managing chickens and vegetables in the hot sun. I could present myself with no shame, to anyone I might meet.

At Nyack I disembarked the *Tappan* and walked to the main street where greater and lesser hotels clustered, and stayed a quiet night there. I returned to the station early to meet my train for the next portion of the journey. I was not such country mouse anymore that travel was so daunting. I had seen the bright gas lights in the City, had heard factory gears turning; I had sat next to strangers on a horsecar and seen foreigners from around the globe eating ears of buttered corn or buying a bunch of onions on my very street. I arranged this journey by myself. The train was due in half an hour and that gave me time to walk the board sidewalk and perhaps ask for a cup of *Kaffee* from the German coffeehouse near the station.

I bought my *Tasse* of coffee and perched on the edge of my iron chair, its curlicued back uncomfortable to lean against even if I could, my stays unyielding to such a slouch. The hot brew tasted good, felt good, perking me awake for the new day's portion of the journey. When the train arrived at a quarter to eight, I took my satchel up the step of the second-class car, stowed it beneath my seat, and placed the folded woolen shawl for a cushion beneath me. A wooden bench and a rattling car would soon become wearisome without padding, I had learned on just hour-long streetcar rides. At five minutes past the hour, the train pulled away from Nyack, and I was onward again.

I wished I could see Ira, sit and talk with him, the young man he had become. His battery was yet in Virginia this summer, skirmishing up and down the Shenandoah Valley, inching east toward Richmond. They had lost some men and horses, but thus far, Ira stood strong. His letters were bold with good cheer and confidence, and he seemed to have found his place as a soldier. The war went on, a stupid thing, idiotic to think they would spend how much blood and money to keep the Union together. Just in April, the papers had said, some 13,000 Union men had lost their lives at Shiloh, and praise be that Ira was nowhere near there.

I had seen his likeness—handsome in his uniform, wearing stockings I had knitted and a shirt I had sewn. I had sent him money to get his photograph made, and when he sent the thin *carte de visite* to me, I sobbed to see his dark lanky hair, his eyes large in his thin face, beautiful Bram come to life again with a young soldier's mien. The photograph folder was tucked in paper inside my carpetbag; I hoped to get Sarah and George to sit for a photographer in Galesburg. Perhaps we would all sit together, a family portrait, it was called; quite fashionable for folk especially since the war began. I had read about such in a recent issue of *Godey's Ladies Book* at the boarding house.

Ira hadn't asked for much, but I sent him the extras anyway: a scroll of writing paper and powdered ink, a tin cup with a thong to tie it to his pack, his completed four-patch, and a sewing kit so he could patch his own holes and darn his own stockings. The newspapers were full of what to send and the need for extras for the men. I'd read that Confederate soldiers didn't have it so good; there was no money for uniforms for foot soldiers of the South, though officers had their apparel tailored same as Union gentlemen did. The homespun garments of Confederate soldiers faded in the sun so that their Rebel-gray turned golden-brown; Ira called them *Butternuts* in his letters, saying they blended in with the dry grass or leaves, giving them advantage, while the Union Blues stood out in the field on patrol.

> *Sarah sent me a red neck handkerchief that looks high-falutin inside my collar. Georgie sent me a 4-leafed clover that he found and encased in horn, so it will last me forever for GOOD LUCK! We march and load cannon*

and handle the horses. When they say 'Hold yor Hosses,' I am the one. I put up a tent at nite and they call me Billy Yank, well, everyone from New York is Billy Yank. Maybe from else where too.

I got frends from Rochester and Lockport in my Battery but now I have POSSUMS (that's frends) there's Tommy Reed from Michigand and Morty Johnson from Nebraskah. I don't want to alarm you Mother dear but I believe I have made a special frend in Lockport and we are sending letters. Her name is Miss Mary Gaffney and she is pretty as a fawn. Her eyes like them blue flax flowers that grow in Newberg farm. I wish you could meet her one day...

Such a man now, such a boy.

The train chugged northwest through New York at the shocking pace of twenty-five miles per hour, stopping after fourteen hours at Lockport, of all places, for the night, before next day's long journey. I passed by the grand white hotels catering to those many excursionists to Niagara Falls, the first-class passengers; I walked farther down the street and around to the cheaper hostels, to Van Buren House, where Ira and his ilk had supped. Ira's lass was a servant there, and it was a mother's prerogative to peek at a prospective sweetheart, if I could do nothing else to be near my son. I might once have quelled at a serving girl for his sweetheart, but now I thought it likely the girl was a hard worker and would bear him many strong sons. It would be a gracious gift to see grandchildren before I die; going onto thirty-four this year, I was falling behind, and hoped Sarah would marry in the next few years, bring out a grandie or two for me to dandle and dote on. I miss holding my babies.

Mr. Frazer at the desk gave me a key and said, "Ma'am,

we're serving supper in fifteen minutes for the lately arrived passengers, if you'd care to join them."

I did care. Up the wooden stairs and down a papered hallway padded with a carpet runner, I carried a skeleton key; my carpetbag was in the hand of a sturdy bellboy about twelve years old. He hoisted my satchel without returning my greeting or thanks. I realized that he was deaf and probably could not speak, and my heart ached a little to think of George, my little mute, when he had been a wee boy. He had, Sarah said, been more or less cured of his silence, no matter what I thought of their methods.

Through the painted, paneled door, the boy put my bag on the floor and shuffled backward from the room. I gave him a penny in hopes of cadging a smile from him, but the boy wouldn't warm up to me. He backed from the room and closed the door harder than I liked, perhaps unaware of how loud it sounded in the echoing boardinghouse hallway. I washed my hands and face in the basin, erasing a layer of soot from my skin, wanting to brush out my hair but knowing it must wait until bedtime. I used the clothes whisk to brush up the train soot and rinsed out my handkerchief to freshen for tomorrow; I would damp-press it under my pillow overnight, all I could do, lacking a sadiron and some starch. I took my other clean handkerchief and locked the room, put my key in my reticule and descended the stairs to supper.

The dining room was paneled halfway up the walls in dark walnut, plastered and whitewashed above. A whale-oil lamp hung from the center of the ceiling on a chain, and many glass reflector beads hung in swags around it. The effect was fairly bright; the fatty smell of burning whale oil hung over all. It reminded me of the Newburgh farmhouse, and I took my place at table, appreciating the familiar scent without undue nostalgia. There were but two ladies at table; the rest were men of varying ages, some country folk, some citified, all traveling who knew where? There was no Mrs. Lander to lead grace at table; the guests took fork and knife in hand and set to the moist pink ham, boiled potatoes in their jackets, molasses-crusted baked beans, and savory potherbs on the pretty dishes put before them. Each diner had a sauce dish of sliced red tomatoes sprinkled with vinegar and sugar, and there were clove-spiced beets and pickled onion in bowls at either end of the long table. A basket of hot rolls and a bowl of creamy butter passed down the table.

As I quietly ate my supper, a serving girl entered the room through a swing door from the kitchen, a pot of tea in one hand and coffee in the other. "Coffee 'r tea?" she asked each guest, pouring with a quick reach and no spills. The girl had a rose-petals-and-cream complexion, almost-black curly hair, deep blue eyes fringed with black lashes, and two pert arched brows. She was the very picture of an Irish lass. I wondered if this were Ira's fawn.

"Tea 'r coffee?"

I quickly answered, "Coffee," not to hold up the girl in her rounds. But I longed to talk with her, with someone who had seen Ira more recently than I had. I finished my supper, including the piece of buttermilk pie with tender crust and fragrant gratings of nutmeg on top, that appeared at my elbow as I sipped my hot coffee. I stayed at table after the menfolk and the other woman had gone, hoping to catch the girl alone.

That curly head popped around the swing door, catching my eye. "Ha' ye done eatin', ma'am?" Her accent was as bright as I had expected.

"Oh, yes, I thank you. I still have my coffee. Please, don't wait on me. Please, go on."

"I have to clear away, ye see." The girl came in with a tray and stacked the remaining dishes on it. She took the vinegar cruet and mustard pot, and wiped crumbs from the table rapidly—into her hand, not onto the floor. I approved. "Ye can take it into the parlor if ye like?"

"I shall." I rose from my chair. "Are you Miss Mary Gaffney?"

The girl raised her brows. "Who's askin'?"

"My son Ira Lozier told me he had a friend in Lockport."

The girl's face changed from suspicious to confused to pleased to nervous in a grand moment of metamorphosis. She was as transparent as a lace curtain. "Beg yer pardon, ma'am, I wasn't expectin' to make yer acquaintance so soon!" She bobbed a little curtsey that surprised and charmed me.

"Please tell me, how was Ira when you saw him last?" I gripped the back of my chair, a wave of shyness flashing through me. This was Ira's first girl—and I couldn't help but drink in the girl's beauty and all her presence. "I receive his letters, but it isn't the same."

"Oh, he's right as rain, that'un. He's bound to knock them Rebels from their palfreys. But he'll be back here again, one day. I know it."

"He has always wanted to be a soldier." I reflected on how many times the boy had played this game.

"He's one now, and he's happy as a butcher's dog." Mary wiped the table one last time and lifted her tray.

"I worry about him. I want him to be safe." More than anything.

"He'll be safe. I sent him with a little medal of St. Christopher—the patron saint of travelers. God will watch over Ira every step of the way. I've got a candle lit and I pray for him. Every day without fail. Pardon me, ma'am, I'm behind in me work, a cow's tail." She hoisted the tray to her shoulder and left me standing in the empty dining room with my coffee.

I took a sip of the lukewarm brew, then left it, stepping outside for a cool breeze, wiping the perspiration from my upper lip and dabbing at my throat with hankie. Mary's talk of saints and idolatry—everything I disliked about Catholics—and yet, this single girl had enough faith in her religion, in her god, that she feared no evil for Ira. She prayed every day for Bram's son. How could I fault Ira for sparking a Papist, when, to be sure, marrying a man of my own faith had not saved me—or even himself—from travail. My religion had little to do with how my life had turned out after all.

Mulling these thoughts, I sat in a willow chair on the front porch of the boarding house, a striped blue ticking pillow behind me, the sound of crickets chirping heavily in the velvet dark. The very air smelled like Newburgh had used to. Hudson's River was far to the east, but I could smell the Niagara River, fancied I could even hear its low rush in the night air.

Horses pulled a creaking wagon on the main street and I could hear men's laughter and someone playing "Darling Nelly Gray" on a piano not too distant. A dog set up barking and another dog or two joined in the chorus. A man shouted down the near dog and at last it was still again. It was late, I was overtired, and I must early rise, but I waited until Mary came outside after a half an hour or so.

"I mayn't sit here, ma'am; Mrs. Frazer wouldn't like it." With her apron off and nothing in her hands, the girl looked defenseless, less sure of herself.

"May we stand at the end of the porch, or just down there?" I looked over the railing to the scythed grass below. "We might speak a moment longer."

"Aye, Missus."

We descended the wide steps of the porch and strolled a few steps away, wrapped in the heavy air and the sounds of a town at night.

"How old are you, Mary?"

"I'm sixteen."

"Where are your people?" Was it a fair question, one that I would easily answer?

"Me family'r back in Cork. I came on me own. I worked to save me passage and I work now to pay me own way." She smoothed her black curls. "I don't want to starve like me family back home. That's why I come."

"Times are hard here, too," I said without inflection.

"I know ye struggled. I know ye've had it bad, you and the childr'n. But it's better here by miles, than seeing yer own kin gray and starvin' under their skin. I'll do what I must to keep us fed," the girl said.

"Ira's still a boy."

"He's a soldier. He's a man already, in the eyes of the Union. He'll fight for them and he'll be back. The war can't last but another year, they say. Ira'll be sixteen by then, and lots of boys marry that age." The girl lifted her chin. "He says he's coming back for me. And I doubt not his word. Do you, Mrs. Lozier?"

My eldest son, so smart, so determined. Had he ever not done what he'd vowed to do?

"If he said he was coming back, he'll be back," I agreed. "He may be young, but he knows his mind. Pray for him, every day, as you say, my girl. Will you?"

"I will, Missus."

I offered my hand to the girl, who took it, and we clasped hands for a moment, two women agreeing to love the young man, however his story should end.

"I am traveling to Ohio tomorrow, thence to Illinois, to my daughter and my other boys. Will you send word if you hear anything? I'll give you Sarah's direction in the morning. We'll be there, waiting for him, when the war is done."

"Aye, Missus. You have my pledge."

I gave the girl's hand a squeeze. "Then I shall say good night to you, dear."

"Goodnight, Ira's mam."

It made me smile.

I rose early and swallowed my coffee and a hot meal of fried mush and eggs, relishing the moist greasy food in my mouth as the flavors of my old home in upstate. I passed Mary a note with Sarah's address written and the words, "May the Lord Bless You, from M. S. Lozier." Ira was still a boy, but soldiering had made him a man, and as such, I could hardly tell him to whom he could pledge his troth. I trusted that he knew what he wanted, and I saw a core of strength in Mary Gaffney that inspired faith. I could do nothing but hope that all would be well, until the war was over, and Ira and Mary would see if their hearts were still attached.

The train left Lockport promptly at eight o'clock forenoon and I was in my seat in the carriage. I saw flashes of blue lakes from my perch above the bridges we crossed, roads and farms as we passed; canal traffic seemed always nearby. Lockport was soon behind us and before the morning had much elapsed, I could truly hear the thunder of the great Niagara waterfall, but we didn't swing near enough to see it. We flew alongside at an astonishing thirty miles per hour, the conductor said, farther than a horse could trot in one day. Sometimes we sat on a siding at a town and waited while another train came behind us and passed. But I felt that, compared to my many years of rattling across Orange County on corduroy roads, modern travel was speedy and elegant. I thought about Bram, never having had the chance to ride on a train. He might not have liked it, dashing along at such a speed. He wasn't plodding like an ox; he was surefooted like a plow horse, and steady, but not slow. However, the fleetness of the train seemed beyond him, in his deep graveyard slumber near his father and our babies.

We coasted along the shores of Lake Erie unto the very town by the same name, in Pennsylvania at the nooning. Some queer religious folk were there, Mennonites, dressed in black, as was I, but they were not mourning. Conductor said Mennonites were backward in their practices, unchanged since the *Mayflower*, but they had tasty food for sale. I bought a chunk of cheese, a tart apple, a small loaf of gingerbread, and a handful of cracked walnuts from the back of a wagon; I was able to take a drink of water at the common dipper at the station, and use the necessary behind it. The half-hour stop was scant enough time for my business, and I and the other passengers scurried to board again. I had no choice but to consume my dinner aboard the train, but did so as neatly as I could, all things considered. Luckily, other passengers were also eating, and a fellow traveler lent me his penknife to slice the gingerbread and cheese.

The arc of the lakeshore seemed to go on forever after Erie, but slowly, we stopped in Painesville, Willoughby, then the busy town of Cleveland at last at about five o'clock. I was to change trains there, for a smaller local in the morning. After a night in another boardinghouse, I met the morning train at nine o'clock, fluttering inside over seeing Homer that day, that very day. How very big he must be, three years heading to four, wearing short breeches and chattering like my other children in their time—except for George, I corrected myself. I tried to imagine Homer's face as a child instead of a baby and could only impose Ira or George in place of the one I had held in my arms. His baby face I could not forget, but did he still resemble the child I had last held on my hip, had handed to Sarah to carry away? My hands trembled with excitement, but I smoothed them down my skirt and forced myself to sit quietly, to fold my hands and count cows in fields, count blackbirds on fences, apple orchards, men working, how many horses I saw, anything to divert my lurching heart.

The slow local train took half the day to go thirty-four miles, and I was worn out from high nerves and travel by the time the train chugged into the station. Of course there was no one there to meet me. I knew not a soul in Oberlin but the name of my child and the occupation of his foster father. I asked the station agent to hold my satchel for me in the baggage room; if all went well, I would have the baby and be able to take the later train to Toledo tonight and onward to Galesburg, three of my four children within my grasp.

We would pray for Ira's safe deliverance through the battles before him, and we would reunite in glory after the war was over, perhaps with pretty Mary Gaffney to join our circle. The plains to the West might be our new home: a farm, rolling acres of wheat and corn, a new landhold for George and Homer, and for Ira when he returned. President Tyler's Land Act could help us, or some such; land grants were easy to come by for a widow and three strong sons. I would work and save for the day that Ira returned, and we would all head west, start again. Tie up our few belongings in a wagon, unfurl a canvas cover, and we'd roll out in convoy, make a new life.

Oberlin station was newly built and offered separate waiting rooms for ladies and for gentlemen. I took advantage of the relatively private room to wash my hands and brush the soot from my clothes as best I could. I adjusted my scoop bonnet and dabbed a bit of grime off my cheeks and nose. Train travel was so filthy; I longed for a respite where I could feel clean and settled; tonight Homer and I would be in Toledo and they'd have standing baths at the least! I was grateful, again, for the forgiving color of black; a woman in mourning, still appearing clean when I'd been wearing the dress for several days of sooty travel. I felt absurdly giddy, anticipating my reunion with Homer, butterflies in my middle and a shakiness of hand. I took a drink of water from the dipper and was ready.

I left the station and walked up Main Street, following the station master's direction to the town hall a long block north. I could see the many-windowed walls and tower of Oberlin College, the orange brick still new and bright and unadorned with ivy, ahead of me. The square turret and solid brick promised warmth and knowledge inside their walls. The town was still rising from the plains, but the buildings in the town were beautifully crafted—there wasn't a single log cabin to be seen, but many homes of local brick and buildings of yellow Ohio stone.

As I neared the town hall, I quailed a little. Perhaps I should not just walk into the man's office and demand to see my son. In fact, what ought I to say to the keeper of my child? My throat felt very dry and I stopped on the wooden sidewalk. Nearby I saw a building which declared itself home of the *Oberlin Journal* newspaper, publisher and notary public.

I hesitated, then decided. The heavy paneled door was well oiled and pushed in away from me. A man about forty or so with a pipe in his teeth wearing a tweedy suit looked over his newspaper at me from his desk. He wore an eyeshade and sleeve garters and had a friendly face. He might be the publisher.

"Good morning, madam."

"Good morning." I got hold of myself. "I'm looking for the fire chief—I don't recall his name, but I understand he lives in town with his family—he has a baby boy, I believe?"

A young man with a red pencil behind his ear stuck his head around a door, curious, and listened in. "Gaston? He's fire chief now."

From the back room came a clattering sound, perhaps the newspaper press.

"Marshall Gaston—is that who you mean?" The man at the desk sat up as if to stretch his back and shoulders, but remembered he was in company. He cleared his throat. "He has a boy, couple years old by now. And a daughter."

"Gaston, yes, that was the name," I said. "Will you please tell me where I can find him?"

The publisher pulled at his collar. "He'd be at the firehouse down the road a piece, most days. But I happened to see him go down to the station this morning, off to Cleveland for some business."

"His business is fire," said the youth with the pencil. "What the deuce—sorry, ma'am—could he want in Cleveland?" The boy was attempting his first beard and the downy whiskers seemed too soft with his bright brown eyes.

"Watch yourself, pup. He's after a fire pump or a new-fangled engine of some sort—steam-powered or some such, land sakes, Thompson, how do I know? Ask him yourself when he gets back. Make it front-page news." The publisher turned back to me. "My apologies for the stupidity of my newsboy. He's a regular donkey some days, ma'am."

I followed the conversation with interested confusion. "He is not at home, then," I concluded. "Perhaps I might speak to his wife." I saw them looking at me with curiosity.

"It's a family matter," I added, looking down at my dress, the pleats fanning down before me like a waterfall. I had spent hours pinching those pleats and finger-pressing them. I was respectable in my black dress, on this mother's errand. I had nothing to fear. "I've come from New York City to speak with her."

"New York City! That's a far piece of railroading, ma'am."

"If you'd please, I'd like to be on my way?"

The publisher came to the door with me, young Thompson crowding behind to help.

"I'll point it out for you so's you don't get lost," the boy said. Out on the boardwalk, young Thompson directed me two blocks north and two blocks east.

The publisher elaborated. "Turn right at the college square. His house has a white fence and an octagon-shaped tower room. His wife is particular about that fence. Can't miss it, Missus—?"

"Lozier," I told him. "Mrs. Abram Lozier of New York."

So what if I told him my name and from where I'd come? I wasn't going back that way again, and Mrs. Gaston should know my name soon enough from my own lips. I thanked the newspapermen and continued along the sidewalk, crossing the first street, until I had the town square in my sights. The day was warming up and I felt the heat against my dark dress, the short hairs curling at my neck. I stopped at the corner to look at the college. It would be cooler under the trees, walking along the cool brick walkway, than along this dusty street. The square was Old World-elegant, with trees that arched gracefully overhead. Young people strolled together, and I caught snippets of some of their conversations as they passed by—abolition and manumission, the war, *Great Expectations* and *Silas Marner*, the poetry of Mr. and Mrs. Browning. Men as well as women, even Negro men and women, walked along, quite engaged in their banter and badinage, their arguments unceasing. What a thing to go to university—perhaps Homer would go some day. Still I dreamed for him, visions of grandeur for my youngest son, when I was without a job, a home, roots that bound me anywhere.

I felt cool and calm as I turned from the square and pushed onward past small brick buildings with a bakery, a furniture store, a tailor, then a grocer at the corner. The next corner held a bookstore, and what a delight it must be to walk right in and buy as many books as one could carry! I saw students on benches along the street, and at a Reading Room, "open to all who would read the Word," according to the sign in the window. I crossed the last street, approaching the house. The stable behind the home had its half-door open and a brown horse's head peered out, over a pile of straw with a fork in it.

I slowed my pace until I saw before me the white fence aforementioned, its pickets bright with a new coat of paint, enclosing the front area from the street. The white house behind it was a tall frame house with a brick porch and chimney, and an octagonal-shaped room on the second floor—a charming nursery or parlor for the children, I guessed. An orange brick path led from the dirt road to the steps of the porch, with a willow tree to one side and a plane tree to the other side.

From under the willow tree ran a little brown-haired boy, a big girl of maybe ten years with darker hair chasing after him, laughing. She swooped him up and trotted over to a wooden swing hanging by two ropes from the plane tree. She sat him in her lap and leaned back to pump and swing. Her green dress hem dragged in the grass, white-stockinged legs in polished high-buttoned shoes, pumping strongly. Her dark hair was bound in a simple braid down her back, a straw hat falling down her back by its limp red ribbon.

"Hold on tight, Willie! Whee! We swing!"

"Whee!" his little voice called out.

My skin pimpled with chill, I drew toward them like a leaf in a current, unable to stay myself at the road. I stopped at the fence. My throat was dry again, stopped of all speech. I swallowed the dryness, cleared my throat.

"My goodness, Homer," I said, my voice a creaky door. The boy took no notice of me. The girl looked at me and kept swinging.

"Homer," I said, a little louder. I raised my hand a little, but faltered, both shy and hesitant. Could he see me, outside the fence of his little world?

The girl held the boy safely with one arm and slowed down, dragging her feet on the grass until they stopped.

"More swing! Please, Celie? Swing me!"

I stepped forward, my hand on the pickets. "Pardon me, dear," I addressed the girl. "Is this the Gaston home?"

"Yes, ma'am," the girl replied evenly. She sat in the swing, her feet on the ground, holding the boy with her one arm. Suddenly she put her other arm around him and held him close. The boy nestled in her arms as if used to such open displays of affection.

"Is your mama home?"

"She's lying down now. She has the sick headache. I took Willie outside so she can rest in the dark."

"I am sorry to hear Mama is not feeling well," I said. "Is this—Willie?" My baby boy, so grown now, with sandy brown hair, lightened by the sun, and Bram's blue eyes. No more sweet curls. He looked more like Sarah, not much like Ira and George. How children could bloom.

"My brother." She held the boy close.

"Is that his real name? Willie? Is it not—Homer?"

"Homer? Oh, no," the girl smiled. "His name is William Gaston. My papa named him."

"May I come in?" I had the gate open and was walking slowly toward the children, my eyes on Homer, looking for any sort of confirmation—recognition from my son. He would smell like my child, I knew it. "What is your name, dear?"

"I'm Rocelia, but my papa calls me Celia, and so does Willie. Or he tries to say it. Say Celia, darling."

"Celie! Swing me!" The boy had eyes only for his playmate, not for the approaching stranger. He laughed, a sound that rang in my ears like Ira's had once, and perhaps Sarah's, but it had been so long, and I couldn't quite grasp the memory.

"How old are you, Rocelia?"

"I'm going on eleven."

"Any other sisters or brothers?" The boy's nose was definitely a Seybolt nose. I looked at his left foot to see the freckle, but it was hidden by a little stocking and a brown leather laced-up boot.

"I had two little sisters but they both went to Heaven. My mama was so sad," Celia said somberly. "That was before we had Willie."

I absorbed the information, understanding at last why Homer was here with this family. "I'm so sorry, my dear. I've lost little ones, too. May I greet your little brother?"

"Say how do you do, Willie!" But the boy twisted around, his face in Celia's neck and wouldn't speak.

"He's a fine boy. How old is he?" I coaxed with my voice, gentle as with a motherless lamb.

"Three years old, ma'am."

I put out my hands to the boy. "Homer, Homer, it's Mama, do you remember me? Homey, do you remember Sarah? And Ira? And George? Do you see me, Homer?"

Celia stood on her feet quickly, still holding the boy. "His name is Willie." She started toward the steps of the porch.

"Homer, do you see me?"

His eyes were closed into Celia's neck, and I saw the whorl of fine hair at the back of his neck, his brown locks falling over his ears. He opened his eyes and looked right at me. I stretched out my hands to him. "Homer. It's Mama."

The boy started to scream and scream. He wailed like a dog stepped on by a boot, a deep and ragged cry—"Maaaa!" He squeezed his eyes shut and screamed.

I followed the girl as she ran up the steps. The boy screeched like he was fit to be slaughtered, the rage and anguish that only a tiny child can exude, to the surprise of all around him.

A woman appeared at the screened door, her hand to her forehead. "What is all this noise about? Oh, Willie, what is it, dear heart?" She came out to the porch.

Celia ran to her mother. "Mama, the lady says his name is Homer and he started to squall—" When Celia got to her mother, the woman put out her arms to take the boy. I reached the steps with my arms out to him, tears welling up, scrolling down my cheeks.

"That's my boy," I implored the woman.

Homer, still screaming, melted into the woman's arms, sobbing with all his heart into her shoulder. She caressed his fine hair. The woman looked at me. The boy clawed and clutched, in terror. "Maaaaaaa, maaaaaaa."

"He wants his real mama," Celia said to me.

"Do you want to see the lady?" Mrs. Gaston asked the boy. Fresh wails issued from the depth of his little soul. He shook his head violently, "Noooooo! Maaaaaa!"

I stood at the bottom of the steps in my black dress like a shadow, watching a woman and a girl, strangers, comfort my son, who was theirs by law, if not blood. I knew he was just a babe, just a wee child, and he didn't know what was right. He had been so young, he was confused. He didn't remember, he could not know all I had been through for his sake, how much I had lost and given up to secure his safety. Homer did not know me.

If he had recognized me, if he had wanted me at all, I would have taken him and run. But all the fight went out of me then. I wiped my cheeks with my fingers.

"Forgive me. I had to try," I said, my voice almost too soft to hear. "Be good to him."

"Thank you, Mrs. Lozier," Mrs. Gaston said. "Good day to you."

Mrs. Gaston took my sobbing boy into the house, with Celia hanging back to close the door. A moment later the lace curtains moved and I knew I was being watched. I wiped my eyes on my handkerchief and turned away, heartsick, toward Main Street. I could still catch the afternoon train to Toledo, and from there, go on to Galesburg.

Sarah and George were waiting for me there.

Chapter 19

Galesburg, Illinois 1866

I dreaded nothing more than my arrival to face my children, Sarah most of all. I arrived unannounced and betook myself from the railroad station to the Ferris home on foot after days by train and nights along the way. I wanted my children, to hold them close and help me forget the shame of losing Homer. I could not bear thinking about my baby. His scream rang in my ears for nights, blood-curdling, for days, "Noooo, Maaaaa," as if I were killing him, when, in fact, it was killing me.

I stopped before the big plank house and admired its clean lines and broad porch, seeing with my own eyes the rolling lawn and the porch swing where Sarah wrote her letters to me. I smelled flowers in the air and saw roses growing in the yard, and a picket fence like the Gastons'. I stood at the gate, reliving in my mind the horror of rejection, the sharpness of my loss, when the front door screen burst open and a willowy young lady with golden hair was running down the little path toward me, a barking liver-spotted spaniel at her heels, and then a big boy lumbering after her, approaching cautiously, peering sideways to see me under my bonnet.

Sarah caught me in a great hug, nearly bowling me over, squealing and crying, "Mama, Mama!"

George, relieved, put his arms around me and said, "I love you, Mama," and he sounded just a little slow, but like an old man who's worked hard all day and just wants to drink a glass of cider. He was so sturdy at ten years old that I thought he was older.

Sarah, who reminded me to call her Della, was a young lady with a grown-up figure, and the spaniel, named Candy, was her very own dog, a gift from the Ferrises.

"George named him," Della said. "When we asked him the best name for a dog, he said, 'I like candy.' So we called him Candy and George loves him almost as much as he loves real candy."

George became shy of speaking then, and he fell on the ground and rolled with Candy and was happy as a boy with a dog could be.

"Mama, Mrs. Ferris is indoors waiting and I want to introduce you to her properly. But please. Where is Homer?" She took my hands and looked deep into my eyes. "Tell me."

I looked back at her and my eyes filled. I thought of how to begin, how to tell her I wasn't wanted, I had lost him forever.

"He's too far gone. He didn't remember me. He will never remember me." That's all I could say. What more could I say but, "I'm sorry."

Della and I held each other and wept, then, and that's how that story ends.

• • •

But our lives went on.

Della had a beau named Jerome, a farmer boy with yellow hair and a red face. He stood back shyly as we met upon the front porch. The Ferris home was large and gracious, and felt very modern and new, made of boards, not at all like Malcolm's big stone house. The prairie air was so fresh, and the little town of Galesburg so clean and modern. It was a pleasure to be with my children again, and a very hospitable Mrs. Ferris kindly let me stay as a guest until I found a small house to rent. And the Ferrises allowed the children to come with me, releasing their indentures.

Our little house had a shop at the front where I could sell hats and dresses, in the latest New York styles. Those in Galesburg didn't know my every secret; they knew I was a dressmaker from New York City and that I could turn my hand to any pattern or style they wished. With Ira's bounty money, we put down a year's rent and fitted up my shop, and were able to live, the three of us, very nicely in town. George tried another year of school but he wasn't meant for the classroom. He was still a serious boy, rarely laughing, and liked to keep to himself, watching the chickens for hours and tending a hutch of pet rabbits out back.

The next year Jerome asked for Della's hand and they were married at the Methodist Church. Jerome moved us with them to a house in Fairbury and started his own business in town, a gun and tool store on the main street. Candy came, too. We followed along the war news, waiting to read of each battle, and absorb Ira's letters, where he went next. My young man fought at every major battleground in the East throughout the war and wasn't injured once—until the very last bit, in Atlanta, chasing the last Rebs to the sea. He got a head wound, though he wouldn't tell us how. It was bad enough that he didn't have to fight anymore, but not so bad it ever bothered him again—the best kind of war wound to have. By the time the War Between the States ended, he had already taken himself back to Lockport and married his sweetheart. I had earned back his money by then and held it safe at the bank.

Mary and Ira arrived on the train in Galesburg and took a little place for themselves outside of Peoria, starting a bakery. Mary knew how to bake for a crowd and together they built up a thriving business. Their first little girl, Hattie, was a joy and a treasure to me, and their next child, a boy, they named William Homer Lozier. He was the apple of their eye and mine as well. By then, Della had a little boy of her own, Lyman, and now, with three grandchildren, I am just glad to be here to hold them and croon them to sleep.

I thought perhaps I might change the color of my dress, go to half-mourning, discard these widow's weeds at last. Sometimes Della nudged me, saying, "That green print would make a beautiful gown for you. Or that wine-colored calico. Didn't you promise to wear cherry-red one day?"

"I did, but not yet."

The truth is that I never stopped mourning my losses. I missed Bram and his fierce protection, and the love we had made together. I grieved so many relatives and friends along the way. Everyone we knew had lost a brother, a son, or a friend in the War. There was still so much to mourn that I couldn't slip my colors just yet.

But most of all, I missed my little son Homer—not as a death, but as a dandelion puff blown on the wind, impossible to catch or follow. I missed his learning to run and starting to talk, his first loose tooth and his first taste of candy, his tears and his nightmares and his skinned knees. I missed it all; he cried in Mrs. Gaston's arms, grew into Mrs. Gaston's young man. I'm glad Homer was too young to go to the war. I hoped his new family would send him to school, perhaps to that Oberlin College, and he would grow up to be a fine gentleman, with a walking stick and a monocle and a silk hat. There's no sin in praying for the best for somebody.

The truth is I never stopped feeling him in my empty arms, and I never stopped blaming myself for letting him—them all—go. Until I could stop feeling that blame, that shame, I would wear a black gown—as new and as fashionable as I cared to sew, perhaps. But widow's weeds, nonetheless.

There is always something for the bereaved to mourn.

Author's Note

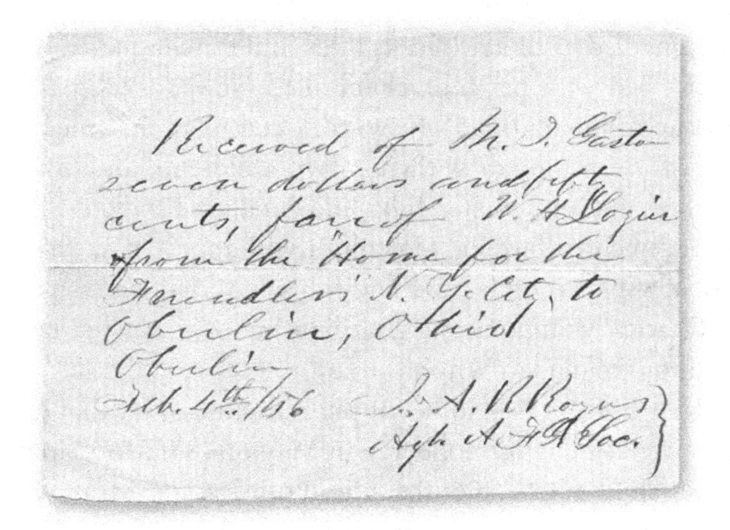

Received of M. J. Gaston
seven dollars and fifty
cents, fare of W. H. Lozier
from the "Home for the
Friendless" N. Y. City, to
Oberlin, Ohio
Oberlin
Feb. 4th 1856 J. A. R. Rogers
Agt. A. F. A. Soc.

DISCOVERING MARTHA HAS BEEN THE JOURNEY of several years for me.

William Homer Lozier was taken in by Marshall and Valetta Gaston in 1856 in Oberlin, Ohio, and legally adopted some years later. Willie lived with them and his beloved new sister, Rocelia, with whom he was very close. Will, who signed his name W. L. Gaston, became a successful salesman for a pressed glass and dishes company. He married and had two daughters. Will Gaston was my second great-grandfather, and my father remembers him well.

All we knew about Grandpa Gaston's origins was from

a blue slip of paper, a receipt for $7.50 for the train fare from New York to Oberlin in January 1856. That piece of paper was as much as he knew about himself. He believed he was French (The L in his name was for Lozier, indeed a French name), and that his mother had died in New York and left him a foundling. Will/Homer never knew what his birth mother, Martha, did to get him back.

The facts: Martha lost her husband, Abraham Lozier, in Newburgh, New York, in October 1853. Her father-in-law Malcolm died just a few weeks later, and for cause unknown, Martha fled with her four children to New York City. She turns up in the mid-1855 New York census in the tenement on East Twenty Sixth with just two children, Sarah and a little boy, and roommates Julia and Amanda Pendleton. The advertisement regarding Malcolm's will appeared in the Albany newspaper; each child had inherited $100 and was under Charles Montgomery's guardianship. But Martha never asked for the money. Why?

Records from the Home for the Friendless show that Martha surrendered Ira and George in May of 1855, and Homer and Sarah about six months later. Both Ira and Sarah were sent out to their respective foster homes almost immediately, but Homer and George went to Oberlin together in January 1856, with Mr. Rogers, agent, alongside. George was indeed a little slow, rejected by his Ohio foster family, and sent to live in Galesburg with Sarah. Ira was punished and a chronic runaway; he finally joined the Union Army in Lockport at about age fifteen, fighting in every major battle throughout the war, virtually unscathed until the end. Martha wrote again and again to the Home for the Friendless asking for her children back, but in the notes from the Home, it was written that "[we] do not choose to do it."

In essence, all the facts of this novel are true—but the why and the how are fiction. I am grateful to author Christina Baker Kline for writing her novel, *The Orphan Train*, for, in reading it, I wondered if the so-called Orphan Train was the same train that had brought my Grandpa Gaston to Ohio. The train receipt was just a mysterious relic in our box of family papers. I wrote to the Orphan Train Museum in Concordia, Kansas, and the excellent historians there found the records of Sarah, Ira, George, and Homer, and the story, in notes and scraps, of what had happened to their mother. Until then, I didn't know about the siblings or Martha. I made a trip to Kansas to see Martha's surrender documents with my own eyes in 2016, and I donated the train receipt to their permanent display. There is a brass memorial plaque at the museum now dedicated to the Lozier children as riders of the Orphan Train, affixed to one of the seats in an actual vintage train car from that era.

I have followed my family tree as far back behind Martha and Abraham as I could go, and as far down the contemporary lines as I could get. I correspond with some of the Lozier descendants, and I have been to the graveyard in Fairbury, Illinois, where Sarah, Jerome, their two children, and Martha were laid to rest. I rode the ferry down the Hudson River to watch Newburgh slip away behind us. I found the Seybolt farm in Otisville, and the Greenleaf graves nearby. I have walked the streets in Kip's Bay where Martha walked, including the mysterious Broad Way Alley, and stood in the sanctuary of the Marble Collegiate Church (Dutch Reformed) on Fifth Avenue and E 29th, where Martha may have worshiped. The Home for the Friendless has been replaced by a skyscraper but it was walking distance from her tenement.

I think Will had a happy life with his adopted family. He named his firstborn daughter for Valetta Gaston, the only mother he remembered. And he carried a photo of Celia, then passed it on to his descendants. Celia was a forgotten face in the photo album until I rediscovered who she was. I now possess several items that were Will's, including many photographs of himself and his wife and children, their wedding silver tea service, and a crocheted doily that his wife made.

The rest of the Lozier family also did well enough—Ira lived a very long and colorful life, outliving two wives; he died in Canada, five children to his name. The fact that he named his first son William Homer Lozier sounds as if they all loved and missed their little brother. Sarah had two children and maintained close ties with Ira's children for decades. Martha lived with Sarah and Jerome the rest of her life, dying sometime before the 1910 census. George had two wives and four children, and a varied career that ended with him as a chauffeur in Los Angeles. Coincidentally, George Lozier and Will Gaston ended up living within 40 miles of each other in California, and are buried near to each other, between Glendale and Pomona.

When I went to visit Martha's grave in Fairbury, I took along photos of Homer as a young boy, as a young man, and a father and a grandfather. I hope she knows how well Homer turned out, and all his descendants (more than 70 so far), and I like to think of mother and son meeting again in a different place. My husband and I lost our 21-year-old son to suicide in 2019; Ira is modeled somewhat on our son Austin. As a bereaved mother myself, I like to hold Martha in my heart, and know how much love was always there for her lost boy.

Enjoy more about

The Bereaved

Meet the Author

Check out author appearances

Explore special features

About the Author

Julia Park Tracey is an award-winning author, journalist, and poet. She is the author of three previous novels, two women's history compilations and a collection of poetry. She was Poet Laureate of Alameda, CA, from 2014-2017. Her work has appeared in the *San Francisco Chronicle, Huffington Post, Salon, Good Housekeeping, Scary Mommy* and *Thrillist*. Her poetry has appeared in *Hecate, Sugared Water, Autumn House Review, California Quarterly, Sledgehammer Lit*, and *Yellow Chair Review*. She has been blogging since 2003 and has been recognized by the California Newspaper Publishers Association for her editing and writing. Julia lives in the low Sierra Nevada after a childhood in the Wine Country and a career in the San Francisco Bay Area. She lives with her husband, cats, and sometimes bees and chickens, in a restored Victorian at the edge of town. She loves hot summers, occasional snow days, history, and the library. For more information, visit: **juliaparktracey.com.**

Acknowledgements

I WOULD LIKE TO THANK the dedicated research team at the National Orphan Train Complex Museum and Research Center in Concordia, Kansas. They worked with me to discover who my adopted great-grandfather William L. Gaston really was—Homer Lozier. And that opened a world of stories and information our family never had before. Thanks especially to Lorelei Thomas Halfhide and former curator Shaley George. (www.orphantraindepot.org)

Thanks also to the generosity of strangers like Kim Sebastian-Ryan, director of membership at Marble Collegiate Church in Manhattan; Erin Algeo, manager and curator at the LACIS Museum of Lace and Textiles in Berkeley, Jill Enfield and Richard Rabinowitz for their kind hospitality in Newburgh, NY; the Newburgh Public Library; and the Fairbury, IL, Historical Society and Prairie Central High School students for their help in finding Martha and Sarah's burial plot.

Thanks so much to my 2016 comrades from Group 10 of the Community of Writers at Palisades, Lake Tahoe: Leta McCollough Seletzky, Andrea Avery, Elison Alcovendaz, Janine Kovac, Molly Welton, Michelle Wallace, Margaret Allen, Lauren Hough, Angel Jennings, and Jon Steinberg; my angels from the Community of Writers at Palisades, Lake

Tahoe, Group 8 in 2018: Geri Ulrey, Joella Teresa Aragon, Jessi Phillips, Charlene Anderson, Sally Henry, Jim Hill, Kristina Horton-Flaherty, Ronald Paul Lewis, and Shaun Miller; Jason Roberts, Julia Flynn Siler, Sands Hall, Brett Hall-Jones, roomies Elizabeth Ann Cavazos, Kathryn Machi, and Reggie Kolbe; writer pals Christian Kiefer, Erika Mailman, Max Wong, Rebecca Lawton and Lisa Lewis; my business partner and lifelong friend Vicki DeArmon; partners Alicia Feltman and Anna Termine for their genius; daughters Mia, Simone, Staizh and Savanna for patience in hearing all about Martha (their own ancestor), and the everlasting love and support of my beloved husband, Patrick Tracey.

And I'm grateful that William Homer Gaston wondered enough at his past to save the receipt for his train fare of 1856, so that his great-grandson, my father, William Park, would find it and together we'd dig a little deeper. Mystery solved at last.

Thank you, all.

Book Group Questions

Do you think Martha should have stayed in Newburgh and taken her chances with their children's guardian? What difference could that have made for Martha and the children?

What are your thoughts about Martha's understanding of the Irish, from the Prologue to the end of the book? How does she evolve?

What role do sewing and crafting play in Martha's life? How does she use her skills to better herself and her circumstances? What are her fallbacks when she can't find work?

What do you think of Martha's decision to place her children with the Home for the Friendless? Is this the choice you would have made?

Why do you think that the Home for the Friendless would not give Martha's children back to her? Share some thoughts about the plight of unmarried/widowed women in an era before women worked much in the workforce outside of home. How much has that changed over the decades or centuries?

The underlying thread of women's work shows itself again and again, from caring for the sick or the deceased, to bringing food to the table. How might Martha's life been different if Bram had not died?

Women's friendships and solidarity are another thread through the novel. Talk about some of the ways in which women show up for each other, and some ways where women fail each other.

Sibylline
PRESS

Sibylline Press is proud to publish the brilliant work of women authors over 50. We are a woman-owned publishing company and, like our authors, represent women of a certain age. In our first season we have three outstanding fiction (historical fiction and mystery) and three incredible memoirs to share with readers of all ages.

HISTORICAL FICTION

The Bereaved: A Novel
BY JULIA PARK TRACEY

Paperback ISBN: 978-1-7367954-2-2
5 3/8 x 8 3/4 | 274 pages | $18
ePub ISBN: 978-1-9605730-0-1 | $12.60

Based on the author's research into her grandfather's past as an adopted child, and the surprising discovery of his family of origin and how he came to be adopted, Julia Park Tracey has created a mesmerizing work of historical fiction illuminating the darkest side of the Orphan Train.

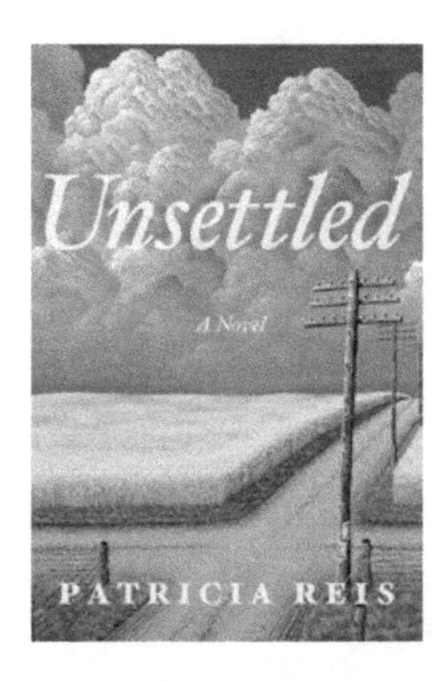

Unsettled: A Novel
BY PATRICIA REIS

Paperback ISBN: 978-1-7367954-8-4
5 3/8 x 8 3/4 | 378 pages | $19
ePUB ISBN: 978-1-960573-05-6 | $13.30

In this lyrical historical fiction with alternating points of view, a repressed woman begins an ancestral quest through the prairies of Iowa, awakening family secrets and herself, while in the late 1800s, a repressed ancestor, Tante Kate, creates those secrets.

MYSTERY

The Rotting Whale: A Hugo Sandoval Eco-Mystery

BY JANN EYRICH

Paperback ISBN: 978-1-7367954-3-9
5 3/8 x 8 3/8 | 212 pages | $17
ePub ISBN: 978-1-960573-03-2 | $11.90

In this first case in the new Hugo Sandoval Eco-Mystery series, an old-school San Francisco building inspector with his trademark Borsalino fedora, must reluctantly venture outside his beloved city and find his sea legs before he can solve the mystery of how a 90-ton blue whale became stranded, twice, in a remote inlet off the North Coast.

MORE TITLES IN THIS ECO-MYSTERY SERIES TO COME:
Spring '24: ***The Blind Key*** | ISBN: 978-1-7367954-5-3
Fall '24: ***The Singing Lighthouse*** | ISBN: 978-1-7367954-6-0

MEMOIR

These Broken Roads: Scammed and Vindicated, One Woman's Story

BY DONNA MARIE HAYES

Tradepaper ISBN: 978-1-7367954-4-6
5 3/8 x 8 3/8 | 226 pages | $17
ePUB ISBN: 978-1-960573-04-9 | $11.90

In this gripping and honest memoir, Jamaican immigrant Donna Marie Hayes recounts how at the peak of her American success in New York City, she is scammed and robbed of her life's savings by the "love of her life" met on an online dating site and how she vindicates herself to overcome a lifetime of bad choices.

Maeve Rising: Coming Out Trans in Corporate America
BY MAEVE DUVALLY

Paperback ISBN: 978-1-7367954-1-5
5 3/8 x 8 3/8 | 284 pages | $18
ePub ISBN: 978-1-960573-01-8 | $12.60

In this searingly honest LBGQT+ memoir, Maeve DuVally tells the story of coming out transgender in one of the most high-profile financial institutions in America, Goldman Sachs.

Reading Jane: A Daughter's Memoir
BY SUSANNAH KENNEDY

Paperback ISBN: 978-1-7367954-7-7
5 3/8 x 8 3/8 | 306 pages | $19
ePub ISBN: 978-1-960573-02-5 | $13.30

After the calculated suicide of her domineering and narcissistic mother, Susannah Kennedy grapples with the ties between mothers and daughters and the choices parents make in this gripping memoir that shows what freedom looks like when we choose to examine the uncomfortable past.

For more information about Sibylline Press and our authors, please visit us at **www.sibyllinepress.com**

Printed in the USA
CPSIA information can be obtained
at www.ICGtesting.com
JSHW082041040923
47807JS00004B/32